Monster Love

CAROL TOPOLSKI

FIG TREE
an imprint of
PENGUIN BOOKS

FIG TREE

Published by the Penguin Group
Penguin Books Ltd, 80 Strand, London WC2R ORL, England
Penguin Group (USA) Inc., 375 Hudson Street, New York, New York 10014, USA
Penguin Group (Canada), 90 Eglinton Avenue East, Suite 700, Toronto, Ontario, Canada M4P 2Y3
(a division of Pearson Penguin Canada Inc.)
Penguin Ireland, 25 St Stephen's Green, Dublin 2, Ireland
(a division of Penguin Books Ltd)
Penguin Group (Australia), 250 Camberwell Road, Camberwell, Victoria 3124, Australia
(a division of Pearson Australia Group Pty Ltd)
Penguin Books India Pvt Ltd, 11 Community Centre, Panchsheel Park, New Delhi – 110 017, India
Penguin Group (NZ), 67 Apollo Drive, Rosedale, North Shore 0632, New Zealand
(a division of Pearson New Zealand Ltd)
Penguin Books (South Africa) (Pty) Ltd, 24 Sturdee Avenue, Rosebank, Johannesburg 2196, South Africa

Penguin Books Ltd, Registered Offices: 80 Strand, London WC2R ORL, England

www.penguin.com

First published 2008
1

Copyright © Carol Topolski, 2008

The moral rights of the author and translator have been asserted

Set in 12/14.75 pt Monotype Dante
Typeset by Rowland Phototypesetting Ltd, Bury St Edmunds, Suffolk
Printed in Great Britain by Clays Ltd, St Ives plc

A CIP catalogue record for this book is available from the British Library

HARDBACK
ISBN: 978-1-905-49026-4

TRADE PAPERBACK
ISBN: 978-1-905-49027-1

For Michael, Cassie, Clea and Alessia, the steady pulse of my life

and Kit Pedler (1927–1981), my dad

O dark, dark, dark, amid the blaze of noon,
Irrecoverably dark, total Eclipse
Without all hope of day!

Samson Agonistes, John Milton

Charlotte

The baby was a dear little thing. Sherilyn had an extraordinary pram cum buggy for her – I'd never seen anything like it. It was state of the art, all aerodynamic lines and huge plastic wheels and so silent they'd be on you before you realised they were there. It was dreadfully distracting – you were so busy admiring this expensive carriage, you had to remind yourself there was a real live baby in it. Mind you, she was so quiet and still she could have been make-believe, like the dolls they give little children in nativity plays in case they drop baby Jesus. I'd never subscribed to any religion, but after they found her I had this niggly question batting around in my mind: would it have made it any easier if I'd had a faith to cling on to? If I'd believed in all that nonsense, would the idea of a credible evil have helped? I didn't think so. I'd always rather prided myself on never having slid into religious faith as insurance as I got older, so I wasn't about to become a docile penitent, even in the face of this appalling tragedy.

Samantha was always beautifully dressed. Everything matched: coat, hat, frock, gloves, and if she was wearing lilac, the pram cover would be dark lilac, if pink, then lighter pink and so on. The planning that went into that made the Iron Lady look chaotic. One might have expected Sherilyn to be in another shade of the same colour, like a mummy 'n' baby matching set, but she was determinedly different, as though she'd divested herself of any association with her daughter. She often wore black in the early months: immaculate, tailored, designer black, as though she were just on the way to her important job. Or in mourning. I'm reasonably fastidious about the way I look, but she made me feel like a bag lady sometimes. I do try to make time for going to the hairdresser's and shopping around for smart clothes, but there are other priorities, like the gardening, so I keep my nails short and practical. Hers were like talons – put me in mind of those mandarins who never cut theirs so everyone would know they were too damn important to have to do manual work – and I wondered how she managed all those tender maternal tasks with her nails that long.

I try not to be too judgemental – Lord knows, a career teaching in inner-city schools exposed me to wildly different lifestyles and cultures – but something didn't fit. You can see a woman with her child and she may be wholly uneducated, but she knows how to mother. She knows how to respond to her child, how to read her child, how to gratify or deny her child but it was as if Sherilyn were playing a role in someone else's life story. She'd be clacking down the street in those vertiginously high heels she wore, and you'd stop her and say How's Samantha? And she'd smile tightly and say Oh, she's sleeping through the night now, she's such a good baby. Or, She's started eating solids – it's such a relief not to have to sterilise all those bottles. But it was as if she were talking about someone she knew nothing about, regurgitating something she'd come across in a book without having digested its meaning.

And I never saw her touching the baby. Not once. She'd tweak her bedclothes or raise the hood of the babymobile when it started to rain, but she never stroked her face or patted her curls or made any of those busy loving gestures you see in new mums. Samantha was always stoppered, and when her dummy fell out Sherilyn would stick it straight back in then pull out a tissue to wipe her own fingers. Once the baby had a cold and was pouring mucus from her nose. When Sherilyn noticed, she gave an involuntary grimace. I said Poor little sausage and wiped her nose with one of my own tissues. Sherilyn's sharp little face

2

cracked just for an instant and she shot me a look of such gratitude I felt slightly breathless. But I couldn't capitalise on it. With anyone else, I'd have said Come in for a coffee, you look like you could do with a sit, but her face closed down immediately. It was like when you're looking at one of those lowering skies pregnant with rain and there's a sudden split in the clouds – you get a momentary glimpse of some other weather beyond, then it snaps back again. You have to insist that it really happened because it's become incredible.

She must have got pregnant shortly after they moved in and because her frame was so delicate you could pretty much tell straight away. I'd see them going off to work together in their fancy BMW and while she'd obviously had to buy new clothes to accommodate her growing baby, the bump always looked as though it were strapped on to her like an added extra. As though it really wasn't part of her at all. As though her body absolved itself of any responsibility for it.

I was sad when the Bennetts moved out because Lamorna was a good friend, but I thought the Gutteridges would enhance life in the Crescent; they looked as though they'd got life sorted. They painted the outside of their house as soon as they moved in, and had the front and back gardens done by professional gardeners. It was all a bit formal for my taste – I like plants to roam around and ramble into each other – but each to his own. Like the way Sherilyn dressed, it was precisely colour-coordinated. No room for any happy accident. I have a much admired camellia in my back garden – the soil's limey, so my rhodies and azaleas are pretty spectacular too – and I offered them a cutting. How very kind, they said, How thoughtful, but no thank you. We decided against red in our garden. They were frightfully well mannered, always. I'm in favour of that. Rather swam against the tide at school by insisting that the kids please'd and thank you'd alongside learning the fundamentals of grammar. I was much derided. But their manners were too good, as though they weren't there to demonstrate concern for the other person, but to repulse contact. I try not to be wise with hindsight, but Annie from number 17 remembers me saying that when I'd spoken to one or other of them, I felt like I'd been talking to an iceberg. Very beautiful, very frozen and very hidden. Very lethal, I might say now.

But you can't be close friends with everybody and they were never rude. When my husband, Russell, died unexpectedly five years ago, there was a tremendous rallying round. My daughter, Olivia, had already gone off to Australia with Stefan, but she jumped on a plane straight away. Even Marcus, my son, came over from Denmark for his dad's funeral. We'd rather lost touch with him since he'd emptied one of our bank accounts, but the Danish police tracked him down and he turned up at the crematorium in his robes. I was glad he'd found some roots, even if it was with the cult. Being adopted, he was probably always looking for a way of belonging.

All my friends in the Crescent popped in and out with food and flowers and the cards arrived in droves. All Russell's and my colleagues sent condolences, and the jungle drums boomed around both our families. Cousins and second cousins I'd almost forgotten I had got in touch, so for a short while I was positively swaddled with love. One might have thought the Gutteridges would have noticed the comings and goings and have asked one of the neighbours what was going on, but they didn't. And I'd welcomed them to the road with a little basket of goodies when they arrived: crab-apple jelly from my tree, the burdock wine Russell used to make, and a big bunch of flowers from the garden. I suspect there were too many colours in the bunch for them. But they didn't send a card or stand at the kerb's edge like the other neighbours when the hearse left. Maureen from number 24 pointed it out. I hadn't noticed, but then grief temporarily blinds you.

A lot of the support dropped away after a few weeks. It wasn't that people stopped caring, more that you're supposed to have got over it a couple of months down the line. Actually, it's then that it really starts hitting home that you're on your own. That there's twenty, thirty years to go without your life's companion. I was quite low and was already debating whether to carry on teaching, so when Olivia called me in the middle of the night to say she was pregnant, that settled it. I handed in my resignation. I didn't need the money – Russell's life insurance was very generous and thirty years' teaching produced a reasonable pension – so I got into training for grannyhood. Shortly afterwards I noticed Sherilyn's strap-on bump and while Olivia was assiduous about keeping me up to speed about her pregnancy, I couldn't just pop round and see, so I might have been slightly overkeen on following my neighbour's progress. I remember passing her in the street once and saying How's it going? And she said What? as though I'd asked her about the presidential election in Guatemala or the millet harvest in Moldavia. Your pregnancy, I said, My daughter's pregnant but she's in Australia so I'm going to be spending a lot of time on planes. But I'm delighted, I said, Bet your mum is too. There was a slight pause and then she said Oh yes, she likes babies and then she said Sorry, I'm in a bit of a rush to meet friends, and that was the end of that.

I didn't think I was nosy, I was just interested in people. When my neighbours were away and I looked after their cats and plants, I tried to put on metaphorical blinkers as I went round the house. Frank and Amelia's fluorescent condoms on the bedside table made me smile though: he was such a formal man and she could barely cross the road on her own. I noticed hooks in their bedroom ceiling too. Once I'd given up work, I kept an eye on things in the Crescent just as a matter of neighbourliness. When the Blewitts at number 12 started building a raised terrace all round their house, I said to Jenny at number 10 that she should speak to her solicitor because it meant they'd overlook her patio. He wrote them a letter, so they altered their plans and built a very pretty wall in between. It was all very amicable and Jenny gave me a lovely urn to say thank you.

There wasn't a lot of crime in Tamley – last burglary was about seven years ago, Alice and Thomas at number 3 – but nonetheless it was wise to be alert. The Gutteridges installed a Banham alarm system shortly after they moved in, which surprised me because we'd none of us gone in for that sort of thing, but they were new to the area, from London, so I thought maybe they felt more vulnerable than us. They may have cost a fortune, those modern houses, but they were nothing like as sturdy as the older ones in the rest of the Crescent; the Victorians were empire builders, after all. Their house looked pretty impregnable – I noticed they'd fitted locks on their windows, top and bottom, and bars on the front and back doors. You can see their back door from Jessie and Tim's patio, at number 11. They'd made it impossible to get in there, I thought. And it was much the same with them. Nothing was going in and nothing was coming out. Brendan was perfectly amiable when you met him on the street, but it was nearly a year before I discovered what he did for a living.

When they moved in, I said to them Any time you're away, just give me a bell and I'll pop over and feed the cat – they had this exquisite long-haired cat with blue eyes. I never did find out what it was called. And they said Thank you, how kind. We will. But they never did, though before she had the baby I saw them shut the house up from time to time for the weekend, so they obviously did go away. They didn't seem to need anything from anyone else and to some degree I found that self-sufficiency quite enviable: that delicious sense of being utterly wrapped up in another person. Russell and I were like that before we had Marcus, but after you've had children your mind necessarily divides itself between all the people in your life and that bubble of intimacy pops.

My friends often say Oh Charlotte, you're always giving, giving, giving, do let us give something back to you, but I find it hard to ask, and anyway I find it much more satisfying being useful to other people. But when I went to Canberra after Amy's birth, I had to ask for help, and Amelia and Maureen took care of my indoor plants and my garden between them. My calla lilies weren't very well when I came back, but they did their best.

I fell in love with Amy at first sight. I cried when Olivia handed her to me because she reminded me of Marcus when first we got him. That's idiotic of course, because we didn't actually conceive him, but it made me think of how long we'd waited and how desperately we'd loved him so I wrote to him from Australia telling him again how precious a gift he'd been. He didn't reply. Olivia had had a difficult delivery and was struggling to breastfeed the baby, but she said I must have brought serenity with me in my coat pockets because she and Amy settled soon after I arrived.

It was such a wrench leaving them; it was almost as though my womb had been filled again and was suddenly evacuated when I got on the plane. That's a little fanciful, but I'm sure that's why I kept my eye on Sherilyn's pregnancy and their baby, who was born seven weeks after I got back from Australia. I popped a card through their letterbox when I heard and left a potted plant on their step, because they weren't answering the door. I didn't see her or the baby for nearly three months after she was born, although I saw Brendan going off to work and coming back as usual. Then I started seeing him coming back during the day and picking her and the baby up. She was smartly dressed in suits, as though she were going off to a business meeting; he carried the baby to the car like a bag of shopping. I never saw her face.

I had rather to push Sherilyn for her name when I started seeing them occasionally in the street. She referred to her as 'the baby' when I asked after her, and even when I established that she was called Samantha, she didn't use her name and looked slightly discomfited when I did. I showed her the pictures of Amy I kept in my bag – I'd become a shameless granny-bore – and she looked at them politely for a moment as though she were looking at someone's new roof, changed the subject to something neutral and took herself off. I wondered if she had a touch of the baby blues, but any gentle enquiry just pinged off her carapace, so I had to hope that her mum was around.

I'd see the three of them out together sometimes when Samantha was a toddler. I was going over to Australia every two or three months by then and Amy knew who I was. She called me Nannie-Lottie, and Olivia and Stefan took the opportunity to go away for long weekends while I was there, so I had plenty of granny-time with her. She and I used to potter around the garden together and sometimes she'd help me plant things; she was passionate about ladybirds, which she called 'babylirds'. But I never saw Samantha walking, even when she was of the age. Rain or shine she was always strapped into the buggy.

I know I'm partial, but Amy's language was very well developed by then so I used to squat down to chat to Samantha when we met in the street. She was a solemn little thing and nothing I said evoked a cheery response: it was quite eerie. When she was that sort of age, everybody used to say Olivia charmed the birds from the trees, though they found Marcus harder to know. I'd say to her Hi Sammy, are you going to the shops with Mummy and Daddy? What are you going to buy? And she'd look at me and say We buying food for pussy cat 'cause he hungry.

And I'd say How lovely, lucky pussy, and how about you? Maybe Mummy and Daddy will buy you an ice cream, what do you think? And she'd look very serious and say I do be good girl, I be very very good girl. Not bad girl. I remember Brendan saying We try to be careful with her sugar intake, actually. It's so bad for her teeth. I knew he was being responsible, but I thought Oh give her a treat for heaven's sake, it won't kill her.

Then she dropped off the map. I'd seen her out of the house only rarely anyway, so it took a while for it to sink in that I hadn't laid eyes on her for six months or so. I asked Jessie and Tim if they'd seen her playing in the back garden and they said they hadn't, but sometimes they heard her crying and Brendan's voice shouting in what was obviously her bedroom. That was strange, because she'd always seemed like such a well-behaved child from babyhood on. Unnervingly well behaved I might have said, for such a little one. Some time later, I asked them again and Jessie said she hadn't heard Samantha crying for a while, but she and Tim were having a marital blip just then so they were probably preoccupied. Turns out Jessie had been having an affair with a woman at work for some months.

When the two of them went away to the West Indies for a reconciliation holiday, I said I'd look after their house for them. They were very grateful. We know it'll be in safe hands, Tim said, Wish us luck, Charlotte. The master bedroom was in the back in those houses, and theirs was pink and floral. Poor old Tim, I thought, because it was rather assertively girly-girly. When I looked down from there at the Gutteridges' garden, I was quite taken aback because I hadn't seen it from above before. The big house that had been on that site had had a lovely garden, huge and rambling, but it had been dug up when they demolished the house to make way for those five new ones. It was about nine years ago and I remember saying to Russell at the time that I hoped the new houses fitted in. They didn't, but there wasn't a lot we could do about it. Each household inscribed their own horticultural signature on the land, and four of them: the Pinkers (they're gone now – off to Egypt with her job), the Bulls, the Smedleys and Jessie and Tim went in for quite traditional gardens, though the Pinkers added a conservatory in which they grew a not very successful grapevine. The Bennetts went in for a lot of lawn. But the Gutteridges had had this formal garden made, with geometric shapes edged with box, and different-coloured gravel and paving. It had probably cost a fortune, but had all the organic energy of a plastic box. It was ridiculously grandiose too – this was Tamley, for heaven's sake, not Blenheim – and there was no room for any plant to do its own thing. It was a well-mannered garden, like them: very ordered, very correct and very unyielding.

Most days I sat on the pink window seat in Jessie and Tim's bedroom, just observing. I wasn't prying but I was intrigued by this polite garden and wondered how they used it. It wasn't the kind of garden a little girl could kick a ball around, or turn somersaults in, but then I never saw Samantha out there that whole fortnight. Sometimes one goes into a house or sees one in a magazine and it's clear straight away that there aren't any children living there; that's how this garden looked. No nooks and crannies for hide and seek, nowhere for a sandpit or a paddling pool – no room for any of the ordinary messes that children make. It made me rather sad. Russell was forever saying things like Oh, what's a broken standard rose between friends? Marcus is turning into a fine batsman. Forget it, Char! And he was right, though losing my beloved Princess Alexandra was a bit galling.

I'd see the two of them out there though – it was a balmy late August, as I recall – and they'd sit and chat on their patio every evening, Brendan in his shirtsleeves and Sherilyn in some tight little wisp of silk. She'd have brought out a bottle of wine in a chiller, two or three sorts of nibbles in matching bowls, he'd

uncork the bottle – it often seemed to be sparkling, champagne
for all I know – and they'd settle in like a pair of bookends.
They were never lost for words, unlike some couples you see
who make you wonder quite why they ever got together:
these two were like yin and yang. It contrasted so strangely with
how they were when you came across them in the street: in
private there was a fluency between them and a playful good
humour that was very attractive. I realised afterwards that I'd
never seen either of them laugh before, not in that hearty throw
back your head way. You'd get a pinched little smile when you
made a joke, but you knew they were simply applying the proper
formula: joke + response = smile. But on that patio, night after
night, they laughed and chuckled and giggled and chortled; they
seemed to find each other endlessly entertaining. Despite the
fact that they looked such a mismatched pair, he with his burly
rugger-bugger frame and she with her porcelain-doll fragility,
there was such a rapport between them, they could have been a
pair of ivies winding around each other in happy symbiosis.

One evening when she brought out the drinks, she had a red
stethoscope around her neck. Brendan looked utterly delighted
and clapped his hands. She put the tray down on the table and
went over to sit on his lap. She must have been whispering
something in his ear, because his head was cocked towards her.
A few minutes later they got up, went inside, and didn't come
back for an hour or so. I thought maybe they'd gone to make
Samantha her tea, maybe bath her and bring her outside to sit
with them in her pyjamas, but she didn't appear.

Tim and Jessie had told me which room was hers and I'd sit
in the equivalent room in their house at various times of the
day, listening and watching. By that stage I was a little worried.
I value the way the English respect privacy and I'm chary of
intruding on anyone, but I suppose I was probably more sensitive
than usual because of Amy. And Marcus had just written the

week before saying his wife had had a baby. I didn't even know he was married, let alone that she was pregnant.

I'd sit there early in the morning thinking I'd hear them getting her up for breakfast, but there was nothing. Then lunchtime: nothing. Sherilyn went out shopping: nothing. Bathtime: nothing. The curtains on the window opposite stayed resolutely shut like a pair of blind eyes. I saw Sherilyn in the back garden one afternoon when I was watering the lawn and I said Just looking after the house for Tim and Jessie while they're away. Caribbean, lucky so-and-sos. She said Oh you're such a good neighbour and I said Do the same for you any time, how's Samantha? Without a blink she said Gone to play with my friend's little girl. Frannie, she said, They're bosom buddies the two of them. I said Terribly important to have friends, isn't it, especially if you're an only child. I've got a pond in my garden, I said, With goldfish and frogs. Would the little girls like to come round and see them? They could help me with the feeding. She said That's very kind of you. Thank you. We'll knock on your door sometime. Which house is it? The one with the mature acer in the garden, I said, Rather dishevelled wisteria up the front. Thank you, she said, We'll definitely be round. I thought I probably wouldn't hold my breath.

I've kicked myself that I didn't do anything about it then. I've often thought, What if I had? Would she have been alive now? What if I'd broken the usual protocols of letting people be? Sleeping dogs lie. Dead children rot. But the bald fact is I didn't.

Soon after talking to Sherilyn in the garden I suddenly became very busy because Marcus's wife developed a potentially fatal infection and he asked me to go to Denmark to help. It meant that he wanted me in his life again, so I dropped everything and ran. She jolly nearly died, so it was a good thing I went because it was my insistence that they took her to a conventional doctor that saved her life. They seemed to think that chanting and

seaweed were going to do it. I had to keep telling myself that
everyone had a right to their own beliefs, but I was spitting teeth
– how *dare* they risk my grandson growing up motherless for the
sake of some cockeyed God-bothering mumbo-jumbo!

By the time I'd trekked to Denmark and back a few times, and
taken quite a long break in Australia – Amy'd just started nursery
and Olivia went back to university to research a doctorate – it
must have been nine months or so before I finally decided to do
something about Samantha's disappearance. One of my colleagues at school, rather an odd woman who taught sociology,
had her children taken into care when it became clear she was
a serious drug user, so I was well aware that neglect goes on
among the middle classes as much as on council estates. But
truthfully I had been dithering. All their excuses were plausible
enough: Samantha was asleep/ill/staying with her grandparents/
her cousins, but despite her busy social life, you'd expect to see
her occasionally.

I wasn't ashamed of what I was doing, so I gave the NSPCC
my name and phone number when I called to alert them.
Probably nothing I said, But you just want to be sure, don't you?
The woman agreed. I wasn't simple-minded about authorities –
Lord knows, I was a figure of authority myself for years – but I
was happy to hand over responsibility to a specialist organisation.
I didn't tell anyone in the Crescent what I'd done. If it was
nothing, I didn't want to poison anyone's mind against the
Gutteridges; they had to carry on living among us after all. I told
Olivia though, and she thought I'd done the right thing. Someone
from Social Services called me a few days later and said they'd
be following it up. She said I'd done the right thing too.

Once I'd reported them, it was as though I could let my
imagination run off the leash and I was quite plagued by bleak
imaginings. Mostly I imagined Samantha ill or even injured by
her father, because Jessie had said his shouting sounded quite

hysterical, but I never imagined the cage. Rationally, you know human beings do unconscionable things to each other, but you never think, Here. Next door. In my street. That's what people always say, but people always say it because it's true.

I asked the social worker if they'd let me know the upshot of their investigation, but she said no, and while I knew that was right I did feel a little frustrated. I didn't think about what had happened to Samantha every day, but it was obviously simmering away on the back burner because she came into my dreams. She was always dead in my dreams. That probably upped the ante, so when their burglar alarm started going off I called Tim. He said he'd seen them going off with quantities of luggage some time before – just the two of them – so I called the police. No emergency, I said, But I'd be grateful if you'd come and check the house.

I saw the patrol car arrive and the two police officers get out, so I walked over and spoke to the man. He had a sweet, open, podgy face and said Not to worry, madam, we'll just have a look around. Leave it with us. We'll let you know if there's anything untoward – you just pop on home. I did, but I kept my eyes on the house, so I saw all the other police cars and the ambulances turn up a bit later. They brought out the policeman first. He seemed to have shrunk. He was a rotund man, but he looked like one of those inflatable clown punchbags whose plug had been pulled. He had to be helped into the ambulance by two paramedics.

The police cars had different letters on their roofs, and men in disposable overalls swarmed out of the vans and into the house. They brought her out in a white box. Not a coffin, just a box you might keep odds and ends in. Her remains. Like leftovers on a plate. Detritus littering the ground after a picnic. I prefer 'body'. Dead body. Murdered little girl. Daughter. I wanted to rub my own nose in it, so I imagined being Brendan or Sherilyn.

Imagined what it must feel like to so hate your child you'd want to put her in a cage and leave her to die. Though perhaps hate didn't come into it. They didn't seem hateful towards her when I met them on the street, just indifferent.

Even having that idea in my head made it ache, so I tried to shut down the thoughts, but they were compulsive. I had an almost continuous sub-migraine for weeks. When the police interviewed me, I dosed myself up with so many painkillers I must have come across as a bit of a zombie. But a zombie doesn't feel anything and I was feeling too much. So when they asked me What did you see? and I said Nothing. What did you hear? Nothing. What did you do? and I said Nothing again, I burst into tears. It was in that Nothing, that black hole of Nothing, that Samantha had disappeared.

You couldn't move for the press. They descended almost immediately, like a swarm of unholy locusts frantically gobbling up anything in their path. I became pretty housebound for a short while because they'd pounce on you as soon as you showed your face at the door, but you weren't even safe inside because they'd stuff notes through the letterbox offering sums of money for an interview. Quite large sums, and I could imagine the temptation for someone less comfortably off than me. I thought Maureen had succumbed, though she denied it. She was anonymously quoted in one of the newspaper features, but she'd just lost her part-time job, so she might have taken the blood money. I tried not to blame her.

Then I thought, Buck up, Charlotte, you were Head of Department for heaven's sake and these people are just maggots doing their maggoty job, so I tried to resume my normal life. And I did to a large extent, though in some ways nothing was ever normal again. I went to the shops two weeks later, but it felt different because I was going to the shops having experienced this. This was never *not* going to have happened. This outrageous piece of history lodged in my present and future like a piece of shrapnel in my flesh and so skewed things that I couldn't look at parents with their children and not wonder, fleetingly, what was going on behind their front door. Wonder if those pretty trousers were hiding dynasties of bruises. If the child's jolly smile was hiding terrible anguish.

When the press interest died down, life in the Crescent resumed, but it walked with a limp. I'd begun drinking a little without noticing it: it started off with a second sherry here and there and then I found myself consuming a whole bottle of wine with my dinner most nights. I was quite ashamed of myself, but not enough to stop. In a weird way, it linked me back to Russell, which was comforting. He drank far too much.

But while the first dramatic stages were over I knew it would all crank up again when the Gutteridges came to trial, so I arranged to go to Denmark. I thought the Danish press would be less interested in it than the Aussie vultures, but Denmark was having one of its periodic Lutheran lurches and so it was all over the national media. The decadent heart of the uptight Brits, that sort of thing. Strangely, the Robed Chosen Ones devoured it too. They had one wonky television in a tiny anteroom and they all piled in night after night watching the reports, so there was no escape. Marcus acquired a kind of notoriety by association with me, so he didn't stop his fellow cult members banging on about what had happened, tacitly accusing me of culpability in Samantha's death. He needed to feel special, and this was one – albeit perverse – way of being centre stage.

I couldn't bear the sanctimony, so I left. I rented a tiny house on a practically uninhabited Danish island and wrote terrible poetry. It was odd to be so isolated, but in that contemplative mood I learned something about my almost imperative need to know everything about everyone, which truthfully does bleed into nosiness. I might once have called it community spirit.

Now I'm back at home and trying to take things slowly. I considered training for Childline and went to a couple of preliminary meetings, but I recognised early enough that I wanted to do it as expiation, which was quite the wrong motivation, so I withdrew. I've put the house on the market and I'm conducting an archaeological dig through the twenty years of living here before I ship myself over to Australia. If I choose to work again there are apparently plenty of jobs going teaching Aboriginal children, but I may not apply. Life has acquired a terrible sense of brevity, and I want to be around to teach Amy to play cricket in the garden.

Anthony

He was my protégé. It's a word I'm fond of, a staccato word with a legato heart. The human instinct to protect your own. I know we're supposed to sneer at colonialism nowadays, but I take the view that as much as ruling the colonies, we were protecting them too. Mostly from themselves. When I look at the mess Africa's in, I despair; if we'd stayed on we might have prevented them from slitting each other's throats. Metaphorically speaking I suppose Brendan did slit someone's throat, but at least it wasn't on my watch, though I always wondered what I'd missed. How I'd missed it. I consider myself a watchful sort of chap, but I didn't see the signs. Diana tells me I shouldn't blame myself, that she didn't spot anything either, but for her they were nothing more than acquaintances on the periphery of our lives. Just passing through – she was never going to grant them permanent residency. They were what her family called NQOCD – Not Quite Our Class Darling – so even if they'd made millions, they'd always have been below the salt.

By the time I went up to Oxford and met Diana, I'd incorporated my mother's maiden name into my surname, so I was introduced to her as Berwick-Grant. Anthony. Never Tony, which was what my parents called me. I'd laundered any trace of home out of my accent, so I offered her a glahhs of bubbly. A common-as-muck gluss was what Dad drank out of at the Working Men's Club. I met her in my second year at a shooting party at her family home. Her brother, Henry, was up with me and we'd rather bonded on the rugby field – both blues – so when he decided that the best way to celebrate his twenty-first

18

was to kill a few feeble pheasants, I was on the guest list. I was terrified I'd shoot one of the beaters, so I took myself off to the university shooting range and practised until I could more or less split a hair with one shot.

Diana was at boarding school still, but got an exeat for the party, so I met her for the first time when I came down to the drawing room after dressing for dinner on the Friday. The war had been over for a couple of years, but the nation was still being throttled by rationing, so ordinary people – people like my family – were patriotically making do with discards and scraps. Not so the Racines. Even after all these years of living disguised among them, I'm still astonished at the way they elude the exigencies dictating most people's lives. It's as though they're serviced by an invisible horde of Rumpelstiltskins who can conjure gold out of a dead heap of straw, silk purses out of sows' ears. In a sea of parachute silk and calico, Diana floated in a frock that was made of such fine lace she looked positively ethereal. As I came in, she was standing by an ornate fireplace talking to her father. I'd been announced by Evans, the butler, so she knew who I was, and she glided over to me with the grace of a Bolshoi ballerina. She held out a kid-gloved hand and said Anthony, how lovely to meet you at last. Henry has captivated us with tales of your exploits. Do come and meet Daddy. She was taller than me, but she had the art, even at sixteen, of convincing men that she was a rare and fragile creature whom they must protect from the grit of daily life. I executed an awkward bow over her hand and clumped beside her to the stiff-necked bore by the fire. Daddy, this is Anthony Berwick-Grant, she said, Henry's dear friend from Oxford, and turning her amber eyes to me she said Anthony, this is Rupert Racine, my papa.

I was so terrified I'd inadvertently drop an aitch or flatten a vowel, I barely said a word all evening, but when we rejoined the ladies after brandy and cigars, Diana managed to whisper that she was looking forward to meeting me the next day on the shoot. Suddenly slaughtering blameless birds wasn't so repellent.

We had a long courtship because while I'd maintained myself at Oxford on an exhibition and a milk round, supporting myself through accountancy studies was a Sisyphean task. I could no more ask Rupert for his daughter's hand without a profession than I could move the Arctic two inches to the left. At that, so far as he was concerned, accountancy was only a tiptoe above trade. He used to crash on at dinner parties about how his family could be traced back to the Normans, as though that made him interesting. It didn't. Fortunately he was so fascinated by himself, it was a simple matter to keep my own background opaque. I knew he'd have to meet my parents at the wedding, but was pretty sure he'd pay them scant attention, since the guest list consisted almost entirely of Lincolnshire grandees and Wyke-hamist old farts. QOCDs. A beak-nosed vulture from *Harper's Bazaar* was there, so the following month we featured in the society pages. Diana dismissed it as a trifle, but there was a framed photograph from 'Jennifer's Diary' in a prominent position on our Steinway.

It was inconceivable that I'd invite my brothers to our wedding. Phil was an unsuccessful burglar and Bob was what we called 'educationally subnormal' in those days and lived in a Home in Wales. I wanted to avoid any discomfort, so I told Mum and Dad that coming to the wedding was optional. When I'd won the scholarship to Manchester Grammar they'd never come to any school events because they were worried they'd show me up. Dad demurred, saying he thought he might have a job to do on the wedding date, but Mum said Of course we will, you daft 'aporth! I'll stitch mesel' a suit.

I did my best to protect them on the day, but every time I looked over at them some other asinine prig was busy patronising them, and my tough and stalwart dad looked as though he were being hammered into the ground like a tent peg. I longed to be able to spirit them away for pie and peas in a pub, longed to fold the three of us in a family cloak, but I knew by then it was a cloak that could be worn only infrequently – and covertly.

But Diana loved them, as did Toby and Francis, our two boys. We'd visit four times a year, the boys curling round each other like kittens in sleeping bags on the floor of the front parlour, and Diana and I in the guest room. We'd lie in bed under the lilac quilted eiderdown smelling of fresh air and washing days in a hotpot and dumplings-induced coma. Diana said counting the floral sprigs on the eye-curdlingly busy wallpaper was better than counting sheep and I hoped she wasn't mocking Mum's taste. Diana's was as refined as her manners. My parents wouldn't come down to see us, even though I said I'd send a car for them. They always refused. It would be: Dad's got a cold, or Phil's sent a visiting order, or Bob's coming out that weekend, but I continued to ask even after I knew the hope that I could lure them south was forlorn. We never talked about it – talking was for southern jessies – but their experience at our wedding lay between us like the bolster down the middle of a virgin's bed.

I like to think I've been a good provider for my family; unlike Rupert, I've had to put in the graft and have as a result savoured the tastes of achievement. I was a partner in the firm at thirty, senior partner three years later. I sent my parents a letter on the firm's notepaper when first I appeared on it. They sent me a card obviously designed to congratulate someone on passing their driving test: Mum had written, *You make us proud, son* and Dad signed his name but added an uncharacteristic kiss. It made me weep.

I wish I could say the same about my boys, but their lives of plenty have starved them of ambition and in my darker moments I've almost wished my father's life on them. I grew up with the smells of Dad's job at the chemical plant: he'd come home at the end of a shift, his faded blue overalls reeking of deadly gels, the fabric burned and bleached by leaks and splashes, and, pleading homework, I'd have to take myself off to my room until he was washed and changed. I've worn cologne ever since my university days because it's the only way of warding off that part of my past.

Brendan smelled of ambition. When first he joined the firm, before he qualified, I'd pass him in the corridor and he'd say Sir, I need to ask you something – when would you have a moment? He was never obsequious, always polite, and, my God, he was persistent. Sometimes I wondered if he lived in that corridor, if he brought a sleeping bag to work, because he was always there. I didn't mind – though my secretary sometimes complained when talking to him delayed a meeting – because his questions were spawned by a fierce desire to know. It was as though each enquiry was a passport application to my world. He moved around the firm as he slowly qualified, and each head of department would comment on his diligence, his commitment, his professional scruples. His files would come to me from time to time annotated and indexed like textbooks, different-coloured tags flagging up sections and subsections. Robertson in Corporate Finance told me with a mixture of admiration and weariness that he'd get calls at weekends from Brendan wanting to check the minutiae of an offshore loan. He seemed like an honest young man, an ethical chap, the sort of son to make a father proud.

As the firm expanded – and I have to take credit for our tentacular grip on the European financial world – so our corporate life became grander and I was obliged to attend any number of events, always with Diana on my arm. I used to tease her that she was like the vicar's wife, distributing largesse and benefaction around like whipped cream, but she'd say simply It's my job, Anthony – I like to think I do it well. Brendan never brought a guest, which surprised me. He was a personable young man and had the kind of sportsman's physique girls seemed to like. If I'd thought about it at all, I'd have supposed that he was too busy doing the job and fitting the studying around it to run a romantic life too, but when I mentioned it to Diana she said she'd find a suitable girl and introduce them. Matchmaking was another of her talents. It rather surprised me later on when he turned up at an event with a girl from Personnel, Sherilyn Miller. Personnel rather frowned on office romances because they always end in tears and good chaps leave the company – or else the girls droop around in the Ladies sobbing hopelessly. Sherilyn was a pert little thing, rather hard-edged for my taste, but then Diana has become even more beautiful to me since she put on a bit of post-menopausal poundage, so maybe I'm biased. They made an incongruous couple, Brendan with his hulking bulk and her trip-trapping along in high-heeled shoes that made her look like a little girl dressing up in her mother's wardrobe, but they seemed happy enough so far as one could tell.

On the whole I try to keep work life and social life separate, but it would have been churlish to turn down the invitations to Brendan and Sherilyn's drinks parties. There are those who are curious to know how colleagues live their private lives, but I'm not one of them. So long as a chap's doing his job well, I don't need to know the colour of his underwear, and Brendan was doing his job exceptionally well. Being a girl, Diana's more interested in people's home lives, and by then she was proving rather good at doing up our houses so I think her interest was piqued.

I was a little truculent the first time we went to Brendan's for drinks, because the Rugby World Cup final was on that afternoon, and since they lived on the other side of town, I was going to miss a fair amount of the game. Their house was inoffensive enough, part of a rather soulless compound in West London designed by a computer I should think. It had small windows, as though it were squinting to keep an eye on the world going by, a bit like Sherilyn herself, who had a tight wariness about her. I'm sure that made her very good at her job, but sometimes in her company I felt like I was waiting for a snake to blink. The inside of the house was pristine, as though considerable effort had gone into making sure everything matched everything else. I found it quite unnerving. Having been brought up in the country, Diana has a relaxed attitude to domestic interiors, and while the formal drawing room of her family home was dreadfully grand, everywhere else was covered in a fine film of dog hairs, and muddy gumboots leaned tipsily against each other by the external doors. As a result, although our houses are thoughtfully furnished and decorated, if a teacup gets left by the sofa overnight, no one panics. Brendan's house gave nothing away: no family photographs or objects that might have reflected the lives they'd lived, people they'd known; everything seemed to represent itself and its formal relationship to some grand plan rather than the amiable clutter of most people's lives.

There was no question of sitting down at their drinks parties: guests stood around like pins at a bowling alley holding exactly the right glass for exactly the right drink, inclining at exactly the right angle to take one of Sherilyn's canapés from her exactly organised platter. The wine was good, not that I'm much of a connoisseur, but like everything else, it didn't seem to be the result of a jolly experience, more a question of micro-planning. We've found some delightful reds on holidays in Tuscany, mostly for a couple of pounds a bottle, and we bring them back in the boot of the car to serve at our dinner parties in London. Along with the wines come the memories: the time our car got towed away by a pair of comic cops in Santa Croce; the time Toby taught the local children in the village to play cricket; the time Francis learned the Italian for 'I love you' so he could tell the little girl with the bows in her hair how he felt. He was three.

Brendan and Sherilyn could have been matching vases, like the pair on their sideboard that Diana told me were from Conran's and cost a fortune: they were empty vessels placed precisely to harvest maximum advantage. Diana was her usual emollient self and said the right things: she admired the paint finish on their walls, the rugs, their colour schemes, the icy garden, but later said she'd never seen anything quite so uninspired, quite so vacant. I've seen interiors like that in *Homes & Gardens* she said, It's like trying to buy good taste in a tin.

Although we went to their home several times, we never met any of the same people, and no one seemed to know anyone else. It was as though we were doing a rather solemn dance, performing all the steps in the prescribed order with no margin for a spontaneous gesture or witty response. Their invitations were always printed on good card, the sort that some people insist on displaying on mantelpieces as an insouciant boast about their social status. The arrival time was specified, as was the time of departure, and Diana and I used to time our appearance at *exactly* two and half minutes after the party started. We'd stop the car round the corner ten minutes before, having set our watches by the Greenwich pips, and allow forty seconds to slide round to the front of the house and park. We felt like mischievous children deliberately not washing our hands before dinner to see if the grown-ups would notice.

They didn't look like the kind of couple that would ever have children: kids are messy little creatures and you have to learn that the Ribena stain on the carpet is more than compensated for by the moist perfume of a sleepy child fitting around your chest like an extra pelt. In the early days, when Toby and Francis were still in the nest, I used to go to work sometimes with a smear of Marmite on my shirtfront, hugging it to me like membership of a secret fraternity, knowing I'd swelter all day with my jacket on, but never minding, never minding. The

Marmite smear was a promise to me down the decades into my dotage; I'd fed my boys well and in turn they'd feed me when I became frail.

In a curious way, although they were clearly joined not only at the hip but also at the ankle, knee and elbow, I couldn't imagine Brendan and Sherilyn having sex. It staggered me when that thought erupted in my head. I'm not in the habit of speculating about other people's sex lives but the two of them were like tidy outlines that you longed to fill in. Or scribble over. Sex is hardly a decorous activity: at its best, it's a sweaty exhalation, a jubilant shout, a titanic loss of control, and Brendan and Sherilyn came across like experimental specimens in a bell jar. In their presence you felt like you were standing in a controlled environment where some unseen machine filtered out the unwanted or the unexpected, ensuring that the temperature, atmosphere and bacterial flora conformed to some formalised grid. You emerged from the experience in exactly the same state as you entered.

We returned the hospitality, of course, though only in our London home. Gloucestershire was for intimates. Diana's terribly good at imagining how the guests will gel – I tease her she has a degree in social harmony – so they were invited with people who were affable enough, but disinclined to rub noses with their fellow guests. On the way to visit her elderly aunt Ivy, Mum used to warn us to be on our best behaviour, and although I didn't entirely know what best behaviour looked like, I did know it meant not being rambunctious or spilling things. Brendan and Sherilyn were never in danger of spilling things – the beans, for example – or being rambunctious, and I'd vaguely watch Sherilyn tilting her slightly over-blonde head this way and that to her neighbours at dinner, eating with the appetite of a gnat.

Despite Diana's growing up being butlered to death, we didn't stand on ceremony at home and guests helped themselves from the dishes on the table. The second time Brendan and Sherilyn came, Diana shot me a look when Sherilyn was serving herself and I watched – unobtrusively, of course – as she helped herself to peanut-sized portions of food, and organised it around the plate in discrete piles. It was rather as I imagined prison food to look like in its separate compartments – or airline fodder.

They always arrived first, punctually at the time they'd been invited, and brought vintage champagne and eye-wateringly expensive sweetmeats. Diana politely admired a frock Sherilyn wore on one occasion – which was slightly too tight for my taste, but then I'm no expert – and asked for the name of the designer. Diana being Diana, she managed to find frocks in the collection that were graceful and elegant, despite costing the GNP of a small African republic; she bought several and looked wonderful. She said afterwards that she only went into the shop because she was passing and was surprised that the designer was able to make clothes both for someone like her and for someone like Sherilyn.

I never warmed to Sherilyn, which troubled me initially because having been something of a class tourist myself, I reckon to be able to make some sort of contact with most people. With her, it was like reaching for something quite ordinary, like a knife or a fork, and banging your knuckles against a pane of perspex. You have a couple more goes until, blowing on the bruises, you give up and look for the cutlery in another drawer. She was never anything but polite, never challenging or controversial, smiled prettily at one's jokes, but it never felt like a response, more the logical result of a calculation. When I thought about it afterwards, I realised Brendan was the same. I'd been too distracted by his professional eagerness to notice his personal opacity. It didn't matter in business of course – you hardly want to find somebody sobbing at their desk over missing offshore tax breaks – but since I saw him from time to time at his home or mine, after a bit I noticed his impenetrable carapace.

There was only one occasion when his varnish crazed slightly. We were thrashing about in Thatcher's recession – this was the woman to whom I'd doggedly given my vote and who'd shafted us in return – and he was pretty much running the Receivership Department. Derek, the titular head, had gone on extended sick leave suffering from stress, and Brendan had slid effortlessly into his shoes. It was, not surprisingly, the busiest department in the firm at that time, and I made it my business to keep a weather eye on it. I'd frequently drop by unannounced. As I walked into his office that day, his usually well-groomed hair looked awry, as though he'd been holding his head in his hands. I said something banal like What are you working on? and his right hand reached for a rubber that was sitting by his phone. Large building company in Devon, he said, Gone under spectacularly. We've just been appointed receivers. As he spoke, he was shoving the rubber back and forth on the desk and something crept into his voice. He had an unexceptional accent, as most people do – standard middle-class London – but momentarily a West Country burr bent his vowels out of shape. Particular problems with it? I asked. No, no, he said, Just one among many. We'll have no builders left when this is over, I said, Might as well learn how to live in tents. He didn't smile.

We emerged more or less intact from the recession, though our economic base was narrower, but I found myself re-membering Jarrow, remembering Dad taking me to meet the marchers as they passed by. I was ten and inhabited a world where you could pretty much trust grown-ups to be big and strong, so the sight of two hundred gaunt, grey, dusty men tramping down the road in donated boots, their trousers held up with string, shook my world. It was one of the few times I remember my parents rowing, when Mum discovered that Dad had given the rent money to the marchers. In those terrible years there was always food on the table, though sometimes a meal consisted of potatoes and bread, but Mum had to take in sewing from the big house up on the hill.

This time round my family were safe, buttressed by investments and pensions and properties, but I found myself playing sports more than usual, as though I were perpetually on the brink of losing a game. Brendan's athletic build made me suppose that he too was a sportsman, so I invited him to my club to introduce him to real tennis, something I'd never been able to persuade my boys to do. They were far more interested in competitive drinking. I liked the obscurity of the game, liked the feeling that it had long roots, that I was engaging in something ancient and venerable. I suppose I must also confess that participating in the sport was another way of participating in the upper-middle-class world into which I had ascended.

Brendan's gear looked pristine, as though it had only lately emerged from its packaging, and I lent him the second racquet I'd brought along. I knew him to be a quick learner, and he seemed to absorb the rules of the game and its strange terms: the dedans window, the penthouses, the double bounce that provokes a chase. He looked slightly nervous as we went on court, so I said Don't worry, you'll pick it up in no time. He didn't. He played so badly I began to wonder if he was deliberately throwing the game out of some sort of misplaced deference. I took him patiently through the rules again, but he seemed to have no idea how to serve, how to hit a ball, how to track a return, and displayed absolutely no tactical skills. In the ordinary way, there was nothing remarkable about his gait, but on court he lumbered around like a walrus on dry land. I began deliberately to miss the ball from time to time after a bit because I wanted to avoid humiliating him, but his limbs were so uncoordinated they could have belonged to four different men. The match usually continues until one player wins six games even if his opponent has five, but it was too painful to watch Brendan's face blotching with shame, so I called a halt when we'd staggered through four. Well done, I said, putting out my hand, It's a difficult game to play first time. His enormous hand felt boneless. Never was much of a sportsman, he said, and shook his head. Let's go and shower, I said, Then I'll buy you a drink.

He looked slightly shifty when I saw him at work a couple of days later, and I wondered if I should say something, but we were suddenly overwhelmed by a major shipping company sinking, so the moment passed. When the economy started to perk up we breathed a corporate sigh of relief and were able to return to the expansion plans we'd had before we realised Thatcher had never quite grasped what monetarism meant. The plans now included Brendan, since he'd performed so well in extremis, and we wanted to reward him. Up till then, London had handled all our British receiverships, but we decided to open a regional department in Manchester, and the job clearly had Brendan's name on it. If he made a good fist of it, I told him, we intended to offer him a partnership. It's safe to say he was pleased. His girlfriend had also kept her head over that period and Personnel promoted her to a position in the Manchester office so they could move together. I thought they made a formidable team and said as much to Brendan. I'm glad you think so, he said, We're about to make the team official by getting married. We'd be honoured if you and Mrs Berwick-Grant would come to our wedding.

Another card was delivered a month or so later, this time gold-edged and embossed. Strangely for a couple who seemed so punctilious where conventions were concerned, there was no parent formally inviting us, but we thought maybe they were all dead. Diana looked at the Harrods wedding list and snorted. God, it's grandiose, she said, These people really do have ideas above their station. I always hated it when her background burst into the present like a sudden throwback, but I said nothing. I don't know what we gave them, but since Diana was in charge of the choosing, I'm sure it was tasteful.

They married the week before they were due to move north. We were invited to the wedding breakfast, but not the ceremony itself, so we imagined the registry office would probably be crammed with their families. When we arrived at the venue for the reception, we were surprised to find it was an expensive restaurant in Soho, with only just enough room for the few guests they'd invited. There couldn't have been more than thirty of us, but Diana told me later she'd counted twenty-five. She was rather taken aback, but secretly I wished our own wedding had been of such a scale and simplicity. There were a number of colleagues among the guests, one couple who had been at one of their drinks parties (crashing bores, both of them) and a little gaggle of people who moved around in a clump and looked like family. My family, not Diana's.

Like their drinks parties, this was about as spontaneous as a Nuremberg rally, and apart from Brendan toasting his bride, it was speech-free. No best man telling tales about disreputable behaviour – not that I could imagine Brendan doing anything disreputable – no father of the bride dissolving into maudlin reminiscence of his curly-haired darling's first steps – nothing, in short, that might have given us a clue as to what pulsed under their skins. There was vintage rosé champagne to begin, and a procession of quite exquisite canapés served by waitresses dressed like joke French maids. We talked mainly to my colleagues, but just before we sat down for the meal, a member of the family group detached herself and wove over to us, knocking a floral arrangement off one of the tables as she stumbled against it. She was shambolically drunk. I'm not priggish about booze, but that degree of inebriation, especially in a woman, is ugly, and I had difficulty in understanding much of what she was saying. She stood just slightly too close to me, and when I took a discreet step backwards, she followed. Whether by accident or design, the top buttons of her blouse had popped open, exposing a disquieting quantity of cleavage; as fast as I averted my gaze, she shifted position so that her breasts hove into view again. Fortunately after a while she ran out of steam and hiccuped back to the family, who closed around her like a fist. Diana and I went back to our own people.

We left as soon as we could without causing offence, and Diana fulminated all the way home in the cab about 'that ghastly tart', whom she seemed to think I'd done something to encourage. Exactly three days later, we received a thank-you card for our 'generous gift', with best regards from Mr and Mrs Gutteridge. They hoped they might entertain us when next we came to Manchester, and we'd certainly be served coffee in what we'd given them. I assumed it was a china service of some sort.

Brendan did magnificently well in Manchester and we made him a partner two years later. I wondered if he'd write to his parents on the firm's notepaper as I did when first I appeared on it, because a chap needs to feel his family's proud of him, but of course I didn't ask. We communicated largely through his departmental reports, so I had no idea what was happening to him personally, but Diana and I were much taken up at the time with Toby's decision to grow his hair in dreadlocks, declare himself a celibate homosexual and join an animal liberation group. He was also nesting in trees. He seemed to think this would stop the building of new roads. That was a shock to the system, but a stroll in the sunshine compared with the revelation that our receivership partner in Manchester was a child-killer. As was his sharp wife.

It's strange, you wait all your life for a murderer and then two come along all at once.

★

There was a rather fierce woman who ran the corner shop at the end of our street when I was growing up, and one day the shop was boarded up and I had to walk three streets over to spend my pocket money. Mum told me she'd retired and gone off to live by the seaside, but years later when I'd gone off myself to university, she told me she'd been murdered by her son. I remembered him. He was terribly nice to me and let me beat him at tiddlywinks. He caved his mother's head in with a crowbar over some burned toast. Perhaps that should have taught me something.

I set up a formal mentoring scheme some little while later, before I retired, because I was committed to fostering ambition in young men – and young women – whose backgrounds had disadvantaged them. I insisted, however, on psychological profiling before we took them on.

Of course I read about what happened to Brendan and his wife. Mr and Mrs Gutteridge. I saw the photographs.

Kaye

I'd been thinking of jacking it in. Coming to the end of the road. Becoming a market gardener. I'd been living on a steady diet of pain and misery for too many years. Sometimes at the end of an especially trying week I'd be driving past a newspaper billboard bleating about some new atrocity in Palestine and I'd think, So what? And that's disgraceful. That's burnout. Over time, and without you noticing it, your sensitivities get blunted and your responses become mechanical. I'd get home and Alex would have had a bad day and I'd put on Caring Voice Number Seventy-Nine and say Oh my poor darling, how wretched. Give me a minute and I'll come and massage your legs, but I'd be thinking, Oh for Christ's sake, get a grip. I used to joke that at least he had the pleasures of being paralytic without the penance of the hangover, but he'd had a sense of humour bypass by then. He'd been off work for two months and we'd knocked around from one clinic to another but were no nearer to finding out what was causing the paralysis in his legs. He'd been quite chipper at first, but as time dragged on he was becoming increasingly dispirited and I was beginning to think he needed to go on antidepressants. I talked things through with him of course, but it didn't help his state of mind and sometimes I'd think, I'm too knackered for this, just take some tablets, will you? I'd come home after a day of dealing with distress and grief and abuse and there it was in my own home. Perhaps abuse is a bit strong, but sometimes it felt like he was bludgeoning me into the ground with his depression.

And then Gemma was doing her 'A' levels and being about as

bloody as an adolescent can be. Not that I didn't understand, of course I did, but when she went for the jugular for the seventeenth time before breakfast, I'd think, Oh call in Child Protection and take her away, for Christ's sake! That's a laugh. I *am* Child Protection. Perhaps I should set up a Parent Protection team and take myself into care. Dump myself in a Home with other parents of stroppy teenagers and we'd drink Cyprus sherry in the shopping centre and go shoplifting. Have fun behaving badly. I could barely remember what having fun was. We'd probably had fun when we were teachers, before I changed tack and Alex took his first management job in education. That's nineteen years ago. Time flies when you're hacking away at the coalface with your Social Services standard issue pickaxe.

I'd wanted more children, but it just didn't happen. I'm an only child and I didn't want that for Gemma because I understand all too well how isolated a singleton can feel. I understand. I understand. I under *fucking* stand. Sometimes I wish I could live a whole day – a whole week – in an Understanding-Free Zone. I could roll around in pigshit ignorance not thinking about anybody else's feelings or circumstances or future or past. I could live my life at the same fluffy-duffy superficial level as everyone else, relieved of the compulsion to repair every broken human being I encounter.

But the job had its moments, like when you'd worked really hard with a kid and her parents so she could go back to live with them and you were pretty certain it would be OK. Everyone's really grateful for your help and you think, Well, there's one less kid destined for a lifetime's incarceration or addiction. That's the pay-off. It was a shame I hadn't climbed higher at work, but what with raising Gemma and all the moves because of Alex's job, I'd got a bit stuck in the front line. But I knew I was considered to be reliable and experienced, so in a way it was a surprise when I was allocated the Gutteridge case because it was low-level routine. But there were two absentees in the department – one having a breakdown, the other more training – so it dropped into my lap.

I hated Tamley. It's swimming with nouveaux riches busily patronising any poor sod who reminds them of where they came from. Sounds a perverse thing to say now under the circumstances, but when I saw the address I remember thinking that I'd love to find something shitty there, because it would serve them right for their serial snottiness. God knows it's just as likely to happen there as anywhere else. I have to keep trotting this one out to friends and acquaintances, tedious though it is. It doesn't just happen in crappy estates, it could be going on in Windsor Castle too. The Duke of Edinburgh looks like he could give her a slap if she stepped out of line, but if he did, mysteriously he wouldn't find himself pilloried on the front page of the *Daily Mail*.

It's not that I didn't take the case seriously, but there was a lot going on that summer and I suppose it *was* low priority in some ways. I'd had an adoption and two fosterings break down – one really badly, suspected sexual abuse – and on top of that it seemed like I'd suddenly crashed into the menopause. No warning, just criminally punishing hot flushes and odd moods, and I'd put on a stone and a half in a couple of months. There wasn't much time in my schedule for exercise or eating properly, but I was reasonably careful so it was galling looking in the mirror and seeing this big, untidy, middle-aged woman. Especially with Gemma so slender and beautiful – and, I have to say, never failing to point out how fat I was getting. You might have thought she'd have offered some support, but oh dear me no, that's my job. Total Family Support System Inc., that's me.

It was a month or so after I got the papers that I did my first visit because what with these other cases blowing up, a disastrous holiday in France and the Change, my plate was pretty much overflowing. We'd just come back from ten days of non-stop French rain in a crappy gîte, England suddenly decided that it was, in fact, Bermuda, and threw one of those heatwaves that makes you feel that doing your teeth is too much like hard work. Nothing I put on fitted properly, all my clothes felt too bloody heavy, and the Gutteridges were the fourth visit I'd had to do that morning.

She came to the door wearing some floaty silky thing – minute little creature, looking cool and groomed – and after we'd been talking for a bit he loomed up behind her. This is Mr Gutteridge, my husband, she said, He's got a day off today and we're going out for lunch presently. Oh, I said, How lovely. Where are you planning on going? The Hyacinth, she said, We often pop in there. Mario, the maître d', keeps a special table for us. Lunch at The Hyacinth would cost me about a week's salary and I thought of my cheese and pickle sandwich turning to mush in the car. Lucky you, I said and told them why I was there, usual spiel about legal obligations, and she seemed mildly shocked. I looked at my notes again of course, in preparation for the trial, and I'd written, *Mrs Gutteridge looked slightly taken aback when I told her why I was there.* That did alert me – though obviously not enough – because if someone's being told they're suspected of mistreating a child, there's usually a bigger reaction, like, *How could anyone do that?* Or, *That's a dreadful thing to say, I adore Kevin/Rickie/ Mary-Lou.* Or Samantha.

When I look back on it – and Christ knows I look back on it all the time – I wonder at how gullible I was that time, because when I asked them if I could see Samantha, just for the record, she said she was playing at the rec with her friends and I just went Oh, OK. She said she had lots of friends – Not surprising, he said, She's a sunny little girl and her mates come knocking for her all the time. She was only three and a half then so she'd have to have been with much older friends, but for some reason

I didn't pursue it. I can only excuse it by saying my brain must have shut down with the heat and the flushes, though I think at that point the two things were virtually indistinguishable.

I did look into the house down the corridor though, and I'd seen into the living room as I came up the path, so I had some idea of their circumstances. It looked like they'd simply thrown money at it. There was a flimsy chair in the hall that I recognised from some design magazine or other, and the furniture was careful to match the muted colours on the walls. Altogether the decor was determinedly perfect: not a scratch or a smudge or a spot anywhere. I suppose that's what she looked like too: perfectly turned out, not a bleached hair out of place, not beautiful really, but well polished.

I reported back to the allocation meeting, but the whole place was in such terminal chaos the second half of that year, what with murderous cuts in funding and people resigning left right and centre, it was all we could do to supervise the most urgent cases. But there was a quiet nagging at the back of my head about Samantha. Something wasn't quite right, so when I was passing around Christmas, one of my clients having just cancelled on me, I thought I'd pop in. He answered the door this time and was perfectly pleasant and polite. Invited me in because it was perishing outside, so I got into the house and we had a cup of tea in the kitchen. I noticed some very expensive stereo equipment mounted on the wall, but the room didn't have the feel of somewhere that was used very much: all the surfaces were gleaming and containers had been strategically placed to look good, but not anywhere a real cook might have used them. That's probably the kind of thing I notice because I love cooking.

We chatted very amiably – he said he'd been teaching Samantha to read, that she was a clever little thing and he was terribly proud of her. He said most of the neighbours were really nice and loved his daughter to bits, but there was this one woman, lived up the other end, whom nobody liked. Charlotte someone-or-other. She stirred up trouble, he said, and she was always making false allegations about other people in the Crescent. She'd accused the woman next door to them of mistreating her dogs and reported her to the RSPCA. The neighbour didn't have any dogs, he said. We sat on either side of the breakfast bar on these stools with impossibly spindly legs, like overdesigned insects. He was such a big man, it was a miracle that they could support him. My bum was flapping off the edges, but he looked utterly comfortable. His hands grabbed my attention. They were huge meaty things wrapped round the porcelain cup he'd served the tea in, and I was touched by the incongruity of the strength in his fingers and the fragility of the china. You'd be safe in those hands, I thought.

He said Samantha was a very sporty child, although she'd not been very well the last couple of days. She'd taken to sleeping in their bed recently – he loved it, he said, the family all cosied up in bed together – and she'd caught the flu bug that Sherilyn had been fighting off. With Alex drooping around at home like a bit of old lettuce, the combination of strength and tenderness in this man was quite alluring. I began to think it was a pity he was married.

He'd said she was upstairs in bed asleep – called her Sammy – so as I was leaving and passed the stairs, I said I'll just go up and see her, shall I? Then I'll be able to close the file and I won't bother you any more. I don't know how he did it, because he was coming out of the kitchen behind me, but as I went up the first couple of stairs he was suddenly ahead of me. He was a big man, and standing two or three steps above me, he was quite intimidating. He didn't raise his voice, just told me she really wasn't very well and he didn't want to disturb her because she was having broken nights with the high fever she was running. I wasn't going to push past him because I thought it probably made sense not to wake her up and anyway he'd seemed such a loving father in the kitchen. That was the moment I let Samantha down. That's the way I see it. I let her down and she died. She'd have been four the day after I went round.

The department decided in its wisdom to computerise all the records after that Christmas, so for a while we didn't know which end was up. Files went missing – some of them permanently – or turned up muddled with other files, so you'd get three-quarters of one case topped and tailed with a quarter of another. Samantha seemed like she was one of the permanently lost children until a colleague attached to a GP practice found her in the dead files box at the surgery. She *was* dead by then, in fact. It arrived in the morning post at the office and because I was racing off to court I just bundled all of my letters in the car to open later. In a morning adjournment I looked at it and was suddenly reminded of her. It resurrected the faint puzzlement about her parents' reactions so I decided to check up after court.

The house was locked and bolted when I arrived, no one answered the door and when I went down the side just to check, there was one window on the first floor with the curtains drawn. I didn't think anything of it. I was pretty whacked at the time – I'd just started the HRT and it hadn't really kicked in yet – and I remember having this envious fantasy that they were all off on holiday somewhere exotic: Mummy, Daddy and kiddie frolicking together on a sunny beach. Seemed like the kind of thing they'd do and make sure everyone knew about it afterwards.

Then the sky caved in. When she was found, our department was obviously consulted and it didn't take them long to get to me. On the day itself I went into meltdown and was sent home. Alex and Gemma did their best, but I was inconsolable. All those years, all those children, all those successes, and now I'd killed a child. There was some stupid graffiti once, *Save A Child – Kill A Social Worker*, and at that moment I felt like a murderer. I was so scrambled I wasn't making sense to either of them, but I remember Gemma putting her arms around me and crying when she found me howling over the washing basket. I did a lot of that in the following weeks. I really wasn't crying, or not crying you'd recognise anyway – I was howling like some dog gone mad. The facts of the matter were so bald, so unadorned, it was like I'd been flayed and someone was pouring vinegar on my flesh. The past and future vanished and the here and now was poisoning me.

I didn't notice at the time, but when I've looked back at those first ghastly days, Alex made this miraculous recovery. Picked up his bed and walked. Ironically the results of the last neurological tests came through the following week; everything was normal, so we were back to the *'well, it's a virus'* territory. I couldn't have cared less.

Then the phone calls started, and the letters, and the stones through the window. I've heard language like that millions of times before of course. I've *understood* where it's coming from. When the death threats began we changed our number and tried to pack Gemma off to my mum's, but amazingly she wanted to stay. This hissing, spitting, viperish teenager said she wanted to look after me, as though she'd suddenly turned into the mum and I'd become the daughter. My own mother did her best, but I could hear her accusations behind the concern: *Why* didn't you persevere? *Why* didn't you save her? And I had no answer for her or the police when they came to take my statement or Marigold, my boss, when she and I met. She was very good, made all the right noises about We've all been there. We've all done that, but I could tell she was thinking, No I haven't and No I didn't. There'd have to be an internal inquiry of course, in the spirit of openness, but I knew all my colleagues were saying to themselves There but for the grace of God when I walked through the office. Which I didn't do very often, because I was suspended.

The press found out who I was and where I was almost immediately and the nicer neighbours told me they'd been door-stepped but hadn't said anything – honestly. But someone had. They ran features on us: 'Would You Trust Your Children With *This* Woman?' with pictures of me – Christ knows how they got them – looking variously like a camp guard and an itinerant dipso. Another piece hinted that Gemma hung out with a bunch of dropouts who took drugs in the city centre and were into petty crime. When I quizzed her, she said she vaguely knew one of the kids, but *absolutely* didn't hang around with dossers – what kind of girl did I think she was? Before this broke I'd have had my suspicions, but at this point it was vital to stick together so I let it pass. I didn't have the energy to suspect anything anyway.

And then Alex, poor Alex, he was crucified. I tried to make a joke about it like So that's what you get for marrying me, but it all fell horribly flat. 'Malingering Husband In Samantha Case' was one of the milder ones, but they'd got hold of photos of the time he finished a marathon and implied he was throwing this fake paralysis so he could run a business from home. What business would that be exactly? His friend Pete, who *does* run a business, was in and out of the house because he's a good and supportive friend and they threw two and two together and made ninety-five. And the fact that Pete does business in Colombia – tractor parts, actually – somehow added up to the implication that it was drugs. Pete's a lay preacher, for Christ's sake.

We took legal advice, but we neither had the money to sue nor the stomach to fight, so there are probably people out there who still see me as a child-killer, Gemma as a drug-crazed delinquent and Alex as the drug baron who supplied her. A family to breed from, as Rumpole would say.

They held the internal inquiry. I'd given evidence to those before so I knew how they worked, but it's not exactly the same thing when it's you they're investigating. It wasn't just me of course, it was the usual guff about procedures and protocols, but it damn well felt like me. They could have asked me how often I have sex – not a lot, actually – and I wouldn't have blinked. My whole life, my whole raison d'être, was under the microscope. In the end, they concluded I hadn't been derelict, only overworked, that the department hadn't been poorly managed, only underfunded, and everyone's honour was preserved. Except for me. I became an ex-social worker in my mind from the moment they found Samantha. Ex-teacher, ex-social worker, ex-mother next year when Gemma goes off, and what if Alex decides he's had enough? I'm a pain in the tits to live with, boring as hell, fatter and more depressed by the day, only one topic of conversation: I wouldn't blame him. I'd leave me too.

Then I'd be alone. Not quite in Samantha's league, but alone anyway. There'd be no point in going on.

I try not to think like that.

Alun

It was brass monkey's outside, that Monday. Mam used to call me Chilly Willy when I was growing up, even though my name's not Willy. She was right though, I am a chilly morsel, so it's as though my bones remember the weather that day. I was on earlies. I'd been on lates for nearly six months before that, so Sheila and I hardly saw each other, what with her going back to work part-time and everything. But we'd had a family break in Lanzarote, which was fantastic in spite of the hotel mucking up the booking and putting the kids in a room down the corridor. They were ever so apologetic and gave us a couple of bottles of wine, so I said Not to worry then. Sheila looked like she was going to have a go, but I looked at her and I said Your luck might be in, girl, you never know, sort of wiggling my eyebrows suggestively and she calmed down. Her luck *was* in, as a matter of fact. It was like we'd just met for the first time.

I remember that first time, clear as anything. I was on the front desk and this little thing came in looking like a terrified kitten, all huge green eyes and fluffy hair. Because of that first day it's what I call her now when we're alone – my little kitty cat. She hasn't got a nickname for me. I thought she was a punter so I said Hello, madam, can I be of any assistance at all? I was gobsmacked when she said she was DC Harris and she was starting today. I knew I looked surprised so I quickly made a joke of it and said Are you sure, madam? She pulled out her warrant card and I said Only joking and buzzed her in.

That Monday, I jumped on the alarm clock when it went off – didn't want to interrupt Sheila's beauty sleep. I woke up straight

44

away like I always do, no messing about – eyes open, quick stretch, up you get, boyo, straighten the duvet – and looked back down at the wife. She wraps her arms around her head when she sleeps which makes me want to stroke her and stroke her till she purrs. I went round to her side of the bed as usual, kissed her on the head as usual, said Love you as usual and she said Mmmm, bye as usual. Sometimes I wish she'd say Love you too, but never mind.

I don't usually go into the kids' room because they're light sleepers, but that Monday I did because it was Katy's first day in the nursery class at big school. She'd been dead jumpy all weekend and I told her her big brother David would look after her in the playground so she'd be fine. He's a bit of a wild child, David, so I thought it would do him good to take some responsibility. I bent over Katy and kissed her and wished her luck for the day, but I said it in my head so I wouldn't wake her up. I settled the duvet around her – she's very lively like in her sleep – and patted her shoulder. How they do grow up on you! It was a bit of a surprise having kids in my forties, but Sheila's that bit younger and she wanted them. You can't refuse a girl kids.

I made myself coffee for the Thermos – canteen coffee's undrinkable – and checked the uniform and the shoes in the hall mirror on my way out. Mam used to say Look at the shoes, Alun, and you'll see the man. Da's shoes were always filthy.

I'm always at the station fifteen minutes before the shift begins, don't see the point being late myself. I try to set an example to the younger officers because some of them don't seem to care, quite frankly. Wasn't like that when I started. Strange finding myself the older generation, but someone's got to maintain standards. Like bad language, for example. I won't be doing with it and I like to think people watch their mouths when I'm around.

Usual banter when I arrived – Hello Sarge. Hello Alun. Quiet night? Yeah, yeah, just about managed to keep the lid on things.

Couple of rowdies pub chuck-out time – cooling off in the cells, the little darlings – burglar alarm went off at Satchell's midnight and some old nutter phoned, wittering on about how her cat hasn't come in. What we supposed to do about that, eh? Dunno, keeps you on your toes though, doesn't it? Becks in yet? He called, coming in later, says his big end's gone so he's stuck there till he's towed. You've got to be kidding me – Becks's got a big end? Yeah – so I'm sending you out with Suzanne. Righto Sarge.

He's a good laugh, Mike – Sarge. I tried for sergeant a few times ten years ago. Didn't make it, but I like to get out and about helping the public, and I'm due for retirement in a couple of years. Probably go into security work. Bit of variety. Sooz is all right, she can take a joke, so I said How's your big end, Sooz? when she arrived. I'm pretty sure she smiled but she turned to speak to Mike so I couldn't see. Couldn't hear what she was saying, either, she was sort of whispering like, but Mike said No, it's only one day. Put up with it. He's firm but fair, Mike, and I respect that. Cath called out Alun, call on line one – says she's your missus or something. Which one would that be? I said, joking a bit, and we laughed. I picked up the phone and Sheila had Katy with her who just wanted to talk to her da before she set off to big school. I told her she's my special princess and it's going to be lovely there – all she has to do is smile her big Katy smile and they'll love her as much as I do. And don't forget to say please and thank you and excuse me, I said.

Brought a prickle to the back of my eyes, actually. Didn't feel like that when David went off to school, but then boys are different. Don't need your protection like girls. Megan – that's my sister, Megan – she wanted protecting. Mam said Look after her, Alun, she's only a girl. I didn't understand it at first on account of she was five years older than me, but later I did. It's like with Sooz – she was half a head taller than me and she was a big girl like, but I'd still look out for her on patrol.

She doesn't talk much, Sooz, but I was used to that. I'd seen her chatting, very lively like, in the canteen with other officers – even CID – but she didn't chat in the car. Liked to keep her mind clear on patrol probably. Good thing too, because you never know what's going to happen. You've got to be alert. Be prepared, like the Brownies.

When the call came through we were just parked up for a mid-morning break. No sense in going back to the canteen, I said, I've got coffee here, but she wanted tea so she'd gone into this little café. Routine call, burglar alarm going off on a house in Tamley, so I didn't hassle Sooz when she came back to the car even though she'd been gone quite a while. Lovely area, Tamley, very quiet – not that anywhere's very noisy round here – mostly well-off residents. We shot off to investigate – well, not shot off exactly, because it wasn't an emergency call, probably the wind had set it off or something – and pulled up outside the house in Quinley Crescent. What I remember is, just as I got out of the car the sun came out, that lovely sharp blue sunlight that you get in spring sometimes, and my heart lifted. It was the kind of light that says All's right with the world. Just count your blessings, thank your lucky stars, there's plenty worse off in Africa. I smiled at Sooz but she didn't notice, she was off up the front path and looking in the windows of the house. I thought she'd approached the house a bit quick, so I said Be careful, Sooz. I could be wrong, but I think she muttered *Suzanne* under her breath.

As I went towards the house, I noticed there were locks on all the windows and internal bars on the glass door panels. There's people who take their security seriously, I thought. No messing about. They had a good alarm system – Banham's, top of the range – and it shouldn't have gone off for nothing, so it wanted checking. I was just going to join Sooz at the house when this woman came up the path behind me and said Good morning,

Officer, I'm Charlotte Tomlinson, it was me who made the call. Is everything all right? She had one of those BBC voices and was very neat and tidy, apart from her nails, which were short and grubby like a workman's. Looks fine to me, madam, I said, It's a fortress up there – wish everybody was that careful. I was worried, she said, That alarm. It's been going off for thirteen and a half hours. Crikey, I thought, you've been counting, but all I said was Thanks for the info, madam. We're checking it out. You pop on home and we'll let you know if we find anything untoward. I'm sure we won't. Thank you, Officer, she said, Can I get you a cup of tea? Just had some coffee, madam, I said, We'll see you later.

As the woman walked off, Sooz called out Everything OK here, Alun, just going round the back. I picked up a bit of speed and joined her. Went through this garden that looked like a chessboard and as we turned towards the house, there it was. Patio doors opened. It's been forced, Sooz said, somewhat stating the obvious because there was a big dent in the frame, and I said Righto then, let's have a bit of a look-see.

It was a lovely house – my wife would have sold her nan for a house like that and she's very fond of her nan. It was all deep-pile carpets, silky curtains and the kind of soft leather furniture you'd need a second mortgage for; not the sort of house you'd have animals and children in. Not like ours, which is a bit tatty around the edges, what with the kids and the dogs. Burglar must've been disturbed, I said to Sooz as we looked around the lounge, because there was nothing out of place as far as I could see, none of the mess burglars usually leave behind. We went through the lounge and checked out the kitchen. It was all brushed stainless steel, but very new and untouched-looking. I'd noticed some expensive hi-fi equipment in the lounge, and there was more in here too. Must love their music, I said to Sooz, But you wouldn't want to get toast crumbs in there, would you? She grunted and we went out to the hall. There was a downstairs loo there – probably call it a cloakroom in these houses – and a fiddly little chair by the phone table. Wouldn't have survived Sooz's big end, I thought, but I didn't say anything.

Let's check upstairs, said Sooz, Give it a quick once-over and we can shut that posh cow up. I thought her language was a bit OTT – the posh cow hadn't done anything to us and she couldn't help the way she talked – but I didn't say anything. Sooz can be rather fierce sometimes and we had the rest of the shift to get through. But as we went up the stairs something changed. Sooz and I looked at each other, professional instinct kicking in. This isn't right, she said. It must have been the smell. Downstairs it had been quite clean-smelling, like polish or air freshener, though even there there'd been a sort of undertone of something else, but up here there was a smell that got stronger as we got to the top landing. When I wrote my statement later I did my best to describe it, but there aren't any good enough words for it. I know I'm not good with words, but it was the stink of evil. Of the devil. It smelled like when you find a piece of meat you've bought days ago and forgot to put in the fridge. I noticed the locks straight away – I suppose even a civilian would, it's pretty strange to have bolts and padlocks on an internal door – and pointed them out to Sooz. Yup, she said, I saw them. We'd better check all the rooms up here, she said, You start at that end, I'll start down there and we'll meet in the middle. The padlocked door was in the middle.

My end was easy: study with loads of expensive computer equipment in it, double bedroom – looked like a spare room – shower. When we met outside the middle door Sooz told me she'd found a large bedroom and an en suite bathroom, all immaculate. The smell was overpowering right there and I pulled out my hankie to put it over my nose. I offered it to Sooz first, but she shook her head and covered her nose with her hand.

We'd better get in there, she said, Shall we call Fire? No, I said, Just call for backup, because I'd remembered the bolt cutters in the car. I'd got them in a boot sale a couple of weeks before and Charlie at the garage said he'd sharpen them up for me. They might do the trick, I thought, so I said Just a sec, I'm popping out to get something from the car. There was another Mrs Noseybags, some other bloody neighbour I suppose, by the car. Is everything all right, Officer? she said. Everything under control, madam, I said, trying to keep my voice even, but I think it was wobbling a bit and my heart was doing its best to escape from my chest. As I went to the boot, I said Move along now, madam, and I knew I wasn't sounding polite, but I didn't have time for good manners.

The cutters were a bit manky and I couldn't make them work at first. Couldn't quite get the right angle or maybe my hands were too sweaty to hold them level, so Sooz said Let me have a go and she got through them, bam, bam, bam, bam. Four padlocks on four industrial-sized bolts. She was in the room first because she'd done the cutting. I didn't plan it that way. If I'd been thinking straight I'd have made sure I was the first one in because it might have been dangerous, but the stink was muddling my brain. She sort of gasped and groaned all at once so I pushed past her to see what was going on. There wasn't much light in the room because the curtains were drawn, but they weren't pulled right across on one side. And I saw this little girl. What had been a little girl. In this wooden cage thing, like some animal. A tiny, stinking, rotting animal. Her legs were drawn up to her chest and her bony arms were around her knees like she was hugging them to keep warm. Her hair was all matted and her toenails and fingernails had curled over or broken off. She wasn't wearing much. I must have been in shock because I didn't notice Sooz going over to the window to open the curtains, but the sound of the rings on the pole felt like someone dragging a knife across my head. I think I took a step forwards because then I saw the child's face more clearly and that's what did me in. Her head was resting back against the cage so that her mouth had fallen open and she looked like she was screaming. Like she was screaming for someone, anyone, her mam, her da, anyone, to come and rescue her. And someone, some bastard, some *cunt*, had left her there. Had put her in the cage, locked the door and fucked off. Sooz was beginning to ask if I was all right, but I was gone. Passed out. Right there. I've never fainted before, sort of thought it was what girls did, but it was like my brains were scooped out, like it was too much to keep on looking, keep on smelling, keep on feeling, so I just lost it.

By the time I came round, Sooz had been down to the kitchen to fetch me a glass of water. I needed to drink something but it felt like broken glass going down my throat because it came from the monsters who'd done this. You didn't have to be a CID genius to work out it had to be the parents. I sat there on the floor, *cunt cunt cunt cunt* going through my head like a train. I never normally used that word, but it was like all the ordinary rules were out the window. If this could happen, anything goes. I think I was moaning – don't know really, my brains and my body had got separated – and Sooz came over and held me. I'd always thought of her as a bit of a tough nut, not much of a lady like Sheila or my mam, but I think I was rocking backwards and forwards and she put her arms around my shoulders. I was close enough to smell her perfume and feel her chest and it was very soft and I started sobbing without tears, just sobbing like out-of-control hiccups.

Then all hell broke loose: more of our lot, forensic, SOCOs, medics, ambulances, everyone and their bloody aunty swarming through the house and cordoning off the garden. Two ambulances, one for her, one for me. I've been in lots of ambulances before – when Mam got ill, taking Sheila to have her babies, going to hospital with RTA casualties – but not on my own account. Never for me. Thought I was invincible. They took me to St Matthew's. Sheila turned up shortly after. I was still in Casualty in a screened-off bit and when she came in she said, Alun, I heard all about it, love, and that set me off again and I kept saying Katy, Katy, Katy and she said She's fine, Alun, she's fine, Sally's picking her up from school and you'll come home and we'll have tea together and she'll tell you all about her day. Bet she's had the time of her life, you know what a sociable little thing she is. But I didn't go home, not then anyway, because they wanted to keep me under observation for a bit. I hate the smell of hospitals, but at least it temporarily blocked out the smell of that room.

I insisted on going back in to the station a few days later, against doctor's orders, because I needed to be part of it all. I couldn't be, not really, because I'd been signed off sick, but I wanted to be around something solid, somewhere my feet touched the ground. That's how come I was there when they brought them in. They'd found them in South America. There wasn't any extradition treaty but they came back voluntarily, everyone was amazed. They said when they picked them up they behaved as though there was nothing wrong. What's the problem, Officer? they said. They strolled into the station, brown as berries, fit and well: they could have been popping into a bar for a cocktail. She was tiny, like a teenager, and well got-up, as Mam would say. Blonde hair all piled up at the top, and elegant clothes just that bit too tight, but expensive-looking. Her lipstick was bright red and sticky like she was going Watch your step, boyo, or I'll have you for breakfast. And he was huge – you'd have taken him for a football hooligan except he was dressed in this tasteful suit that practically smelled of money. Bob and Cheryl were on either side of them as they came in holding hands like young lovers, looking straight ahead as though they were in a world of their own. Like nothing could touch them. My head felt like a balloon suddenly pumped up too full of water and I must have jumped to my feet because someone – it might have been Suzanne, actually, she'd been around a lot – held my arm and pushed me down and said Steady, Alun, let it go.

I couldn't let it go. You can't let go of something that's stapled to your brain. I managed to give evidence at the trial, fuck knows how. Doctor stuffed me full of pills that wiped out my emotions but left me with enough brain cells to give my evidence in chief and deal with the bastard briefs defending Samantha's killers. Saying her name always set me off again because it meant she existed, she was just a little girl like Katy and they snuffed her out. I stayed on in court after I'd given evidence and watched them. They held hands all the way through like they were Siamese twins. Like they couldn't be divided, even when the jury found them guilty. Didn't take long. Six hours and they were back – bang – guilty. Life sentence, no problem, but how long's that really going to be? Samantha's life was four years, three months and two days.

My life's over. The job was my life, and that's down the shithole. Early retirement on medical grounds. They got me a nice shrink – older lady with lots of grey hair, let me talk. Talking's fine, but it doesn't alter the fact that I couldn't do anything for Samantha, and it doesn't stop the dreams. The worst are when I'm the killer. I've got Katy around the throat and her life's in my hands and I'm going to end it. And I wake up thinking it's all my fault, and Sheila's always there, don't know how she sticks me, she's always there, saying It's OK, ducky, it's OK, I love you. But it's not OK.

Brendan and Sherilyn

I loved him the first time I saw him.

It was as shocking as cresting a sand dune in the desert and seeing your reflection in the cobalt-blue waters of a lagoon. As disconcerting as a teetotaller discovering a taste for alcohol. I'd read the books, seen the films, heard the idle chatter around the water cooler at work, but they could have been discussing extraterrestrial life forms. Love wasn't part of my vocabulary, nor was there any need to slip it in. I'd observe other people's relationships like laboratory cultures in a petrie dish: I could see the swirls and spikes but they were of scientific interest only. People seemed yoked together by difference and all I needed was me. I was the same as me. When I saw Brendan striding out of the lift at work like a giant with a wash of pigmies in his wake, I recognised him as one of me. I smelled his singularity – my singularity. I tasted his self-sufficiency – my self-sufficiency. I saw the shape of his solitude. Mine. For the first time in my life I wanted to join up with someone, allow him close enough to breathe my breath.

The first few years were blissful.

I loved her the first time I saw her.

It was from behind, and although she was wearing a skirt, it was quite tight and I could see the shape of her bum – taut, high cheeks like a boy. She moved with the grace and power of an athlete, as though she could jump hurdles, hurl javelins, exterminate competition, without breaking sweat. Met a man in a bar once who told me he liked women to walk up and down his back in high heels. At the time I thought he was a pervert, but when I saw her I knew what he meant. She looked like she'd go for whatever she wanted with no deviations, no passing 'Go', no stopping off to collect £200: she'd scythe the air like an arrow heading for the bullseye. It wasn't so much that she was strong – my dad's third wife was strong – more that Sherilyn knew her own mind.

The first few years were blissful.

We were soulmates. Better than mates – our souls fused. We had the obvious things in common – both of us ambitious, well dressed, with an understated gold habit – but there was something more profound, as though we each had a secret space inside that exactly mirrored the space inside the other. Like one of those underground caves crammed with stalactites and stalagmites that no one knows is there. We'd been walking around like padlocked diaries all our lives and when we found each other, we opened our clenched fists and there was the key. We sometimes wondered what would have become of us if we hadn't met. We'd have carried on being the Living Dead probably.

I never wanted children.

No point to them, I thought. They'd get in the way of living my life and turn me from Sherilyn back into Linda. I wanted to slough off the provincial skin and climb ladders my family didn't even know were there. I suppose that's the way I've tried to make sense of it, just to see Mum and Dad as ignorant, because if they'd known what they were doing, they'd have been monsters. Their minds were simply too narrow to imagine a rainbow world beyond their monochrome small-town lives. My sister was prettier than me, and in a narrow-minded universe the only things that count for a girl are her looks. Sometimes I wondered if they even saw me as a girl. I loved Ann Marie at first because

I stank of loneliness, and anyway it was obvious that we were all supposed to worship at her shrine. *Look at your little sister, Linda – she's smiling at you! (So am I, Mum – look at me smiling. I'm over here – Mum?) And she's walking! (Hey Dad, I'm walking too – can you see me?)* I used to watch Mum feeding her with such tenderness I would feel famished. I longed for her eyes to take me into her like she took in her baby while she stroked her cheeks, her neck, her feet. I thought if I did the right thing, some of that might come my way, so I fed Ann Marie, resenting every spoonful I shoved in her mouth, changed her stinking nappies, dandled her on my knee, but there was only one daughter in the Miller house. Everything she did was as though it was the first time, as though I'd left no impression, as though I'd just been passing through Mum and Dad's lives like a breeze. Mum came to life when she looked at her baby and when he looked at the two of them there was a levity about Dad that I'd never seen before. The three of them made the perfect triangle. They were never going to see the beauty of a square.

I felt like the odd one out all my life until I met Brendan.

I never wanted children.

I used to look at them in advertising campaigns – always cute, never older than about seven, usually girls. I was seven and a half when Dad remarried for the first time, so probably I'd passed my cuteness sell-by date. The new family closed around itself like a space capsule. There they were inside, the perfect flying unit, and there I was outside, struggling to do a space walk without oxygen. But I'd been on my own for so long, I was happy when Dad met Shirley. She was very pretty and did her best to make me like her. She used to tickle me until I cried and sometimes she took my side when Dad was in one of his evil moods. I barely met her kids before the wedding, but I remember thinking, Good. Good, I'll have brothers and we can all muck about together. And Shirley said she was really sorry about Mum dying so young and everything, but she'd like to be my mum now, if that was OK with me. It was. All that cosying up vanished after the honeymoon. It was the same with Dad's next wife, Rita, as though the honeymoon was over for me too. I was sandwiched between Shirley's two boys: Steve was two years older than me and Wayne three years younger and still cute. I was always the odd one out.

I felt like the odd one out all my life until I met Sherilyn.

We were all we needed, but we'd mastered the choreography of the social dance. We went to parties when it was strictly necessary, did the kind of brittle chat you do with people who don't interest you – even had the occasional drinks party at home to pay people back. The parties were an investment in our future, but every time we steeled ourselves to hold one, it felt like a heathen invasion of a sacred space. It made strategic sense to invite people who could be of use to us professionally, so Anthony and his wife always came. He was a senior partner in our firm and a great admirer of our work, but we also wanted him to see us as sophisticates, as a couple with quietly refined tastes. Diana, Anthony's wife, loved our furniture and decor – we had *Homes & Gardens* to thank for that – and asked us for the name of our decorator so she could have her walls sponged like ours. Didn't tell her we did it ourselves. She was struck by the way we dressed too, so we told her about the exclusive designer we'd discovered; a week later she dropped several thousand pounds in one go and wrote a charming thank-you note. Her manners were impeccable. We'd bought several books about good vintages so we knew how to choose fine wines, and we matched them up with nibbles from a criminally expensive delicatessen in Kensington. Diana was brought up on some big country estate, but you could see her thinking, These people know how to do things. They've got class. She invited us to dinner several times at their London house, along with people who came from the same sort of background as them. We always took vintage champagne. Some of the other guests were so wealthy they didn't have to work, but generations of inbreeding had made them rather thick, so conversation was just a matter of winding them up and letting them rattle on about blood sports and vintage ports. We were Hoovers sucking up tips on how to breathe in the rarefied air of privilege, but when we got home at the end of an evening, we'd wet ourselves laughing about them. They thought we were like them, but we were miming, mouthing the words in a script.

I wasn't stupid.

I was top of the class in most subjects at school, though maths was my favourite. Ann Marie flunked everything. Maths always made sense to me because you went through the steps, logic leading each one to the next, and there was no mucking about, no opinions, no arguments. No messy maybes. When I got to the end of a calculation, I felt comforted, as though someone had patted my arm and said There, lovey, you see? There *is* an answer, after all. I especially liked algebra because there were all these mysteries, all these a's and b's and x's and when you'd finished, the mysteries had gone. You'd solved them. I hated mysteries. Languages were something else altogether. Although I excelled in them, I never saw the point of learning all that gobbledegook just so you could talk to foreigners. It wasn't going to make you any more French or German. Might as well be a gerbil as far as they were concerned. At home I was Linda the gerbil over here and they were all cosied up over there in their mouse nest talking mousey to each other. Ronald and Marilyn Mouse and their daughter, the lovely Ann Marie Mouse, in their beautiful Norwich mouse hole. I'd be doing all the right things – working hard, being polite: *please thank you oh excuse me I'm sorry*, all that stuff

– but I'd still be a gerbil. As soon as I left home I changed my name to Sherilyn so that Linda would never again feel like a different species. I established a new species with one member and one language, but I longed for someone to say Yes, yes, I understand what you're saying. Brendan spoke my language.

He knew me.

I wasn't stupid.

I used to like school, though I didn't go in for friends much, but Wayne and Steve came along and spoiled it. At least until then my Exeter primary was *my* school, but once they joined we morphed into The Boys. *Have The Boys gone off without their caps? Have you made The Boys' lunches? It's The Boys' sports day on Wednesday – bugger it, we'll have to go.* That was the worst. Sports. It was like a Scout badge and if you didn't have it, if you didn't like sports, you weren't a proper boy. I was always big for my age so it was assumed I'd happily choose to be out in the freezing cold kicking a bit of leather around with the other boys. Assumed I'd welcome the humiliation of no one passing to me. *Oh look, Brendan's missed the ball again. What a nonce.* They didn't know about the collection, thankfully, or they'd have had a go at that too. *Scabby weirdo, sticking feathers into a book. What a spaz.* Shirley used to say Get out there with The Boys, Bren, get some fresh air, and Wayne and Steve would look like they'd been asked to swallow sick. When I said No, I've got something to do in my room, thank you, the relief on their faces was priceless. No one ever asked me what it was that kept me up there all those hours. No one ever asked me where my pocket money went. I didn't cross their minds. My secret was the talisman I stroked to ward off the evil aliens when they attacked. If Dad had found out, he'd have gone for me like he did when he found out I slept with Mum's old stocking wrapped around my chest. He called me a nancy boy and pulled down my pyjama bottoms in front of the others. His eyes exploded like fireworks. Look, he crowed, Look at that tiddler – my fag's bigger than that! and he flicked my dick with an unlit cigarette. I crept downstairs when he'd gone to sleep and retrieved the stocking from the dustbin. I always wore it under my pyjamas after that: tight against my skin I could believe Mum was holding on to my heart. Sherilyn understood right away. She cradled my heart in her hands.

She knew me.

We met at the big accountancy firm where we worked: between the two of us we had the Receivership Department and Personnel covered. We were both regarded as loners but colleagues seemed to like us well enough. We celebrated the anniversary of that meeting every year, along with a slew of other anniversaries: our wedding day, the vasectomy, buying our first house, our first BMW, the cat's birthday and so on. We always managed to speak to each other at the exact time on the day we met; magically it was 10.21 on October 21st. We never missed it. Never. Other couples – ordinary couples – finish each other's sentences and boast about their harmony. They know nothing. We were echoes bouncing around a canyon, humming the same notes, thinking the same thoughts. We didn't believe in fate or luck. We believed you created your own destiny and made whatever sacrifices or compromises it took to fly high. Getting together made us twice the size.

He was big. That was the first thing I noticed.

Once I'd seen him by the lift, I saw him everywhere and I started thinking of ways to meet him: I never left anything to chance. My opportunity came when one of his secretaries resigned – silly girl got herself pregnant – and I said I'd handle the vacancy. Usually you'd get the job spec, read the report from the head of department and contact the agencies, but this time I pretended I'd found an error and had to go down to the second floor to sort it out. I walked in and he was bent over his desk. All I could see was a broad back in a seagull-grey jacket. Then I noticed he was stroking the hair over his ear with his ring finger over and over, and that was it. Here was this big man who looked as though he could take on an entire rugby team and he was soothing himself like a small child. He said no one had ever seen that in him before, but I saw it right off. He had these broad beefy hands that wouldn't hurt a fly. Powerful arms to keep me safe. When he held me, I was in his castle with the drawbridge pulled up. He sometimes put both my hands in the palm of one of his and closed his fingers around them like a tiger holding a feather in his mouth. He liked me being petite, but he never knew what hard work it was staying that way. He made a joke sometimes when I went to the toilet after a meal – *Was it something I said?* – but I'd got it down to a fine art. He never smelled the sick on my breath afterwards.

We were both efficient, meticulous Virgos.

She was tiny. That was the first thing I noticed.

She always wore high heels, but even when she was wearing the highest ones – the Dior sandals with the silver heels and chains – she only came up to my chest. I noticed her for the first time when I had to go up to the fourth floor, which was where her office was, and as I came out of the lift, I saw this little doll clicking down the corridor carrying a pile of files. She dropped one and as she turned round to pick it up, I saw her face. She had quite a long chin but she shaded it to look shorter and defined her face with a pearly peachy blusher. She had an artist's skill with powders and paints and did this cunning thing with her eyes – tiny dots of brown along the lashes – that made them look hazel, even though they were somewhere between blue and grey. Or green. She went much blonder later, but at that time her hair looked like a dull-gold cap on a precisely sculpted bottle of scent. Everything about her was immaculate, from her make-up to her lacquered toenails. Even after we got together I never saw her without make-up because she always made sure she got up before me to put on what she called her 'early-morning gloss'. She said it was just for me. I used to wish I knew what she looked like without any make-up so I could have seen her like no one else ever had, but she said it was impossible. I respected that. Sometimes I'd wake in the night and I'd hear her sucking her thumb. I never turned the light on because it would have been a betrayal to look at her naked face, but she made these tiny mewling noises so I stroked the back of her neck until she stopped. I wasn't really on the lookout when we met because I'd been seeing this Scottish guy, Frank, for a bit and while it wasn't serious, he was a good fuck. Before him, I'd had six months with Emily, but she started going on about babies, so I had to let her go. At least guys don't go on about babies. Nor did Sherilyn.

We were both efficient, meticulous Virgos.

It must have been on the third date – grand opening of an ex-client's restaurant – that we discovered that neither of us wanted kids. There was no sacrifice involved, no compromise, we were both adamant: kids hold you up, slow you down. All our lives we'd been prospectors for gold, panning and sifting and searching for the nugget that was going to give us a pulse, and suddenly there it was: us. Brendan and Sherilyn. The year after we met, the recession blasted a hole in the economy that thousands of companies fell through, including ours, and we became frantically busy. Between us we must have overseen hundreds of receiverships and redundancies and we were both promoted because we just got our heads down and did our jobs. The sound of livelihoods shattering bothered some of our colleagues, but we understood market forces and knew that the efficiently run outfits would rise again. We got married on the crest of a wave. As it was our last social event in London before moving north with the firm, we used it to cut the flimsy ties to our acquaintances too. Small wedding, but expensive. All five parents impressed, Ann Marie envious. That spiced up the day. In the pictures, even the ones with guests intruding, you could see we only had eyes for each other – like in a film when everything around the couple shimmers into a blur. We set up our wedding list at Harrods – the families ignored that and bought us their usual trash instead – but our wedding gifts to each other were priceless: a vasectomy and a cat. A beautiful long-haired white cat with blue eyes called Snowie. A pedigree.

I was Mrs Gutteridge, wife of Brendan.

All through the night before our wedding, I had to keep getting up and touching my dress, my fingertips tripping over the tiny seed pearls around the scoop neck, riffling the flirty frill at the hem. I knew that when I slipped it over my head the next morning, slid it across my skin, I would inch by inch transform into something unavoidable: me. Growing up a Miller, I could have been a glass of water on the table, shivering a little when someone kicked a toe against the leg, shunted sideways when room had to be found for the mashed potato. Mum would look through me to gaze at Ann Marie's loveliness, Dad would take a sip of me to slake his thirst, Ann Marie would flick bits of me at the wall in sheer devilment. If they'd knocked me over, I'd have been nothing but a temporary mark on the tablecloth evaporating my droplets into the air they breathed. I had a name that was borrowed from somebody else, an appearance that echoed neither of my parents, temporary membership of a family that could be rescinded at any time and was predicated on my usefulness. I was useful in highlighting by my unremarkable presence quite how remarkable my sister's beauty was. I was useful in demonstrating that my father was potent, that my mother was fertile. *Two daughters, fancy!* I was useful in allowing Dad to believe that he could have been a contender, that my academic success flowed from his gene pool. I was useful in making up numbers. My roots were too starved of nutrients to flourish in Miller soil, so by leaving home and becoming Sherilyn I hoped to grow visible, audible. I became skilful in the arts of fabrication and disguise, shrugging on layers of identity like so many coats. I learned to paint on my blank canvas of a face a woman of experience, a woman of potential, considerable in the scheme of things. Using three angled mirrors, I spent long hours micro-designing the first impression Sherilyn would make. Each new powder, each new cream, each new brush and sponge was an investment in her future, another shaft dug deep to sink her foundations. I had eyes of indeterminate colour: Lancôme pencils and brushes and shadows deftly created eyes that could be described as hazel. Would be described as hazel in my passport. I had a shapeless face: sable tufted brushes flicked and dabbed and pressed Guerlain colours on my cheeks to give them defi-nition, my cheekbones a presence. I had a long chin: my fingers smeared dark Dior cream under my jaw to stop it short. My mouth ran a lipstick gamut from pearlised to glossy to sticky to matt, and I generously created lips of shapeliness and substance. I rehearsed a panoply of smiles suitable for any event: I could be mildly amused, secretly knowing or intelligently responsive to order. I could have dyed my hair any colour, and I toyed with burgundy, auburn and mahogany before settling on the promise of blonde. There was an advertising slogan when I was growing up, *It's fun to be a blonde, a Hiltone blonde*, and I wanted to know what fun looked like. My mother was a woman perpetually at war with her body, which rolled over waistbands, sagged against buttons, threatened her seams, and I was determined to be not-her. I was slight by nature, but tiny by design, and I organised my wardrobe and appetite to emphasise my form. My small waist, not much bigger than a weightlifter's neck, sported belts, sashes, chains, clinging and clanking to draw the eye to my middle. Below the belts, my narrow hips promised a woman who'd never be distracted by childbearing. I wore tights that gleamed like lightly oiled skin, and my shoes were extravagances that hinted at decadent inclinations I didn't feel. I was a master-piece: a piece of living theatre created to captivate my audience. But Brendan made me real, breathed life into the waxwork I'd moulded. He slipped off my disguise, convincing as it was, and bound my core to his.

Mr and Mrs Gutteridge moved north.

I was Mr Gutteridge, husband of Sherilyn.

My dad had three weddings, but I doubt he had any idea of what 'wedding' really meant. His was a casual, dick-driven hunger for company: as long as she cooked and warmed his bed, one woman would be as serviceable as the next. I always hoped that Mum was different, hoped theirs was a love match, not an itch scratched, because then at least I would have been the result of a passing tenderness. Sometimes I used to think I remembered Mum. Sometimes, when the family was asleep, I'd creep down-stairs and sit on the floor of the scullery, and the cool of the flags and the smell of the washing powder evoked a memory that stopped just short of seeing Mum in the kitchen. Hearing her voice. But the feeling of safety fleetingly rooted me. I'd take it back up to bed and, until I fell asleep, imagine I could take Dad on. Stop him short mid-howl. Marrying Sherilyn felt like taking up permanent residence in the scullery, sitting on the floor knowing that Mum would come when I called. Tend me when I barked my shin or grazed my elbow. When Sherilyn curled into the pit of my belly in bed it was as though there was no

Dad, or Shirley and Rita, no stepbrothers and sisters, but only the history we began writing when we met. I loved her body, a pale glimmer moving across our bedroom to the bathroom, her hips tilting a bony invitation, her bush a hungry beating heart, her breasts pinkly punctuating the sheer drop of her torso. I could fold myself around her as though I were cupping her in my body, my bulk a bulwark against the enemy. Only I knew that she whimpered in her sleep. Only I knew that she'd sit bolt upright sometimes, rigid with alarm. She could never tell me in the morning why her ineffectual little father had haunted her dreams. What he'd done. Only I knew that when she cut herself, she'd get so upset she'd sob in frightened child gulps at the sight of her own blood. Only I could comfort her. She said she'd never cried as a child, even when she fell over, so she had tears to shed, she said, that had been dammed for years. She was inconsolable when Snowie fell ill once and the vet told us he might not survive the major surgery he needed. For a week Sherilyn called in sick to work, spoiling her unblemished record of attendance, and I'd come home at the end of the day to find her curled like a comma over the cat in the crook of her arm, feeding him with a bottle. She could have been suckling him. She barely slept the whole week and would come into the bedroom three or four times a night to give me bulletins about his progress. I never minded. We'd got him from a snotty breeder in Buckinghamshire who went on about his family history, clearly not entirely sure we were posh enough to take him home. Unlike us, he had a pedigree. Unlike us, his ancestry was a proud boast. He was a creature to be admired. A creature of beauty and prestige. But he was a Gutteridge too.

Mr and Mrs Gutteridge moved north.

Somebody at work said to us Jolly well done for the new jobs and everything, but aren't you a bit daunted to be moving so far away from home? Won't you miss your family and friends? We said something banal like Oh well, home is where the heart is, isn't it? because that's the sort of thing people understand: we weren't about to unlock our mysteries for people who were, after all, passers-by. The removal company quoted for packing and unpacking, but we told them we'd do it ourselves – Just move it up the motorway, please, we said, We'll take care of the rest. The idea of outsiders rummaging around in our things, gawping at our lives, was as unthinkable as volunteering to be raped. There was no debate about what was coming with us and what we'd discard, because we were of one mind. We were on the rise – new city, new status, new responsibilities – and some of the clothes we'd worn, the objects we'd chosen, belonged to the old life, so had to be destroyed. We didn't send them to the charity shop because we didn't want anyone slipping their arms into our sleeves, so we had a funeral pyre in the garden and smashed the Conran vases on our kitchen floor. We'd be buying vases from designers from now on, art from galleries, and the sound of glass shattering, the curves drowned in a sea of jagged fragments, was music to our ears. Move on, we thought, always move on – don't look back. We never forgot our passports. We'd chosen our new house carefully. There'd only been one owner before, and we expunged the traces of their lives as soon as we moved in. They'd gone in for bright colours on the walls – especially in the kids' room, which had a lingering stink of vomit – and wallpaper borders sneaked around the walls like floral snail-trails. We had those scraped off and chose classy neutrals instead. The garden was a horticultural coma – lawn, lawn and more lawn – and they'd left some battered plastic toys around the sand pit, whose contents spilled incontinently over its edges. We consulted with a very expensive garden designer who came up with a way of ordering the space into coloured compartments. We'd been mugging up on art history so we could pepper our conversation with cultural references and were much taken with Mondrian at the time. When all the workers had finished scurrying around interrupting our peace, we sat on our buttery-leather sofa and toasted each other in twenty-year-old Dom Perignon. The wine guides had gone on the bonfire along with our old clothes. Our new clothes caressed each other's elegance in the wardrobes upstairs, the study hummed with the latest technology, the state-of-the-art kitchen was a minimalist's wet dream and there we were, ensconced in our fiefdom. We cele-brated our arrival by putting on *The Sound of Music* and singing along triumphantly to 'The Hills Are Alive'. The neighbours came round early on – Tim and Jessie, a rather unkempt couple – to tell us about milk and paper deliveries, local shops and the names of our other neighbours. We didn't invite them in. Sorry, we said, Everything's such a mess at the moment, what with the builders and decorators – you know how it is, and they pressed us to come and have a drink with them. It's ghastly when you first move, isn't it? they said – Everything's so horribly chaotic and you can never find anything you need. Come over and have a bit of a breather – escape the builders' detritus. We looked up 'detritus' when they'd gone. It was a useful word. We thanked them and said we'd come over sometime, but not right now because we still had lots to sort. We managed to avoid going round the whole time we lived there, which was quite a feat because they invited us with the maddening repetitiveness of a jackhammer. We were endlessly creative with our excuses. They had standard English accents, but the Mancunian accent came at us from all angles. Even some of the partners had it, which surprised us because you'd think they wouldn't want to advertise where they came from, but it didn't seem to bother them. Nobody – *nobody* – would be able to place us by our accents. Nobody would be able to tell that we came, essentially, from peasant stock. They'd look at our clothes, our jewellery, our car, our address, hear our voices and they'd positively smell our success. Nothing could dislodge us.

Then I fell pregnant.

It was like the bit at the beginning of *Alice in Wonderland*, where she's falling down a tunnel and she sees things going past and she can't grab hold of them. It felt like that. As though I couldn't grab hold of my life. As though a balloon full of poison had been dumped in me that no surgeon in the world could cut out. I brushed my teeth pregnant. I went to bed pregnant. I woke up in the morning pregnant. I was fit-to-burst pregnant in my dreams. Mad hornet thoughts buzzed around my head: I'd obviously been raped; Bren had obviously wanted a baby all along and lied about the snip; I'd obviously got pregnant from that manky toilet seat at Slough station. I knew he thought I'd screwed someone else, but we were so blown apart there was no way of telling him that I hadn't. We'd had our language, our Brendan-and-Sherilyn-speak, but it failed us; its vocabulary wasn't elastic enough for this catastrophe. I'd been offered this chance, this one chance, to be loved, and now the offer had been retracted. As though I'd never deserved it. When I was younger I'd gone to the doctor's once because my periods were all over the place. He told me that unless I put on at least a stone and a half, I'd never have a regular cycle. Another twenty-one pounds and I'd have been a Zeppelin. Like my mother. I didn't go back and I learned to deal with my periods when occasionally they showed up. As a result of that and the vasectomy, I didn't think anything about it when I didn't come on for several months in a row, so by the time I realised the alien had taken up residence, it was too late for an abortion. It wouldn't have resolved anything anyway because we'd still have had this big question about how it had happened lying between us. There wasn't anyone else to talk to either. Ann Marie was on her third and Mum and Dad were busy being Mrs Nan and Mr Granddad Of The Century. They'd just have said Well done – see, all that career-girl stuff was rubbish, wasn't it? Every girl needs babies, they'd have said – like breeding mares or dogs. I was sick all day, every day, and as the alien got bigger, I got a trapped nerve in my back and could hardly walk. I didn't know what was more revolting, the idea of sex or the invader turning somersaults in my belly.

And then I saw the article.

Then she fell pregnant.

Fell was right. I felt like I was falling down something deep and dark and dank, like a sewer. Since we met, we'd been standing on solid ground for the first time in our lives, but the tectonic plates had shifted and hurled us on to opposite sides of an unbridgeable chasm. We were so devastated we couldn't speak to each other. The silence marooned us in our own wild imaginings. Marooned me anyway. I didn't know what she was thinking and we never spoke about it afterwards. I felt like I'd been caught out believing in fairies. The baby obviously wasn't mine because of the snip, so she must have fucked somebody else and that blew me away. I walked around feeling like there was a huge elastic band around my head and I couldn't think, couldn't bear to think about what it all meant. So I started cottaging – not very often, but enough to loosen the elastic band and release the pressure. One guy's smell reminded me of my first lover, Paul. I remembered the name of his aftershave and wore it for a while. It comforted me. Cut my arms and thighs a few times too. I'd forgotten the relief when you do that. Sex obviously stopped between me and Sherilyn – apart from the fact of her infidelity, I couldn't root around somewhere where there was a baby growing.

And then she saw the article.

★

Babies leach calcium from your body, so there were repeat visits
to the dentist: the article was in a magazine in the waiting room.
It was one of those 'true-life' pieces – 'I Fell In Love With My
Best Friend's Ferret', that sort of thing – about a couple who'd
split up when the husband's vasectomy had failed. It was our
story but we rewrote it. Ours had a happy ending. We came
together to fight the hospital: it was us against them, little David
wielding his lethal slingshot at Goliath. All those meetings –
lawyers, doctors, psychiatrists – all those reports, court hearings,
conferences, gave us an exhilarating sense of purpose. Put us
back in control. Us. We were all that mattered. And as the baby
grew, so the case grew clearer. We. Don't. Want. Children.
Simple. But a court case has a beginning and end, and a child
goes on forever. Once a mum and dad, always a mum and dad,
and for us that meant no more Bren and Lyn. We learned a lot
about the legal system during the preparation of the case, and
we'd compare notes after conferences with our lawyers. We
wanted to make sure we hadn't been hoodwinked. We bought
some textbooks on this area of the law and studied together at
night because we knew they'd want to make us look like fools.
We'd learn about paragraph this and clause that and test each
other afterwards. We couldn't work in the study, which would
have been the most appropriate place, because we'd had to put
the girl in there when she was born. It was the furthest room
from our bedroom. We'd settle in the living room, the books on
the brushed-steel Aram coffee table, our toes in the hand-tufted
rug and a crystal glass of cognac by our elbows. We used to joke
that we could always have second careers as lawyers if the
financial world collapsed, but none of this was funny. It was life
or death, a matter of survival. We'd considered adoption of
course, but it would have compromised our case. The legal
eagles had to see us as victims. Had to agree that the Health
Authority had condemned us to a lifetime of misery. Had to

compensate us for the ruination of a dream. The case ran for two years but the court found in our favour. We walked out of that courtroom, our lawyers fluttering behind us like self-important bats, and hugged each other on the steps outside. We wished there'd been cameras there to capture the moment, but the case strangely hadn't excited any interest. You'd think that NHS negligence on this scale might have been headline material. You'd think foisting a child on to a perfect couple in an effort to split them up might have been seen for the wantonly destructive act that it was, but there was more interest in the destruction of the rain forest than the attack on us. It didn't matter. We knew we'd won. Winning quashed the conviction that we were losers and that it was only a matter of time before we were exposed.

We felt like we'd had the biggest simultaneous orgasm in the world.

By that time the girl was walking and talking.

Although I felt like I was drowning in motherhood, I could just about hack it till then – she could always be put to bed or stuck in a playpen, and I quite liked dressing her up when we were forced to take her out with us. But every time someone said What a pretty girl, I wanted to smash her face in. I had dreams where she had African tribal markings on her face, but the cuts were still bleeding. Sometimes it was Ann Marie's face. I bought latex gloves by the gross and kept them by the changing table. At least that put something between me and her when she needed changing, and we bought state-of-the-art equipment to neutralise her stink. Sometimes the smell of her vomit and shit made my head swim and I'd leave her on the table while I left the room to gulp down some clean air. Sadly she never fell off. Bren did his best to help, but when he changed her nappy for the first time, he went pale and looked strangely frightened. It happened again the next couple of times and I could see he was becoming more and more agitated, so reluctantly I said I'd do that bit as long as he made up the bottles. Despite being so super-numerate, he never quite got the hang of the formula so the milk would turn out either like pee or like syrup, and I didn't correct him. I didn't hit her at first, just bent her hands back a bit in the bath when she splashed. When she did a really shitty nappy, I twisted her feet. Her alien hands and feet. When she was born with webbing between her fingers and toes, I chucked up three times. They said it was the pethidine, but I knew it wasn't. The doctors and nurses put on these idiot sympathetic faces and said Don't worry, Mrs Gutteridge, this is easily fixed. I barely contained myself. Chopping a bit of skin off her hands and feet was *not* going to fix the fact that we were condemned to her. For life. Brendan was less stuck than me because at least he was free of her while he was at work. The company made it virtually impossible for me to go back, so I was in solitary between 7.30 a.m. and 8 p.m. every day, with no time off for good behaviour. It was as though the umbilical cord had never been cut. I used to watch Bren getting dressed in the morning and imagine crawling up his front like a baby monkey so we could swing away through the jungle, my fingers lost in the mummy monkey's fur. Snowie took to sleeping on the girl in the cot and I didn't shoo him off because I thought there was always a chance that he'd roll over on her face – *Oh, Officer, there's been a terrible accident – come quick!* – but mostly he was rather sweet to her. When she touched him he'd purr, but every now and again he'd turn and give her a little nip. I'd have encouraged that if I'd known how. Now he'd made partnership, Bren was working long hours. We'd speak seven, eight times a day on the phone, but it felt as though I was talking to a prison visitor through glass, like in American films. He was telling me about a world from which I'd been exiled. I'd bring you to work with me in my pocket if I could, he said, because we both knew

I'd been catapulted on to a distant planet where I didn't speak the language, didn't understand the customs, didn't eat the food. When he came home in the evening, we'd try to revive the old life together. I'd get special food from the restaurant down the road, light candles, play our favourite music, but the alien always interrupted the meal by wanting food or a drink *right* then, like she'd planned it. Planned to break us up. But I wasn't having it. I'd shove her back in the cot, put the reins on and shout at her. Her first words were 'bad girl'.

The idea came to us one Tuesday evening.

By that time, the girl was walking and talking.

The early months had been torture. All she ever did was want something: it was like endlessly going to the dump and chucking stuff in, but it never filled, it was never finished. I started thinking, If I stuck a bit of duct tape over her mouth, it might give us – me – a moment's space so we could be alone again. I could feel my mind settling when I was getting ready for work in the morning, but Sherilyn would be sitting on the bed looking at me like a tethered bird looks at the sky. I would have to look away because the yearning would hook itself into my flesh. Sometimes I'd sit at my desk at work rubbing my pen across my knuckles, as though each rub returned me to myself, scrubbed the stench of fatherhood from my skin. When I got home in the evening I tried to help Sherilyn with the mechanics – I made up the odd bottle, though I never seemed to get the consistency right – and at first I tried changing the girl's nappies. I had to give that up because when she wet herself the smell brought back Shirley's rages when I wet the bed and the way she'd go for me suddenly, like a cat pouncing on a fledgling. Sometimes I'd wet myself just thinking about it. It was the one thing I never told Lyn about. She knew everything – every tiny thing – about me, but I couldn't tell her how I stank of humiliation and piss, how losing control flushed me out of my cover and left me flapping helplessly in Shirley's sights. And I couldn't stick the girl's littleness, her appalling vulnerability. It felt as though if I got too close she'd infect me with her weakness. I always liked the fact that I was physically so much bigger than Sherilyn because I thought if she were in trouble I could always scoop her up and rescue her. I used to have daydreams about her being swept down the rapids: I'd see myself wading in and pulling her out and her clinging to me like a half-drowned puppy, whimpering with gratitude. Day after day, I could see the girl's demands crushing her and I thought, I've got to do something about this. Got to make it OK again. When Sherilyn was low, before the girl intruded, all I had to do was tell her how beautiful she was, how she was my goddess, how I worshipped her. That used to buoy her up, but becoming a mother, hosting a parasite, stopped it working. She told me she felt like an old apple core, all dried up and gnarly, and while she was as well groomed as ever, it was as though she were painting colours on to a pitted surface. She'd always loved clothes – we both did – but she was dressing herself automatically in the morning, like putting the winter covers on garden furniture; everything matched perfectly well, but there was no joy in it. No pleasure in choosing understated tailoring on Monday, fluid drapes on Tuesday, natty detailing on Wednesday, no satisfaction when you find a novel combination of colour or texture or style. I tried treating her to new outfits, picking them up in my lunch hour from boutiques where they virtually charged you to walk through the door. I'd bring them home at the end of the working day and watch her face as a dress rustled out of its tissue paper nest. One time she held the beaded jacket I'd bought to her chest in a desperate embrace. I feel like I'm looking at ancient history, she said, Looking at a me that's gone into suspended animation. It's not that it's not beautiful, Brendan, it is. It's just that there's nothing there to dress. If I put it on, it'll be hanging over empty space. She was slowly fading away before my eyes. God knows, we tried to get back some of the old magic, but the girl was a cuckoo in our nest, sucking up the light, syphoning the colours from our lives. When she wouldn't stop screaming, I hit her. Mostly with the flat of my hand, but sometimes with a fist. I would *not* let her jam herself between us.

The idea came to us one Tuesday evening.

Eureka. That was it. No more mess, no more interruptions. We'd be back in our underground cave speaking our underground language. We'd sometimes said If only we could lock her up in a box and throw away the key, life would be normal again. We made one in the third bedroom. Genius. We thought we'd probably need to see what the girl was doing when we popped our heads round the door, so we left gaps in the slats around the sides. That made it look more like a cage, but she wasn't a pet, so we always referred to it as The Box. We got a real buzz out of constructing it, like doing a *Blue Peter* project but without the sticky-backed plastic. While we sawed and hammered and drilled, we sang our favourite show tunes, changing the lyrics to suit the occasion. 'I'm Gonna Wash That Kid Right Outta My Hair' was our favourite. We were neither of us great carpenters, but we applied ourselves and learned on the job. It was like everything else: you look around for someone who'll teach you something to help you get through life and all you see is a big nothing, a big no one, so you roll your sleeves up and teach yourself. Until we met, our whole lives had been DIY. We were the perfect team. We bought the best quality wood because it was going to have to last a long time and it needed to look good. We had a smart house and didn't want to spoil it.

We had to work out a way of keeping the girl clean because while we could control her food intake we couldn't stop her shitting and pissing. Two years of changing nappies were quite enough. We installed a sink by the door – taught ourselves plumbing too – got a commode from a junk shop and sat her on it three times a day. We put a television in the corner opposite the commode, because we thought it would distract her and stop her causing ructions. It was only on during the day because the stuff that was on in the evening sometimes shocked even us. The girl soon discovered there was no point in complaining. If we came in and she was yelling, we shut her up. It didn't matter leaving a mark by then because we didn't have to take her out with us any more. We put Snowie in there with her sometimes because he kept her quiet and it meant we knew he was safe. We worried that he'd wander off as cats do, even though he knew how much we adored him.

With The Boxroom locked up, we could go out together again in the evening. The partnership salary paid for us to see all the latest shows and we'd buy the music so we could have our own private performance at home whenever we liked. We kept up with the restaurant reviews so we'd know where to eat out afterwards and sometimes we'd find ourselves sitting next to celebrities. We'd time our meal so we'd be leaving the restaurant at the same time as them and sometimes we'd get ourselves in the background of the paparazzi photographs. Often we were the better dressed – some of the stars were surprisingly scruffy. We'd managed to sever the last tenuous links with our families: the Exeter lot were preoccupied by the ill health consequent on a lifetime of neglect and indulgence, and the bumbling East Anglians could always be fobbed off. They sent presents and cards for Christmas and the girl's birthdays, but she was an also-ran for them. Ann Marie's brood took up all their energy, so remembering her once or twice a year was all they could manage.

We forgot about her ninety per cent of the time. We fine-tuned the system so we only had to go in three times a day. It was as though she were in one of the glass cabinets scientists use when they have to handle something dangerous; they put their hands in the gloves in the front so they can perform the task safely. We'd put our hands in only when it was absolutely necessary and feed her or clean her. She went through a revolting vomitty phase once and we'd have left her caked in it, but it made us feel nauseous ourselves, so we cleared it up and hit her instead. When she gave up yelling, she started being polite and grateful. Began to understand that please and thank you were very important words. And sorry. Not that she could be sorry enough for separating us.

The first couple of years had drained the joy from our life but The Box meant that we could go back to having fun. We started playing games, really silly games, especially at night. We played pillow fights and hide and seek and sometimes three-legged races on the landing. And doctors and nurses. We went to a well-known theatrical costumiers and got them to custom-make us outfits. They hired out stuff, but we didn't want to put on clothes that someone else had worn in case we caught something. We were Dr Sher and Nurse Breda and the sound of our outfits sliding out of their plastic carriers was enough to turn us on. Dr Sher's was a tight-fitting white coat in babyskin-soft leather, which ended mid-thigh with a lacy frill. Nurse Breda's was blue silk with a slight slub and pearl buttons like tiny nipples down the front. The apron, brilliant white with subtle silver threads through it, swished deliciously against the skirt, whispering promises to Dr Sher's leather coat. We had special underwear for the games, which we kept between perfumed tissue in a drawer. We'd had to hunt high and low for Nurse Breda's, because of the size, but we found them eventually: they were dark pink, with little embroidered bits at the edges, and ruffles. Dr Sher's were made of tight black rubber with a zip up the front. The sweat they produced was ambrosial. The stethoscope was red, like a poisonous snake or a tongue, and the sight of it lazily uncurling from the pocket precipitated erections so hard they were painful. It could be trailed between buttocks, slowly inserted, or used to bind wrists and ankles. We were endlessly inventive.

When we tried the uniforms on in the shop, we saw the staff stifling giggles, which surprised us. We'd thought they'd be used to that kind of thing with all those theatrical types traipsing their weirdness in and out, but we let it wash over us. Let them snigger. In our underground cave we were bound by nobody's rules. In our underground cave there was only us, our desires, our fantasies. In our underground cave the answer to every request was yes.

There was no need to kill the girl because she barely impinged on our life: she was simply another daily task which we performed as efficiently as everything else. We could have done it with our eyes shut. She never tried to weasel any extras out of us because we trained her to need only the basics: washing, potting, water and food. Nothing fancy – we couldn't be bothered to cook – so she got used to eating whatever we put in front of her. We had a mild Häagen-Dazs addiction going on for a while but we could never quite finish a tub, so when she behaved herself we gave the girl the leftovers. We used to joke that it was the ideal way to be pregnant – satisfying the cravings without being saddled with a baby. One night we hadn't got around to feeding her at the usual time because we'd been sliding down the stairs on our duvets pretending we were tobogganing. When we remembered, we discovered that we'd run out of the usual tinned and frozen stuff. It was too late to nip out to the shops and anyway it was freezing cold outside, so we fed her Snowie's food. We always bought him the gourmet cat food in flat tins – super expensive, but worth every penny for the delight he brought us. The girl gobbled it down and said thank you afterwards. It was a useful experiment because it meant we always had a back-up when the store cupboard was empty. We never ran out of cat food.

Apart from the nasty vomiting phase, the girl had the good sense not to get ill, or not so we noticed. We'd told her that if she started chucking up again, we'd go away and never come back and she seemed to have heeded the warning – except for the incident with the pills. Our GP had prescribed them for a persistent back problem, but alarmingly they contained steroids. There'd been scare stories in the press about how steroids could turn you into a monster, so we were wary of them even though the pain was chronic. It made sense to test them out on the girl because it was carrying her that had done the damage, so we gave her half a dose to begin with. She was a bit sleepy for twenty-four hours but that was all, so we gave her the full dose. She became unconscious almost immediately, but we managed to revive her by making her sick with salty water. We flushed the pills down the toilet, furious that the pain would have to carry on.

It must have been that snobby bitch in the house with the acer in the front garden. Naturally we'd had our house painted inside and out when we moved in, but hers looked like it hadn't been touched since it was built. It was one of a cluster of Victorian houses further along the Crescent whose gardens had been allowed to run amok. The houses leaned into each other like a gaggle of decrepit old ladies trying to hang on to the dignity of a distant heyday, as though they hadn't noticed we'd moved in and the world had moved on. The snob had obviously not pruned her wisteria for years and it had taken over the facade and side of the house, blinding one or two of the windows. Even that hadn't stymied her incurable nosiness. Her name was Charlotte and she kept telling us how long she'd lived there, as though twenty years was some sort of record. She was a one-woman Neighbourhood Watch Scheme, her beady eyes monitoring everyone's movements like CCTV with a heartbeat, and she persistently asked after the girl. She had a granddaughter about the same age, she said, but she lived in Australia and she missed her terribly. Lovely to see them growing up, she said, I feel very deprived. She pestered us like a hungry mosquito you can't squash and we were certain she'd made the call. So one Friday this social-worker type turned up on the doorstep without warning. She had a slightly superior air and looked like a jumble sale, all saggy brown clothes and haystack hair as though looking good was only for fools. She said the NSPCC had got a call which they'd passed on to Social Services and they were obliged to follow it up. They knew who the caller was, she said, frightfully sorry but she couldn't tell us. Obviously a neighbour, then, but all we said was OK, no problem. Question of confidentiality, she said. Most important. Quite understand, we said, Got to protect the innocent. She was easy to get rid of. We told her the girl was the most popular kid in the street and she was out playing with friends in the park. We know she's safe though, we said, Because everybody looks out for her. Her life's one long picnic. She said Fine, fine and she was obviously mentally ticking us off her list because you could see that she was dead impressed with the house. You could see her thinking, Not in this house. Not these people. Nonetheless we were extra vigilant after her visit.

We burned the girl a few times round about then when she played up. In an uncharacteristically weak-willed moment we took up smoking for a few months when we discovered the elegance of Sobranie cigarettes, especially at the end of a long cigarette holder. The first time was when the girl had messed herself and we were so angry that stubbing a fag out on her arm was just a reflex action. It made a strange smell, but no worse than her shit, so we sluiced her down in the sink and stuck her back in The Box. There were another three or four occasions after that, none of them particularly significant.

The social worker turned up a second time unannounced but we managed to fob her off, although as she was leaving she tried to go upstairs, the cheeky cow. That was a close shave and since these people are like boomerangs we knew it was only a matter of time till she was whingeing about the girl on our doorstep again. On top of that, we could see Charlotte Snitch's nose flattened against her window, making sure the authorities were harassing us on her say-so. As if that wasn't bad enough, the Education bods started writing to us saying it was time we put the girl into school and did we want help choosing which one? No we didn't. Schooling was not on the agenda. We knew what we had to do without needing to discuss it. One Thursday afternoon there were two passports on the desk, Her Britannic Majesty insisting on our entitlement to Pass Freely Without Let Or Hinderance. The hinderance was safely locked in The Boxroom. One of the passports was for Linda, as though she were still alive.

Staying was not an option. Staying would have been an open invitation to the dark forces that threatened the Brendanandsheri-lyn we'd created. Nothing – not career, reputation, possessions, girl – was ever going to get in our way again. We folded down our jobs, packed our lives into the Vuitton luggage and left.

We had enough invested to stay away indefinitely. We could do what we pleased for the first time in our lives, free of the obligation to please anyone else. We could loll on tropical beaches, walk the Himalayas, see every show on Broadway – there were no plans, no targets, nothing to prove. If we chose to settle elsewhere we'd come back to clear the house and get it fumigated, but that was for a future we had yet to imagine.

We both wept when we put Snowie out for the last time. It would have been unbearable to hand him over to another couple, like committing an act of gross infidelity, so we trusted him to find himself another home. That way we could retain our picture of him at the centre of ours.

We were careful to lock the house up thoroughly. Didn't want to get burgled.

Marilyn

Every month I held my breath, hoping that this way I'd stop up my womb and every month the Curse would mock me on the twenty-eighth day. My insides were drying out, my veins running with dust and I'd flush away any remaining hope along with the STs. Getting pregnant was the only reason I stayed alive, the only reason I let Ronald fill me up night after night in our chilly bed. Everything else – my quiet home, steady job, reliable husband – was incidental.

I consulted doctors, haunted waiting rooms, submitted my body to hands, instruments, needles, searching for a faulty connection, and learned not to cry when they said Nothing wrong with you, Mrs Miller. Or, Go home and relax, Marilyn, it'll happen one day, you'll see. Ronnie was only dimly visible to me across the yawning gap between us. He didn't understand that it wasn't him I wanted, only what he had in him to give me. I gave up work, to see if it helped me relax and I'd have his tea on the table six minutes after he got home. His manager at the bank used to say that he was more punctual than the Greenwich pips, so I never had to wait. Once I mistimed the pudding, so the meal was seventeen minutes late. I kept apologising because by that time I thought if I did anything bad – or even slightly not good – it would set me back another year and I didn't want to be angry with him forever. I was spitting with rage, but he never knew because I spat in his gravy instead, watching the little bubbles perch on the shiny brown surface before I stirred them in. I knew it was him. It must have been him. Every part of me had been prodded, poked, stretched and measured, so he must have been deliberately keeping my baby from me.

Five years after we started trying, the twenty-eighth day came and went with no Curse. So did the twenty-ninth, and I sat frozen on the settee all day. If I sat still, I thought, she'd want to stay, she'd burrow into my womb and grow eyes and legs and a smile. She was always going to be a girl. I knew I could love a girl. I pared the housekeeping down to the minimum so she could settle in peacefully. Ronald was used to a big tea, so when he found himself staring at a plate of salad every night for a month, he must have thought it was strange. But he never complained. There was always salad cream and a pudding and it was summer-time anyway, so there was a good excuse.

I was in the doctor's waiting room as soon as I was overdue enough to take the test. Dr Magnus was RC so he thought women having babies was a jolly good thing. Preferably loads of babies. One'll do me, I said, Just let me have one. When the test came back positive, I fainted. Must have hit my head on some-thing sharp when I went down because when I came to, the front of my dress was covered in blood. I fainted again because I thought I must have come on my period, but by the time I came round the second time, they'd cleaned me up and put a plaster on the cut. It was a shame about the dress, but Maureen next door cut it up and made it into cushion covers.

I wasn't taking any chances. I was sitting down when I told Ronald and when he jumped up and looked like he was going to hug me I said No, Ronnie, not now. Mustn't disturb the baby. I never had to tell him to keep his distance while I grew her inside me because he knew this was something so completely female he was redundant. When I sat down I'd feel her lying against my womb's lining like she was resting against a warm wall in the summer sun. When I lay in bed she'd be floating in her waters singing like a mermaid on a rock. It felt like I'd spent a lifetime

84

visiting other people's houses, borrowing their keys to let myself
in and lock myself out and now I finally had the keys to my own
home. The home my daughter and I would build together. For
the two of us.

I was good at producing her, everybody said so. Well done,
Marilyn, the midwife said, You're good at this. We looked at
each other, Linda and I, and it was like looking in a mirror. I
watched as her dark curls dried to a fuzzy blonde, the blue of
her eyes reflecting my own back to me. I fell in love for the first
time, basking in a pool of tenderness, swimming in smiles. My
visitors looked at Linda in her cot and smiled and stroked her
head when she was feeding and smiled and tucked my bedjacket
around my shoulders and smiled, and my cheeks ached with
smiling, with the stretch of pleasure around my daughter and
me. We received our guests graciously, as happy couples do, but
Linda kept her secret grin just for me when she gummed my
breast and I filled her up.

And I go in in the morning, go over to her cot with the pink
and the frills and the soft, soft inside, and I look at her, look at
my round and curly baby and there's blood and she's dead.

She's dead.

I'm on the floor, my shoulders are pounding my knees, my hands
are gripping the sides of my head and there's this sound inside
outside everywhere, the sound of a beast savage with despair at
the black clouds that have murdered the light. She's left me in
the dark and the life seeps out of me into the earth. I can't look
at her, can't touch her, can't feed her my breath.

Someone's lifting me, someone's trying to stop my howling
grieving but I won't let it go, won't have it stop. This is my life
now. This contamination. This death. Someone's picking up a
bundle of rags from the cot and as they pass my head, a small white

arm flops out, saluting her drowning mother. The voices in my head hiss – *Did you think you could have it? Did you think you deserved it? You fool: we gave you this precious vessel and you dropped it.*

Ronnie's fingers are white. Dead man's fingers. He carries the tiny coffin to the hole in the ground. Vivid green plastic grass. Linda Alison Miller. My daughter.

I am a collection of sticks click-clacking as I walk down the street. The eyes of passers-by fall on the sticks and drift through the gaps. I am an outline. I have no middle, no substance. I have a name, like a badge, but no meaning. I fill up with pregnancy again, but it's a foreign body sucking my blood until it's time to hatch. It's born, or so they say, but I know it's just answering the call of its people. I know it's been waiting for the moment it can burst out and sit on its perch staring at me, its incubator. It's called Linda. That's Ronnie's idea, but he doesn't realise it's not Linda, it's an alien. It doesn't belong to me, to the earth, it belongs to another planet and must be returned to them. To its people. I must leave it where they can find it. Where the mother ship can land. Outside, outside, outside. It must be outside. The garden may be big enough. I put it on the lawn on some baking foil so the aliens will know it's one of theirs and I stand behind the tree and watch for the signs of landing. Listen for the sounds of aliens greeting their own. I wear a black plastic bin bag because it will ward off the Linda thing's radioactive waves. The beams of the Linda thing's people as they slither out of their spaceship to claim her. When the impostor's gone I'll be free again. Free to mourn the real Linda.

The garden doesn't work. They can't see it. There's no room to land. I have to take it somewhere else. The park. There's a bird bath in the park. They'll see it if it's up off the ground. Take off its clothes so they'll know it's one of them. Human clothes will confuse them. They wouldn't want a human and I don't want an alien. I sit on the park bench in my bin bag and I cover myself with leaves. They can't see through leaves. A lady comes and sits beside me and her mouth is opening and closing and making shapes. I turn my back on her because I have to stay on the right wavelength so the mother ship knows where to come. I have to send a signal. There's a blue light flashing. They're coming!

The ambulance takes me to the loony bin.

A giant loony rubbish bin and I'm the rubbish. But the alien's gone, so I'm safe. They take my clothes, the bin people, so they can scrape the alien slime off my body. I don't fuss, because this way I'll get my baby back. They put me in a speckled nightie and luckily it's very loose so there's room underneath for her to crawl up my thighs and she does, she crawls up and she sits on my belly and I look down the front and she's grinning her secret grin and singing her mermaid songs. The bin people have given me pills, so when she's finished singing I fall asleep.

Three months later when I was let out of the bin they let Linda out of the Children's Home. I was more or less OK. OK to do the normal things like cleaning and cooking and washing. Routine comforted me, so I stuck to Sunday roast, Monday washing, Tuesday shopping, but Linda was always there, always looking at me. I wasn't mad then, so I knew she must have been blinking, but sometimes she reminded me of a lizard. My first Linda bounced and waved and kicked, but this one sat as still as a sheet of ice, watching me, watching. Suddenly she'd blink, and I'd jump as though I'd been electrocuted. Then she'd go back to staring again, her eyes like nails. I didn't think she was from another planet any more, but she was never mine. Never a baby I'd grown inside me. But I did my best. I play-acted what a mum's supposed to do. I sang her all the nursery rhymes I could remember, though my voice sounded like a rusty lawnmower.

I'd try saying the words that seemed to go with being a mum, like *Hello poppet, have you got a smile for Mummy?* Or, *Are you sleepy now, little love?* but they echoed in my head like the sound of a spoon banging on a table top. Outwardly I'd be doing all the necessaries, but inside I was suspended above solid ground, just waiting for Ronald to come home. When I heard his key turn in the lock, my life would flick from black and white to colour like a faulty television screen, and I felt real again.

When the health visitor came round one day, she mentioned that a place had come up at the day nursery. Wondered if you could use it, she said, Most mums need a bit of a break from baby sometimes. I'm ashamed to say I burst into tears and she handed me a tissue and said Linda'll be fine, she's such a good girl. That's what the ladies at the nursery said too. Linda's such a good girl. She's never any trouble, not like the other little scamps. Ronald said he'd take her in on his way to work and bring her home on the way back. You can have a bit of a lie down, pet, he said, Don't want you getting ill again. He'd never asked for any favours from work before, so when he said could he leave the bank ten minutes early, his manager hummed and hawed and said he'd have to ask Region. Region said yes, but I know Ronnie felt his reputation had been tarnished. Something else I'd spoiled.

Linda used to come home the same as she was when she left in the morning. Never had dinner slopped down her front, never had scrapes and bruises on her knees, never had paint under her fingernails. I used to watch other little girls in the park giggling and gossiping when they made mud pies and chucked a ball around. Their mums had sensibly dressed them in jeans, but because she was so neat, I could dress Linda in frocks with buttons and buttonholes. I wanted her to look like a proper girl, so mostly I chose pink.

When she was pushing two, I fell pregnant. We'd only recently started sleeping together again, so it was like after that bumpy start, my insides were up and ready to go. I felt strangely cheered because I thought, Third time lucky. Maybe this time I'll get it right. The labour was more painful than before, and when the baby was born, the midwife gasped and called for a doctor. I kept saying What? What's happening? Is everything OK? but they had their backs to me and my legs were tied up in the stirrups so I couldn't go over and see what they were doing. After the longest time, the doctor turned round and said I'm sorry, Mrs Miller, we did everything we could and the nurse brought over a white bundle and I screamed because my baby was dead. Stillborn. They let Ronald in and he stood by the bed with tears pouring down his cheeks. I'd never seen him cry before.

I looked at my son, Kenneth, and he was perfect. Little face, little mouth and nose, fine-boned like his daddy, lots of damp dark hair. I nestled his face in my neck trying to revive him, but he was freezing. Someone produced a camera and took pictures of me and him. It'll help, they said, but when I pull them out now we both look dead, my son and me.

Back in the bin. I'm in the baby-killers' room. There's five other mothers in here who must have murdered their babies too because they wouldn't let me be in the same room otherwise. I'm too dangerous. My tummy's rumbling like a volcano and I know it's the poison churning around inside. I keep swallowing because otherwise it'll spurt out of my mouth and my ears and my cunt and someone else will be dead. I don't want anyone else to be dead. Two dead babies, that's enough. They try to make me eat, but they don't understand. If I open my mouth they'll be dead. If I keep swallowing, maybe the poison will kill me too and I'll join my babies in heaven. I see them in a field of flowers and Kenneth puts out his arms, but spiky fingers drag me off because I don't deserve to be in heaven. Hell's the place for me. Go to hell, Marilyn. But hell lasts forever and I don't want to last forever. In the night I go to the kitchen to get a plastic bag. I lie on the floor and push myself along with my feet slowly because otherwise the poison will leak out of me and someone will slip on it and die. I find the bags in a drawer and take two to be sure. I stuff them down my knickers. It makes me look pregnant, so I take them out and hold them between my knees. I'm halfway down the corridor and there are legs by my head and they're saying Where are you going with those, Marilyn? and they're going to stop me so I push harder with my heels but the legs are too quick and the bags have gone and I'm in a bed in a room by myself and the door won't open. There's a nurse sitting on a chair in the corner of the room like a bad fairy.

They let me home after four months with a pile of pills. Ronald used to have to feed them to me because they zombified me for nearly a year. He seemed to be managing fine with Linda. Dressed her nicely, took her to the park. She had this dress – dark pink, embroidered, frilly collar – that she wore a lot that summer. Seemed to be her favourite. Or maybe it was Ronnie's. She didn't seem to have minded being back in the Children's Home while I was away. The workers there said she never made any fuss. Said to Ronnie that she was just like a little old lady. No trouble at all they said. I did my best to stay away from her because while I wouldn't have harmed her deliberately, I was convinced she'd be affected if she got close enough to smell my madness. She had Ronnie anyway. He was always there.

The only thing she was funny about was food. She'd get this look on her face if her tea wasn't the way she wanted it. The food had to be *exactly* the right quantity, in *exactly* the right combination on *exactly* the right place on the plate. She'd refuse to eat anything if you put carrots and peas together, or if the meat pie had too much gravy, or if she didn't like that brand of baked beans. She could tell the difference between Heinz and Crosse & Blackwell. Hated supermarket own brands. She'd pick up a tiny morsel on the end of her fork and hold it against her lips for minutes at a time until her mouth opened and grudgingly took it in. I could see Ronnie struggling to make her eat normally and I emerged briefly from the fog to tell him not to worry. She wasn't losing weight or getting coughs and colds, so it was pointless fighting with her. I suppose he felt relieved, but I'm not sure I knew what he was feeling really. Sometimes I wonder if I ever did.

When I looked at Linda I'd see my first baby with her blonde curls and blue eyes with lashes like feathers. She'd call to me in her dreamy voice and we'd float off to a sweet-smelling garden by a river and make chains of flowers to wind around our heads. Ronnie used to make me daisy chains when we were courting. I was slim as a pin then. I started packing on the weight after the miscarriages two years and three and a half years after Kenneth, and Ronald and I began to look like one of those seaside postcards. Or Jack Sprat and his wife. I was constantly, fruitlessly, bouncing from diet to diet so we rarely ate together again. Or slept together much, so Ann Marie was a miracle.

Ann Marie. My precious jewel. I fell in love with the curve of her cheeks, her shoulders, her velvety tummy, her bum like uncooked dough. I was a mother for the first time: she smiled the earth's first smile, breathed the earth's first breath, coughed the earth's first cough, took the earth's first step. When she turned her blue eyes to me, I was the only mother there had ever been and she was the only baby. When she suckled at my breast, her pale fist resting against its fullness, it was the first time a baby had ever suckled, the first time a mother had ever satisfied her baby. I would reach the point where I thought I couldn't possibly hold any more love inside me, like a balloon pushed to its thinnest limits, and she'd put her head to one side, blink her feathery lashes and I'd fill up some more. Ronald and Linda were shadowy figures shifting at the periphery of our magic circle. After years and years of being a walking corpse, I was finally alive.

Linda was old enough to change my baby's nappies with a little supervision and when Ann Marie graduated on to solids she'd feed her. You had to keep an eye on her though, because sometimes she'd use a spoon that was too big, or push it in a bit far. She'd play with the baby really sweetly sometimes and I'd say Well done, Linda, good girl – look at your sister's lovely smile. Going downtown with the two of them took forever because we had to keep stopping. Ann Marie was such a head-turner she'd gather these gaggles of people around the buggy who'd stroke her curls and tell me what a cherub she was. As if I didn't know. Linda would stand a little way away, watching what was going on. She never intruded. She had lovely manners, always.

You wouldn't believe that these two peas came out of the same pod. There was Ann Marie, cheery and open and creamy, and there was Linda, serious and secretive and plain. Everybody loved Annie. On our caravan holidays, we'd hardly have unpacked the swimming cossies when she'd have joined a gang of other young tearaways bombing around the site charming sweets and pennies out of the other campers. Linda would spend the whole holiday with her nose in a book. Never magazines or comics. She'd read non-fiction books too, stuff I wouldn't touch with a bargepole. She was top in almost everything at school and we thought she'd definitely go to university. First one in the family. Don't know where it came from. Maybe some ancestor of Ronald's. He's quite intelligent.

Ann Marie was hopeless at lessons, apart from sewing and cooking. She bumped around in the bottom five for the academic subjects, but it didn't matter because she was the most popular girl in the school. I'd go to parents' evenings and the maths teacher would say Oh Mrs Miller, if only Ann Marie would stop giggling and concentrate, but he'd say it with a big grin on his face, like he was eating chocolate-chip ice cream straight from the tub. When I went for Linda, there'd be these rows and rows of ticks, everything A this and A that, but she never seemed to have any friends. Not that I knew of anyway.

Ann Marie developed early, like I had. I remember her coming into the kitchen when she found the first pea-shaped lump on her chest. Poor little scrap, she thought it was a cherry stone she'd swallowed the day before. Or cancer. I put my arms around her and told her she was just growing up into a fine young lady and I was proud of her. When she got her period a little while later, I pulled out the STs from behind the cream crackers in the airing cupboard and showed her how to use them. I don't know when Linda came on for the first time. She must have bought her own STs out of her pocket money, I suppose, because she never asked me for any.

Ann Marie and I had these things we called rummage hunts. We'd be chuckling down the street arm in arm when one of us would shout Rummage alert! and we'd pile into the shop and dive into the clothes rails. Since we both had these big bosoms, we'd get really excited when we found a new brand of bra. It was like we had a private language, the language of the underwired, circle-stitched, padded and strapless, and we'd hook them on to each other in the changing room, oohing and ahhing at the wonderful lacy engineering. Linda was never interested in joining us, although I think I must have invited her, so it was me and Annie against the world. The two musketeers. There were never three.

We had the devil of a job keeping Ann Marie at home once she turned thirteen, but we always knew she was safe because she went out and about with a big group and they'd take care of each other. And she had boyfriends galore – couldn't keep them away – and we always liked them, they were lovely boys. All she ever wanted was to have babies, so when she and Johnnie got together she just popped them out like corks: pop, pop, pop, Donnie, Frannie, Joey. Lights of my life.

There wasn't any evidence of boys around in Linda's life, but she didn't seem bothered. When we went shopping for her school uniform, I'd sometimes say to her Let's go to Boots and I'll buy you some make-up. My treat, OK? but she'd say Not today, thanks Mother, so I stopped offering in the end. Ann Marie didn't need much in the way of make-up because she was naturally gorgeous, but when your basic materials are quite ordinary, like Linda, you've got to work that little bit harder to attract the boys. She didn't experiment like any normal girl with eye shadow or lipstick, you never saw her making the effort to give her rather flat face some sort of shape, but she was always well scrubbed. Almost as though she'd cleaned herself with bleach. There was nothing girly about her. She liked practical clothes in nondescript colours – not too loose, not too tight – and kept her hair short and its own colour. It's actually quite hard to describe the colour of her hair and her eyes, but she was always very slim, I'll give her that. Never had to worry about her weight like Annie and me.

When Linda finished her 'A' levels I assumed she'd applied for university and vaguely wondered if she'd chosen a London college because she went down there several times. I remember saying to her one time when she came back home, Had a nice day, Linda? What've you been up to? And she said Oh nothing much, just went to the British Museum and had a hamburger afterwards. Annie was in the middle of her dancing exams at the time – she did tap and modern – so I was very busy, what with making her costumes and driving her around everywhere. Maybe I should have asked Linda for more details, but I assumed she had it all under control. Then one day she was up in her room all evening, just popped down for her tea, and the next morning there was a suitcase by the door. She came into the kitchen where I was making Ann Marie a cake for doing so well in her exams and she said I'm going to London now, Mother. It's all

arranged, I've got a job in an office and a place to stay. I'll let you
know all the contact details when I'm settled in. I said Oh my
goodness, why didn't you tell me? And she said I just wanted it to
be a nice surprise. I'll be fine, she said. Don't worry about me.
What a lovely cake – hasn't she done well? And she was gone.

I went up to her room, still a bit dazed, and it looked the same
as it always did, like a hospital ward. Or a prison cell. She'd left
most of her clothes and her books, which surprised me. She had
this little collection of novels that I knew she read over and over
because they kept turning up by her bed. I noticed them when I
went in to clean. Big books, they were: *Anne of Green Gables*,
Pollyanna, *The Secret Garden* and *Jane Eyre*. Years later I asked my
granddaughter about them because she's a big reader and she
said they were all about these orphan girls. I said to Annie Why
would she want to read sad stories about orphans when she's got
two parents still alive? And she said Dunno, Mum, perhaps she's
gone up to London to buy herself a new pair, and we laughed.

Annie took over Linda's room once I'd taken her stuff to the
charity shop, and Ronnie painted it purple and pink. In Linda's
time everything was plain white – even the doorknobs. It was
like standing in a pot of cottage cheese. Once Annie had covered
the walls with her Adam Ant posters and filled the shelves with
her china elephants, it was as though Linda had never been there.
We went on with our lives and it didn't feel like anything was
missing. We'd just become a family of three, that's all.

After a bit, Linda sent us her address and phone number on a
postcard with some Beefeaters on it and I put the details in my
address book, but that was all we knew. I could imagine her
doing well in an office because she was so meticulous, but I
didn't know what exactly she did, what kind of business it was
or whether she'd made friends. That was so typical of Linda. I
find myself saying all the time, I don't know, I didn't know,
I couldn't know. I don't think any of us really knew her. It was

as though she was a guest in our family for eighteen years – as though we were doing B&B – and then she came to the end of her stay and went off to her real life, whatever that was. Sometimes I imagined her going off to work in a smart suit and heels, just to give her a bit of a lift, and sometimes I even imagined her with a briefcase, but that's as far as it went. Ronald's got a briefcase that I bought him one Christmas, but he just uses it for his packed lunch and a newspaper.

She moved a couple of times and sent us more postcards, we exchanged presents at Christmas and cards at birthdays through the post, but we didn't speak on the phone. When Ann Marie married her Johnnie, Linda sent this monster Gaggia coffee machine as a wedding present. The coffee it made tasted like licking the soles of your shoes – nothing like a nice cup of Maxwell House. I think it's in a cupboard somewhere, still in its box.

It was a bit of a shock when we got the invite to her wedding on this stiff white card with fancy lettering and gold edges. *Carriages at 6.30*, it said, like we were going to fetch up in a coach and four or something. *Sherilyn Miller*, it said. Took us a while to work out who that was. Sounded like Marilyn. We went of course. Would've been rude not to. Met Brendan for the first time. The only time. Huge bloke but very smart. Met his family. Linda – Sherilyn – wore this plain little designer dress that probably cost as much as our house, and there was this food that wouldn't have fed a hamster. When we got back to the hotel with Brendan's dad and stepmothers, we pigged out on fish and chips. It wasn't called fish and chips of course – had some French or Italian name – but that's what it was. A little while later, another posh card plopped on our mat, announcing the birth of their daughter, Samantha. Our granddaughter, I suppose. I sent a Mothercare outfit.

Next thing was The News.

Shirley

He took up a lot of room, Finn. Not just physically, though he was built like a brick shithouse, but he kind of nudged everything else out of the way in your head when he was around. Even when he wasn't. I'd been really gloomy when my first marriage went down the toilet and I was left struggling on my own with the boys. Rita used to watch them for me when I got a job at the Crown and Greyhound, which I badly needed because my waste-of-space first husband was paying me precisely nothing. It wasn't the liveliest pub in the whole universe, but I could always stash my drink under the bar with the empties, which kept my spirits up. Kept them from going down anyway.

Finn used to come in on his own three, four times a week and sit at the bar with his Jameson. And beer nuts, he always liked beer nuts. He had this funny thin voice which was all at odds with his size, like a Rottweiler mewing or twittering or something, but it endeared him to me because otherwise he'd have come across as a bit of a thug. After a few shots he'd start telling me about his life, which you get used to as a barmaid, but it turned out we had a lot in common. Mainly both being alone with young sons – his Brendan was almost exactly between my Steve and Wayne – but we were both still angry with our partners too. It wasn't Angela's fault that she died of course, but you're not thinking rationally when something like that happens, you're just furious with the person that's left you. It was a brain tumour, he said, it took her four years to die after she'd had Brendan and she was pretty well nuts by the end. He'd moved himself down to Exeter to get away from the memories – And her bloody nosy family, he said. Bloody six sisters, she had – they were all over me like a rash after. He'd had a reasonably profitable building business in London, but it was flying sky-high down here in Devon, so he was financially comfortable. Next to my pathetically useless ex he seemed like a good bet for a boyfriend, so when he asked me out I said yes straight away. It's funny, I went on about my two boys all the time, but once Finn told me he had a son he practically never mentioned him again.

It all went very fast and he asked me to marry him after four months. I never brought him around to mine because I didn't want to confuse the boys if it wasn't going to be serious, but he wasn't bothered about me being around Brendan. I didn't stay the night until we were wed, but Bren came into the bedroom once when we were at it. He had this way of slithering into a room without making a sound, like water seeping under a door, so he was right by the bed without us knowing he'd even come in. Finn hauled himself off me and went mental – I'd never seen him like that before. He snatched this poor little scrap by the back of his pyjamas and shook him like you shake your nail varnish. He was cursing him for barging in, cursing him for being born – he kept shouting You little bastard, you killed her! It should've been you! I wish you were dead! and at that point I thought I'd better intervene. You don't say that to a kiddie. I jumped off the bed and grabbed hold of Brendan. Finn looked shocked, then he started trying to pull him off me and I pulled back and there we were, both of us starkers, having this tug of war with a little boy's body. Finn's face was getting darker and darker and he suddenly dropped Brendan and raised his fist at me. Christ, I thought, He's going to thump me, but he seemed to come to and didn't. Not that time anyway. And all the way through this, all the way through the pushing and pulling, Bren hadn't made a sound. Not a peep. Any normal kid would have been screaming his face off, but Brendan just flopped around between us like a rag doll. I wrapped a sheet around me and took him back to bed. Told him it was all going to be OK, that I knew it was really crap his mum had died, but how would he like to have another mum? And a couple of brothers? And he nodded and I gave him a hug.

All three boys were pages when we got married: my two looked gorgeous in their little suits and frilly shirts, but Brendan just looked awkward, like he really was a spare one at the wedding. He was always out of step, never wanted to do anything with my boys, even though they were really close in age. They'd be off kicking a ball around with the other kids, getting into scrapes like boys do and he'd be up in his room, so quiet I often forgot he was in the house. He was good at school, especially with arithmetic, but he was hopeless at sport, didn't even want to watch it on the telly. Finn and my two were footie mad and he'd take them up to see Man U as often as he could, even though it was a fair old way from Devon. He told me the other fans on the terraces used to assume they were his sons because they were that close, really bonded. He said he liked that.

Brendan looked so much like Angie it was spooky. Finn had this big blow-up photo of her and him as a baby over the front-room fireplace and often I'd find Brendan sitting at the bottom of the stairs, staring at it like he was communing with something. It was pretty weird having to live with a giant pin-up of your husband's dead wife glaring down at you in your front room, but I knew it came with the wedding ring so I never asked him to take it down. About a year after Finn and I were wed, I was dusting the picture and I jogged the frame. To my horror, the hook broke and the damn thing fell off the wall. I caught it, thank Christ – I'd have been dog meat otherwise. I put it face down on the carpet and trotted off to fetch another hook. As I came back into the room, I noticed a mucky envelope taped to the back of the picture. I pulled it off gingerly so I didn't damage it, and turned it over. It said 'Brendan' on the front in wobbly old-lady's handwriting. Obviously I wasn't about to give it to Brendan directly because he was far too young to be getting letters and anyway I was the grown-up, so I opened it. It was from her. Angela. When I got to the end of the first page – and it was a long letter, must have taken her ages – I realised I'd been holding my breath, so I put it down and went off to make myself a cuppa. Can't hold your breath when you're drinking, is what I thought. I came back with the tea, curled up on the settee and started from the beginning again.

Fortunately I was alone in the house, because by the end I was sobbing my heart out. It was a love letter. I've never had one of those – moved in with number one too quick to be writing to each other and Finn didn't exactly have a gift for words – but if somebody'd written like that to me, I'd have been mush. I'd seen all her books upstairs – had to bloody dust the things twice a week along with all her other knick-knacks – so I knew she'd done a lot of reading, but she was quite a writer too.

She knew she was dying and it was like she was mourning something that was dead before it had been properly alive. She was grieving for the Brendan she'd never know. It rocked all my basic assumptions, like assuming I'd see my boys grow up, assuming I'd see them through the dating years and into marriage, assuming I'd get to know my grandchildren. Without those assumptions you wouldn't bother waking up in the morning.

Obviously I knew she was dead, but I hadn't imagined her dying: what it must have been like for her to know there weren't many months left, then weeks left, then days. What it must have been like for Brendan to be losing his mum inch by inch every day. All I knew about Finn was how furious he was, although he loved her so dearly he must have been devastated when she finally passed on. He never told me and I suppose I never asked.

There was a noise from upstairs and the toilet flushed. I'd forgotten I'd kept Brendan off school because he had a temperature, so I thought I'd better nip upstairs and check on him. I stuffed the letter in the pocket of my pinny, wiped my eyes and went up to his bedroom. As I opened the door, the letter felt like a red hot brick against my belly and in a mad sort of way I wondered if he knew it was there.

I didn't tell Finn about it until after tea when we were sat watching telly. The boys were safely in bed – they didn't have to know about the letter, I thought, they were only young. I said Finn, I found something weird today when I was dusting. Behind the picture of Angie. He started flicking through the channels with the remote, which drove me nuts at the best of times and I said Stop it, for Christ's sake! This is important! Shush, he said, Nothing is more important than Man U – they're away to Newcastle tonight. But it's a letter from Angie, I said, A letter from beyond the grave. To Brendan, I said, So I opened it.

Oh God, I shouldn't have said that. Should've pretended it didn't have an envelope, but I couldn't unsay it now. Finn punched the mute button and turned to me so slowly I could almost see each hair on his head moving separately. You. Did. What? he said. You read Angela's private letter? You stuck your nose in my business? You'd best give me the letter now, girl, or else. I got up from the settee and he was suddenly there in front of me, walling me in. But it's in the kitchen, I said, In my pinny. In the pocket. He looked at me as though I was some stranger cluttering up the place. Don't. Fucking. Move, he said, and wheeled round. When he got to the kitchen he made this sound somewhere between a cough and a sob, then he was out the back door.

He stayed away for five days and I was frantic. I told the boys he'd had to go away on business, but Steve picked up a couple of calls from his foreman, so I had to tell him Finn was upset about something, but not to worry, he'd be back. Poor kid, he'd already had one dad walk out on him. I called Finn's drinking buddies but they all claimed not to have seen him. I didn't believe them for a moment because I'd overheard Finn covering up for them tons of times. It's what men do.

When he came back, he stank. He was wearing the same clothes he'd stormed out in and he was covered in mud and blood and snot. He looked like he'd just staggered out of a jungle where he'd been falling out of trees and wrestling pythons, but it was a jungle where the rivers ran with stale beer and fag ends. He didn't look at me, didn't say a word and went straight to the bathroom, where he stayed for two hours. When the boys came home and saw him, I made the zipped-up mouth sign and they trotted up to their rooms. I took them their tea later. That whole evening and the following three days was like at the cinema when the sound fails and you've only got the pictures to tell you what's going on. He went to work, I saw to the kids, picked up his clothes from the floor, washed them, put his tea in front of him, sat at the other end of the table eating mine, watched his face, waited. At the end of the third day, he looked up from his sausages and said Mine. That's mine – y'understand? You don't go there if you know what's good for you. I said I know I shouldn't have read it, Finn, but I didn't want Brendan to see it before I knew what was in it. I give it you, didn't I? I took it off you, he growled. You didn't give it me, I took it, and he went back to his tea.

We had sex that night – or he had sex, more to the point. It felt like he was trying to pulverise me, so I lay still till he'd finished. It was the same the next night, except he called me Angela. It carried on like that for another ten days or so and then he flipped back to normal. That's how it went with him, as though he had this secret switch somewhere under his heart, which could unexpectedly shut everything off and just as shockingly switch it back on again. When Planet Cheery was in the sky, Planet Fury dropped out of the universe and vice versa.

But having made one big mistake, I spent the rest of my time with him making thousands more and paying the price. A month or two after he'd gone back to normal, we were doing some gardening together and we'd had a couple of beers, so I suppose my tongue was a bit looser than sometimes. Brendan had been quite poorly with mumps and when I looked back at the house, his pasty face was pushed up against his bedroom window, watching us. I gave him a wave and as I turned back to Finn I said Poor little mite, he looks like he's been pulled through a hedge backwards. For such a big lad, he takes his time getting better, doesn't he? Finn grunted. I carried on, digging myself this big fat hole which I immediately plopped into. I bet Angie was better than me about illness, I said, Being as how she was ill herself and everything. I suppose I'm just used to having healthy boys around the place. What did you do with that letter, by the way? Did you find a better place to hide it? He muttered something and I said What? What did you say? And suddenly he was shouting. Burned it! he yelled, Turned it to ash, like her! None of your business! I couldn't help it – I've got sons, after all – and I blurted out How could you do that? He needed to see it when he grew up, Finn – he needed to know she loved him! and next thing I knew I was flat on my back in the sweet peas, blood pouring out of my nose. Finn's steel-capped boots were by my head and he stamped his foot into the ground. He didn't deserve her, he said, in a hiss that was far scarier than his yelling, So he didn't deserve the letter. She was mine, not his, and he stomped back into the house. When I sat up, Brendan's face was still at the window. Still watching.

He looked like his mum: same big lips, same grey eyes with yellow flecks and same kink in his hair at the front and I think it drove Finn mad that he was such a clone. When he beat him up, sometimes he'd use one of her books, and he'd be thwacking him around the head and I'd be going Not his head, Finn, you'll give him brain damage, but he'd just turn on me. He never went for my head though, it was usually my stomach or my legs. I wore a lot of long sleeves and floor-length skirts.

You'd see Brendan's little face crumbling when his dad was thumping him, but he'd be struggling not to cry because that would rile Finn even more and he'd cop it worse. He wasn't responsible for his mum's death, but the pregnancy made her tumour bigger – all the hormones I suppose – and Finn never stopped blaming him. I should have known I could never replace Angie because when someone's died so tragically they become a saint and I wasn't that good at sainthood. I had to make sure Brendan had his hair cut regularly because if it got too long, he'd look like her spit and Finn would roar at him for looking girly. Fucking nancy boy, he'd shout, Get him out of my sight! I did my best. Or I think I did, but in the end Brendan got to me too. He was a big lad, like his dad, bigger than both my two until Steve had a sudden rush of blood to the head when he was twelve and shot up, but there was something about him that didn't match his size. Something that was almost asking you to hit him. I *never* hit my boys, but Brendan used to stand there when I was telling him off and he'd be hanging his head so I couldn't see his eyes and I'd feel this rage welling up in me like I'd burst if I didn't smack him, so I did. Especially when he wet the bed. He carried on doing that the whole time I was with his dad and there was nothing I could do to stop him. I tried talking to him, tried one of those alarm things, tried shouting at him, but it felt deliberate, as though he was defying me. That sounds nuts because he was such a wimp, but he'd be standing there and it would be like he was going So what you gonna do about this then? And when you've got three boys and a maniac husband to cope with and when you're picking up stinking sheets and stuffing them in the machine *every day*, you crack. So I hit him, really hard sometimes, especially when his dad had been having a go. I couldn't defend myself against Finn, but I could take it out on his son. I'm not proud of that, but it was like he provoked it.

I didn't tell anyone what was going on for a long time – too ashamed to begin with, and then Finn turned funny and wouldn't let me see anyone. He'd time me when I went down the shops and if I came back more than five minutes after he'd expected me, I'd get a good hiding. It got so's I only went shopping with him and even then I had to keep my eyes on the ground in case he caught me looking at someone. He started intercepting my phone calls, told my family I didn't want to see them any more and gave me the third degree every time one of my friends – female friends, that is – wanted to meet up for a cup of coffee and a fag. It was Rita who noticed the bruises and she nagged me to leave him. Leave him, Shirl, she'd say, Or else let *me* have a go at him, and I'd say No don't, it'll come back on me, and it would have too. I was trapped, because even if I took one of the kids down the doctor's he'd go for me when I came back, accusing me of having other men and all sorts, so I stopped in.

Rita used to sneak in sometimes when he was at work – prison visiting, we called it – and we'd have a laugh. She was my lifeline. I never let my boys see it going on and they *never* saw me crying. When you're in a situation like that you've got a sixth sense so you know when he's going to start up, like smelling a bonfire in the wind. I'd get that vibe and I'd say to my two Up to your room now, boys, have a bit of a play and I'll take you down the park later, and they'd go upstairs as good as gold. But Brendan made himself so invisible I often didn't realise he was still around and I know he saw Finn having a go several times after that time in the garden. One time he had me over the back of the settee and he was hitting me in the kidneys and I saw Brendan down on the floor looking up with these huge eyes and I shouted Finn, Finn, Brendan's down there! and he started howling I don't give a fuck, I don't give a fuck, I don't give a fuck, in time with the punches.

Five years I stuck it out thinking it must have been me, I must have been causing it, then one day I didn't pick up the signal fast enough and Wayne saw Finn giving me a bloody nose. End of story. I left the same night and Rita took us all in. It wasn't long after that that she and Finn got together. When she told me, I nearly died on the spot. I said But he's an evil bastard you always said so, he'll do the same to you, and she had this little glint in her eye and she said I don't think so. And he never did. He turned into this pussycat around her – she even persuaded him to keep paying me and the boys right up to the time when he had that mucked-up operation, so apart from she's my best friend, I've got reason to be grateful to her. After a couple of years of being with her, he and I even got back to being friends. Obviously we never talked about what had gone on, but we had sex occasionally for old time's sake. Rita never knew, of course, and I used to wonder what he'd told her the one time he stayed the night at mine.

I rarely saw Brendan when I went over to see Rita, which was neither here nor there because I didn't see him that much when I was living with his dad. But there was this one time I was over there and her and me were having a giggle in the kitchen when he came in to make himself some coffee. I did this big double take like you see in cartoons and I said Brendan? Is that you? because I really wasn't sure. He said Who else? with a half-smile. He was dressed really smart with this tweedy jacket and beige slacks and *seriously* expensive-looking shoes. And he smelled! I don't mean he ponged or anything – he smelled of aftershave, and not the sort of rubbish you get in Boots either. He could have stepped out of some glossy magazine and bearing in mind this must have been about 1976, he looked years older than my Wayne and Steve. They had these Cherokee haircut things and so many holes punched in their ears I thought they'd probably whistle a tune if the wind blew. I knew they'd grow out of it eventually so I wasn't that concerned, but I was a bit cheesed off when they kept pinching my eyeliner.

I said to Rita when he'd gone What the hell's happened to Bren? And she said Dunno really. Discovered girls probably because he's stopped wetting the bed and he's out two, three times a week. Got this mate Paul knocks for him – dead good-looking, he is, smashing manners, real ladykiller if you ask me – and they go off together. No idea why he'd be friends with Brendan though, she said. Maybe he's got hidden depths we don't know about. Maybe he's won the pools, and she cackled.

He suddenly buggered off up London and she said there was this weird thing when she cleared out his room. She was packing his books in a box ready for the charity shop, and all these feathers tumbled out. She thought maybe he was using them as bookmarks, but there were so many of them it didn't seem likely, so it stayed a mystery like so much about Brendan. He wrote and told Rita and his dad when he passed his accountancy exams, but it didn't seem right to be proud of him. Being proud would have been like laying claim to him, as though any of us had anything to do with how he turned out. To be truthful, I think he'd brought himself up.

When Thatcher's recession stuffed Finn's business, he started boozing seriously. Rita's a strong woman, but she'd be over at mine sometimes dangerously close to tears – and Rita *never* cried. She came over one time and before I'd even put the kettle on, she pulled out this official-looking letter from her handbag and said Look at this, Shirl. I leaned against the stove and read it. By the time I'd finished, I was practically on my knees. It was from the receivers. From Brendan. Carving up his father's firm like a

Sunday roast. Pulling his dad's life apart, his life's work, without blinking an eye. There was nothing personal in the letter. No *I'm sorry about this, Dad*. Or *This must be really tough for you*. It wasn't even signed, just pp'd by his secretary. Killing Finn off was just another bit of business for him. Another file to push around on his desk until it was time to bin it.

As a result Rita had an uphill task persuading Finn to come with us to Brendan's wedding. She said he went around smashing things until he fell into another slump and had to go back on the tablets. Poor man, he barely said more than ten words at the reception, one of which was Crap when he saw the food. It wasn't crap, but it wasn't a meal either. Little dollops of stuff on bits of pastry with weird-coloured dips and sauces. And this stuff in a bowl that looked like black snot. Turns out it was caviar. I got a bit tiddly and tried talking to one of the other guests, but he looked at me like someone had farted, so I went back to Finn and Rita. Snotty sod. I met the Millers. Thought it would be just the one time. Little did I know.

I rather envied Marilyn and Ann Marie for the mother–daughter thing they had going on between them. They sat together the whole afternoon and you could hardly see where Marilyn left off and Ann Marie started up. There was thirty-odd years between them, but if you looked at Marilyn you knew you were seeing what Ann Marie was going to be like thirty years down the line. She was a big girl, Marilyn, very pretty still, but with more wrinkles on her face than you'd expect from a woman her age. I would have said she was no stranger to the cake trolley and the elasticated waistband, but then next to me anyone looked like an elephant. Ann Marie had the shiny hair of a real blonde and enormous blue eyes with lashes so long they pricked the skin under her brows when she smiled. I thought she must have done a lot of smiling in her life, judging from the lines around her eyes, and some of the time she and Marilyn seemed to be involved in a long-running private joke which didn't include Ronald.

He was a funny little man. I quite liked him, but in the same way you quite like blancmange. He was very attentive to Marilyn but I wasn't convinced he was doing it out of love. It looked more like fear to me. He was obviously a good husband and presumably a good father because Ann Marie was lovely, but he didn't look like he'd be an animal in bed exactly. I thought he probably couldn't get it up without the help of pulleys and permission from the teacher. No problems in that department with Finn.

We all stayed right to the end, although quite a few of the other guests buggered off as soon as the food was over. Me, I didn't think it was right for us to leave early because we were the only family they had there, though in the circumstances family is a strange word to use. There was a limo booked for us all so when it was announced we trooped up and said Thank you and Goodbye and Good luck, and they said Thank you for coming. Finn was still slumped in his chair and Brendan shot him a look that puzzled me at the time, but when I thought about it later, I realised it was a strange mixture of hunger and disgust. Like he was starving and he'd been served an enormous meal which turned his stomach. I was glad Finn didn't clock it.

He was dead eighteen months later. Heart attack three months after the wedding, recovered, invalid for fourteen months, second heart attack, intensive care, fuck-up with the operation, dead. Rita didn't bother telling Brendan about the first attack, but she sent him a card inviting him to the funeral. He didn't come, but he could have sent a wreath.

And then this. I don't watch the evening news much – too depressing – but when they found Samantha it was all over the papers and I remember thinking What kind of monsters could do that? It had to be the parents, but for some reason the little girl's surname didn't ring any bells – I'd gone back to my maiden

name twenty-odd years before, Rita'd always hung on to hers
and Finn was just Finn. But when they caught them having some
expensive holiday somewhere and their names and faces were
on the front pages, I didn't know where to put myself. I went
over to Rita's straight away and we talked and drank and cried –
well, I cried anyway – until my Steve turned up and took me
home with him. Wayne came down from Scotland and we
locked the doors and drew the curtains. This herd of press hyenas
started stalking round the front gate and if they so much as saw
a curtain twitch, they'd be shouting out Steve! Shirley! We know
you're in there! Give us an interview! What were they like? The
last thing I wanted to do was talk about it to anyone outside the
family, but in the house there was no other topic of conversation.
I'd be helping my daughter-in-law bath the baby and she'd
suddenly look distraught and say What if I dropped him? What
if I just held him underwater for a moment? and she'd burst into
tears. Or I'd be sat watching telly and there'd be someone on the
screen who'd trigger off all these pictures in my head of Brendan
cowering behind a door when his dad came in from work or my
boys rampaged through the room. Or that time he started having
these cuts on his arms and hands. Never did get to the bottom
of that.

It was like the plague. It infected everything we did, everything
we thought. I used to phone Rita two or three times a day and
we'd try to laugh. We said we'd get ourselves T-shirts printed
with 'Watch Out, Watch Out, Wicked Stepmums About!' on the
front, but it wasn't funny. I didn't need a T-shirt. When the
media moved on and I ventured out, I had to go home four
times out of five because I was sure I heard people whispering
That's her. That's his stepmum. What did she do to him? I knew I
was being para, but because it was filling my head, I assumed
everyone else's was stuffed with it too. And then we had to go
to court. Brendan's solicitor called us and said would we please

attend because it would help his case. I said Why would we want to help his case? And he said You were his stepmother when he was a little boy. You must have known him well. You don't have to say anything in court, just be there for him. And I thought, No I didn't know him well, he was this big question mark. I didn't say it out aloud because then the solicitor would have thought it was all my fault too, so I agreed to go but I wasn't happy. I started seriously obsessing about what to wear and Rita said Black, wear black, but I said Then it'll look like we're already in mourning. Like we care that he's going to be put away for the rest of his life. I didn't want to be responsible for him, didn't want to have this mark of Zorro across my face, but I couldn't escape. I was tied to him by history. Five years of misery with his dad and I was glued to the biggest, fattest, most disgusting crime there'd ever been.

I've never been in a court in my life – apart from the divorce court of course. They should have given me a discount second time round, like 'Buy One, Get One Free', but I've never done anything illegal. I'm so terrified of being told off I've never even exceeded the speed limit, never got a parking ticket, but now I was convicted by my connection to a baby-killer. I like a good courtroom drama on the telly, but when we arrived at the court – all together, Rita and me wearing brown – we found out it was us that was the drama. Everyone else was out there twiddling the knobs, watching us, judging us, mocking us, and they could crank up the brightness any time they liked, turn up the volume any time they liked – or turn us off. They stuck us in a separate box together in the court. It was for our own protection, they said, but it felt like they were putting us in quarantine so we wouldn't contaminate anyone else. They should have just given us bells and have done with it, so we could have wandered around going Unclean, Unclean and the good folk of the town could have steered clear.

I had to keep reminding myself that this giant man in the dock was the little boy I used to look after, because otherwise he was just an animal. I forced myself to listen to all the evidence, but I only managed to look at him twice. I found myself thinking, Maybe he's nuts. Maybe he couldn't help it. That would make it better because if he was nuts then he wouldn't have been responsible for what he did and I'd be off the hook too. I didn't remember him doing anything nasty when I lived with him, like pulling the legs off insects or anything – my boys did – but maybe he was up there in his room doing strange stuff. I never knew what he was up to, but maybe he was making voodoo dolls or something. My head was full of maybes. I was trying to make sense of something that was so awful it could drive you mad if you just accepted it. There had to be reasons.

When he was sent to prison I hoped that would bring it to a close for me. There he was stone cold guilty, he was going to get punished, boom, it's all over, go home and carry on with your life, but it doesn't work that way. I'm better when I've had a drink. Better still when I've had several drinks. I've kept the boozing quiet down the years, and I know it's bad for me, but it knocks the corners off things. Makes it possible to carry on. Doctor says my liver's packing up, but I've not had a bad life, I've got my boys and the grandkids so I know there's a future even if I'm not going to be in it for long.

Angela

My son,

It's October and there's a smell of mulch and melancholy in the air. I regret not having read much poetry over the years, but when the air begins to crisp I'm reminded of the image of 'mellow fruitfulness' in that poem by somebody-or-other. I've always thought of it as an apple, its luscious insides pressing against the skin before exploding in a dying cascade back into the earth. From here in the kitchen I can see you outside in the garden, carefully stacking the brittle leaves from the larch that arches over the raspberry canes. I must cut them back so that they fruit generously next year. Add that to my list. They're your favourite and I want to imagine you feasting on the crop that I've grown for you, even if I'm not there to join in. They're my favourite too. You're such a serious little boy and the look of determination on your face as you make sure no one leaf shakes the symmetry of the pile is pulling your full mouth into a thin line. You potter over to the untidy swirls of leaves on the grass, between the plants, and examine them all until you find the very one for your tower. You reject it if it doesn't settle snugly against its neighbour, and since I've been watching you've crushed four in your podgy fingers, casting the fragments into the breeze. That seems to give you great satisfaction, even though you're not as destructive as some little boys.

Your orderliness has always amused me. You certainly don't get that from me – I drive Daddy mad when I leave my books around, or don't tidy up straight away when I've been cooking – but he's no paragon either. The other day I found you with that construction kit I bought you for your birthday, puzzling and puzzling about how to fit the pieces back in the box in exactly the same position they came in. You'd insisted on keeping all the packaging when you'd opened it, and each piece of polystyrene, each cardboard corner had to be placed back in the box in a particular order. You were tutting and humming with frustration as I watched you, but when I offered to help you, you said, 'Don't be silly, Mummy, I have to do it on my own.' I can't bear to think of you on your own after I've gone, and I've said to Daddy that he has to help you to do things, teach you how to be a boy and then a man, but he's not taking it in. He's not taking in much, if I'm honest.

I made sure he wasn't with me when the neurologist told me what I had. What was causing the headaches and the wobbles, the strange absences of mind that I'd put down to the delirious wonder of having a child. Being a mum. I asked him to spell it out so I could write it down and practise saying it. ANAPLASTIC OLIGOASTROCYTOMA – there it is. You probably haven't been told that. I can say it easily now, except for the days when my memory's behaving like a giant colander, but when I told Daddy I just said brain tumour.

I waited until he'd come home from the site in the evening and had a bath, because he's always a bit grumpy until he's clean. I leaned over him to pop a beer on the table and breathed in his soapiness. I love that smell. It's different from the way you smell when your hair's slightly damp – that's more like wheatfields at the end of the summer, shot through with a hint of Sugar Puffs. Daddy's smell is like he sees the world: you're either dirty or clean; it's either day or night, uncomplicated by dawn or dusk.

When I said 'brain tumour', his head flicked back against the chair as though the words had splintered against his forehead, and he closed his eyes. There was a long silence in which I could hear you snuffling in your sleep upstairs and I wondered what Daddy was thinking. As though he'd ever tell me. It went on so long, I thought perhaps I should get up and see to our tea, but then he opened his eyes and said, 'Well, that's OK then. Mum did all right after the op.' I said, 'But hers was benign, and anyway it was on her leg – doctor says mine is malignant, which is more difficult to treat.' 'Mum did all right,' he repeated, and I knew it was time to get the tea.

His reaction didn't come as a surprise because I knew he was like that from the beginning. I think you're more likely to lasso a herd of flying pigs than hear about how we met from your father, so I wanted you to know the story from me, however old you are when you're reading this. I expect Daddy will give the letter to you when you're twenty-one or so, and I imagine you sitting in an armchair trying to find your way around my wonky handwriting. It wasn't always wonky. Before the tumour, I mean. I got a handwriting prize at primary school, actually – oh, and another one for an essay I wrote about my mum growing up in the East End.

I met him when I was an auxiliary nurse at the Royal Free. I loved it. In those days, matron was like God and a regimental sergeant major all rolled into one, but mine took a shine to me right away. She had one of those fronts that looks like it should be stuck to the prow of a ship, and her nurse's watch hung there looking a little foolish, as though it really needed to grow up into a grandfather clock sharpish. She kept saying I should go off to college and train to be a proper nurse, but I told her it was impossible because my family couldn't have done without my wages. 'Then at least you can learn about my hospital,' she said, and she moved me to a different ward every few months. Daddy was admitted when I'd been working on men's orthopaedic for six weeks or so, navigating my way through the patients' moans and groans. And, my word, they moaned! Much, much worse than women – even women with terminal cancer and small children.

Daddy had fallen off a girder into a basement and had multiple fractures in his left leg and the metatarsals in his right foot. He must have been in agony, but he never so much as peeped. He'd lie there, his leg suspended over the bed, as though he'd been carved out of wax, but I could tell how much it was costing him not to call out from the way his eyes jittered like nervous birds.

I had to break off there because you ran into a garden hoe I stupidly left across the path. I'm sorry, Brendan, Mummy's not thinking straight at the moment. You know people say, 'You'll forget your own name next'? Well, I did. The day before yesterday I was at the doctor's for a repeat prescription and I couldn't tell the receptionist who I was. Luckily, doctor came out and, finding me in floods of tears, told me my name. I repeated it, but I could have been speaking Chinese.

You're just like your daddy. The hoe smacked into your eyebrow – you'll have a ripe old shiner tomorrow – but you didn't shed a tear. You let me cuddle you, your skin damp with pain, but there were no sobs, no milking the situation for extra sweets. Maybe it's in the genes, this sense that there's only one way to be a man, because Daddy's got that running down his middle like a message in a stick of rock. But maybe there are other ways too. There was this other poem I read once, also written by somebody-or-other (he must have been a pretty productive poet!), which goes on about all these qualities you need in life, like not telling lies and not hating, learning how to trust and wait, that sort of thing, and it ends up 'and then you'll be a man, my son' – well, those are good ways of being a man, my son. I wish I could remember the title, but I don't think I could remember it when I could remember things. But how would I know? I can't even remember whether I could remember it back then.

I just had to turn the page back to remember where I was going with this.

I was telling you about Daddy and me.

He was on the ward for weeks, having operation after operation, and I used to sit with him when he came back from theatre, when he was still woozy. The whole time he was there he never had any visitors or cards or flowers, and it broke my heart to see him at visiting time marooned on his bed, the chit-chat and bustle of other patients' families washing around him like the tide. When he was coming out from under the anaesthetic, his Irish accent was so thick I only caught one word in three, but once he seemed to be talking about his 'da' and this little renegade tear slid out of the corner of his closed eye and meandered down to his ear. It's the only time I've seen him cry – if that's what it was. Over the past eighteen months it's been a mystery to me where all my tears have come from. Sometimes I think I must have these saline sacs down by my ankles, with a complicated system of tubes and valves that pumps the liquid up to my eyes then refills the sacs from some anatomically bizarre reservoir. Perhaps in my b.t.m.

You do have weird thoughts like this when you're not very well.

Daddy doesn't know what to do with me when I cry, so I try and control it, but usually it just leaks out of me. I'm full of holes, one way and the other. You're different, but then little children understand about crying. When you catch me weeping, you do these tricks to make me laugh, like putting your head down the toilet pretending to be an ostrich like that one in your book. It usually works, but I worry about you remembering me only as I am now, only shuddering with grief, because you were so young when I got ill and you may have forgotten how joyous I was when you were born. And I was, Brendan. For once in my life I thought it would be OK if the wind changed and my face got stuck, because I'd just be this huge grin on legs, as though nothing bad had ever happened in the world.

My illness seems to make Daddy angry – not with me, he's as nice as pie to me – but you're winding him up like a watch spring. I don't know why. The other day you were mucking about in the scullery, tipping cups of washing powder into the socks, and it was making a bit of a mess but I knew you were there and I hadn't forgotten where the dustpan and brush were. Not then anyway. Daddy came in from the garden to dump his gardening clothes in the basket, and when he saw what was going on his face blistered with rage and he stepped towards you with his fists clenched. I was terrified he was going to hit you and tried to rush to put myself in between you two, but my balance is so hopeless now, I went head over heels and ended up under the kitchen table. At least that distracted Daddy and he helped me to sit back on the chair. It started me crying again, of course, and I said to him, 'Be gentle with him, Finn, he doesn't know what's coming,' and he patted my shoulder and fetched a beer from the fridge. You were frozen to the floor with terror – it took me ages, and a lot of cuddles, to cheer you up. Always be gentle, Brendan, especially to people who are smaller and more vulnerable than you. Especially to your children.

I didn't tell anyone at work when Daddy and I started courting because I wasn't sure if it was quite the done thing to step out with a patient. We were soulmates, Brendan, as though we'd been separated at birth and had been wandering the world looking for each other till now. The Ancient Greeks used to believe that – unless it was the Ancient Romans.

Something ancient, anyway. We had a big ceilidh in Kilburn
when we wed, with pipes and dancing and all sorts, and most
of his huge family came over and five of my six sisters and their
children. Your Auntie Aggie was in Australia at the time. It was
a massive celebration, almost like the coronation a few years
before. He calls me his queen actually – Queenie, he calls me,
but only when we're alone. He'll not tell you that himself, but
when I fell for you I used to tell him that if I was the queen,
then that made you the little prince. Or princess, if you were a
girl. You'd have been Breda if you'd been a girl, but you were
so active in there, I secretly knew you'd be my Brendan.

I used to sing to you when you were inside me. I want to
say, do you remember? But of course you don't. Kathleen
Ferrier was my favourite, and I'd sing 'Blow The Wind
Southerly' to you and 'What Is Life To Me Without You?' I'd
like that played at my funeral, but Daddy won't discuss it, so
I'll have to tell one of my sisters. Add that to the list – my
goodness, it's getting long! I'd given up work, of course, so I
just spent my days with my head in a book, or imagining what
it would be like to feed you or roll my fingers up and down
your baby skin. My dad, your granddad, God rest his soul, used
to call me 'dreamy-drawers' when I was a kid because I'd be
away in the magic stories whirring in my head half the time,
but when I was pregnant I'd read you bits of my books out
loud. You were very partial to Dickens – *Dombey and Son*, you
loved that – and were as astonished as me at the pain and rage
in the writings of this American called James Baldwin. I read
two of his books in a week. I've told Daddy he's to keep up
your membership of the library, but I'm not sure he will. I
suppose I have to resign myself to the fact that all of this will
soon be out of my hands, because I want Daddy to find himself
another lady. Not right away – I've told him I'll get God to
smite him with a lightning bolt if he's too quick off the mark –

but you need a mummy, and I'd like you to have brothers and sisters. I don't know what I'd have done over the last year and a half without my sisters. Especially when I had the op.

Time for tea.

You're such a good little eater – you were from the beginning. You'd dive in and guzzle and snort as though you had to drain me dry because there might never be another meal coming. I used to catch Daddy looking at you sometimes when you were feeding, as though you were stealing something of his, so I'd be sure to give him extra cuddles when I'd put you down. Men are like that. But maybe you won't be. Maybe you'll realise that your wife can love you and your baby equally and – who knows? – maybe you'll be as besotted with the little one as she is. I want you to have this experience, my son. I want you to know what it is to wake up in the middle of the night and watch dreams froth under your baby's translucent eyelids. I want you to bend over his cot and inhale the sweet milkiness of him back into you for safekeeping. I want you to feel twice your size, pumped up with love for him like a Zeppelin. I say 'him', but perhaps you'll have a daughter. Perhaps a daughter who inherits that weird bit of hair you and I have at the front – that's a good thought. Perhaps you might even give her Angela as a middle name.

I haven't had enough time being a mum. I feel I've been cheated, but there's no one to blame.

When you finished your tea – bacon and egg flan with frozen peas and mash – you wanted a story. You helped me clear up by carrying the spoons and plastic beaker to the sink, frowning with concentration – you were determined not to fall over and break something. It upsets you when I fall or stagger – and me a teetotaller! – and the twitching of my arm bothered you at first. I told you it was just the arm dancing, like you and I dance in the kitchen sometimes; I put *South Pacific* on the gramophone and we watched my arm dance to 'I'm Gonna Wash That Man Right Outta My Hair'. You're a great little mover.

After the washing-up, I said you should go up and choose yourself a book, but you wanted to settle me in the chair first. You took your time selecting the cushions you thought I'd need and arranged them in a precise order: dark green, light green, blue. I often wonder what you'll be when you grow up. You're such a kind little boy, maybe you'll do something to help people – be a nurse, perhaps, or even a doctor. You're forever bringing me injured creatures from the garden or the park – a spider with a broken leg, a crushed bat, a stream of injured birds – and I always know they'll die, but we make them little death cells out of egg boxes and shoeboxes. You give me constant bulletins about their progress, as though they're members of the royal family going into a steep decline, and when the inevitable happens, we add their tiny bodies to the cemetery under the larch. We'll have to have an annex soon. You'll have to make one with Daddy. When they die, we look them up in the children's encyclopaedia I bought you last year, and it's so funny listening to you trying to get your tongue around the Latin names: *Columba, Passer, Palumbus, Fringilla*. You've been a good talker from early on (not that I'm boasting or anything), but 'fringilla' rather defeated you. You insist on keeping souvenirs of the creatures, so you've got these boxes of feathers up there in your bedroom, and pathetic little insect legs withering in scrapbooks. I'll tell Daddy not to throw them out.

Perhaps you'll be a vet.

You wanted a *Little Grey Rabbit* book and brought down the one where all the other animals secretly plan her birthday and make her presents. You made me repeat the bit where Squirrel puts together a fan made out of feathers from the woodpecker and the goldfinch and you traced your finger around the picture of her in her pink spotted frock surrounded by birds. You sit on my lap for stories, even though you're getting to be a big lad now (you'll be six feet five when you're a man, according to those calculations you do at two and a half), and you like me to stroke the underside of your arm as I read. Since the op, you sneak your fingers under my hair until you find the scar. You caress it so tenderly, as though it's a dear friend you haven't seen for a while. It's less livid now, but when I first came out of hospital you burst into tears when you saw it. I told you I was sick of my old hairstyle and wanted a change and didn't it make me look just like a wizard?

CRANIOTOMY. You'll know that word by now. Perhaps you'll be a neurologist. Find a cure.

Little Grey Rabbit's a bit saintly for my taste, but she lives in a world where there are no dangers, no predators, and she bustles around busily looking after everybody. You'll know when you have your own children that it's your job to buffer them, to raise them in a world where Mummy and Daddy make it their business to explain things, to calm them when they're hot and bothered, wrap them up in reassurance. I'm no saint, Brendan, and since you're reading this as a grown-up you'll know by now that everybody's flawed. I never bought into all that papal infallibility stuff when I was growing up, though I know it's important to some of my sisters. I've done things in my life that still shame me, said things that were designed to draw blood – Daddy will never tell you this. He's already treating me as though beatification is just around the corner, but I don't think I'd look all that good in the robes, so I'll turn it down when it arrives. Little Grey Rabbit can have it.

I suppose I'll have to choose what to wear at my funeral, because Daddy's got the clothes sense of a camel and he'll put me in my pyjamas or something. I must remember to tell my sisters. Now, where's my list?

And they'll tell you about me. Ask them. They'll tell you about growing up in our shabby house in Kilburn, about your granddad, who was a grafter, and your nan, who was a gifted mimic. They'll tell you about the larks we got up to, the barneys we had and the songs we sang, about making do and mending and how scrag end of lamb can last for a week with the judicious use of marrowbones and potatoes. They'll tell you how they used to tease me about my books and try to get me to come out into the park to climb trees. But I never would, because I was afraid of falling – Humpty Dumpty used to terrify the life out of me. That all seems a bit ironic now, really. I wasn't brave then, Brendan, and I'm not brave now. There'll been none of that 'Passed away after a long illness, bravely borne' – I've been an abject coward. Bravery's for men in the trenches, grimy men down the mines, not someone who was stupid enough to fall ill. Stupid enough not to stick around and watch her son grow up.

I expect you'll have to look at photographs to remember me, because I'll fade quite quickly from your little boy's memory. Especially when Daddy finds you another mummy. He's been obsessional about taking photos of me from day one, and there's loads of me after I had you, which I've put in numbered albums in the cupboard under the stairs. I hope it's not too big-headed to say it, but I always felt he was focusing on me, despite him saying how proud he was to have had a son. He's insisted on having a picture of you and me blown up and hung over the fireplace. He put it in a frame so ornate it could have come from Windsor Castle, and when I protested that it was a bit overblown, he said, 'Queenie, hush. It's where you belong.' The picture was taken before I was diagnosed, although I'd begun to have these strange absences which felt like someone had switched off the radio momentarily. We look so content, you and me. Serene almost, as though nothing could touch us.

I like to remember those days, and the picture helps. I suppose when you've got a new mummy, she'll want to take the picture down – which is quite right and proper, don't get me wrong – but even though I won't be beaming down on you from the lounge, I'll be sending sunbeams down on you from up there. Assuming that's where I'm going, of course.

I don't know how comfortable you'll be for money, although I know Daddy's determined to be more financially secure than his family, but it's not everything. Compassion and learning are more important than pounds, shillings and pence, people are more important than things, family than strangers. Remember that, Brendan.

And remember me, son. Perhaps this letter will help.

I love you,

Mummy

XXXXX

Steve

My real dad was a loser, so when Mum, Wayne and I moved in
with Finn it looked like our luck had turned. His house was a
mansion compared with the one we'd been living in, although
maybe it wouldn't look so big to me now. Mine's probably bigger
now. His building company was doing well, so he had all these
things like gold taps and deep-pile carpet everywhere; I wouldn't
give any of that stuff houseroom, but it must have cost a bomb.
I remember asking Mum if he was a millionaire and she said No,
he just works very hard. You do the same and you'll have a
house like this one day. We'd barely met Brendan before they
got married, but Mum went on and on about how he was our
brother now and how we had to treat him right because he'd
had this tragic loss when he was young, and we thought Oh
bloody hell, he'll probably be grizzling all the time, but he never
cried. Didn't smile much either.

He was bigger than me to begin with, but an utter wimp. He
never wanted to play football or chuck stones at milk bottles or
smash daddy-long-legs like normal boys, and he'd spend hours
up in his room by himself. One day when he was at the dentist,
I sneaked into his room and had a sniff around. Hidden under
the mat in his cupboard I found these numbered scrapbooks with
his name on the front in old English writing. Inside was a huge
collection of feathers, each one with the common and Latin
names for the bird next to it, the part of the bird it had come
from, the date he'd found it and the exact location. Exact as in 'top
right-hand corner of third paving stone to the left of Matthews the
butcher's door, 21, Severn St, bird droppings to its left, 3 fag ends

to the right, one with lipstick on'. I'd call it anal now, but back then I just thought he was a freak. I told Wayne about it and the next week when he was at the dentist again, we strolled in and took every feather out of the books and sprinkled them around his room. We put some under his pillow, others in his books and stuffed his socks so he'd go on finding them for ages afterwards. When we pulled them out of the books some of the pages tore, but we didn't care. Serves him right, I thought, but I didn't exactly know what for.

We closed the door on the mess and sat on our beds when he came home, listening for his reaction. He didn't make a sound. Nothing. We thought he'd go ballistic and run downstairs to snitch on us, but he could have been painting his toenails for all the noise he made. When he came down for tea, we scrutinised him to see if he'd been crying, but he hadn't; he looked as blank and impassive as usual. But he did have these little cuts on the back of his left hand. At the time, I thought maybe the ends of the feathers had scratched him as he was gathering them up, but they were exactly parallel, as neat as his scrapbooks. After that, I'd see them on other parts of his body – his arms and his legs mostly – but I never gave them any thought. We were always covered in scratches and bruises, being boys.

Mum was going to call me Gregory, after Peck, but she said she thought that'd make me sound poofy, so she decided on Steve, after McQueen. She liked what she called manly men, and she said McQueen in *The Great Escape* ticked all the boxes for her. When we were naughty she'd sometimes say That's it, I'm taking you back to the shop and changing you for a girl, but we knew she loved us being ordinary rumbustious little boys. It was different with Bren: I could see her counting to ten with him because he got under her skin like a grain of sand, but sometimes she'd lose it and she'd thump him. It bothered me at first because she never hit us, but I think it was part of the same thing that made us destroy his feather collection: you wanted to shake him until he rattled.

We knew Finn was hitting Mum, although she always made sure we were out of the way and we never saw her crying. Wayne and I would shut ourselves in the toy cupboard in our room and sing nursery rhymes at the top of our voices to drown out the noise downstairs. We'd pretend we were soldiers in hiding, waiting for the right moment to burst out and blow the enemy to smithereens with our mighty weapons. I don't know where Bren was – probably seeing to his collections or reading in his room – but we naturally divided at those moments: this was our family, that was his. He was welcome to his dad.

So was Rita. I'm quite fond of Rita and she's been a really good friend to Mum, but she's a sharp woman with a corrosive tongue, which is probably how she kept Finn in check for so long. Mum was with her when she called me to tell me they'd arrested Bren and what for. I wasn't best pleased that she'd called me at the office, partly because it looks so unprofessional, and partly because I was chasing up a big order that had gone astray in Japan, but I picked up the phone. It was one of those 'Where Were You When Kennedy Was Shot?' moments: I remember what I was wearing, what time it was, what the weather was like and sitting down very suddenly on my desk, knocking off my photo of the baby.

I must have broken every speed limit on the way home. There was a stuck record in my head going Don't let Nat have heard. Don't let Nat have heard. *Please* don't let Nat have heard, and my wheels squealed as I swung into our drive. When I went into the living room, Sophie was sitting on the floor watching *The Little Mermaid* on video and they were singing 'Under The Sea'. She looked up at me and said Hello Daddy – look, it's my favourite! and I scooped her up in my arms. I hugged her tightly and said I love you, Sophs, I love you my precious girl, and she wriggled and said I *know* Daddy – put me down or I'll miss it. Where's Mummy? I said and she said They're upstairs, now shhh.

Nat was in the baby's room changing Gregory on the mat and they were smiling at each other. I said Hello petal, how's my little man? but I knew I was going to lose it any minute so I picked him up and laid him down very gently in his cot. Nat said What? What's going on? and I said Just come into the bedroom a minute, it's OK, everything's OK and when I told her she went white as a sheet and vomited all down me. We stood there for a while in the middle of the room rocking backwards and forwards, drenched in sick and the horror of it all. Fortunately Gregory's a good baby and after we'd cleaned ourselves up, we went into his room and he was lying on his blanket holding his toes, crooning to himself. He gave us a big sappy grin as we approached.

For weeks afterwards I found myself obsessively counting heads. I'd think, Nat's in the kitchen, Sophie's in the toilet, Gregory's having a nap or, Sophie's singing to Gregory in the bath, Nat's holding him tight, he's not going to drown. No one's going to die. No one's going to hurt them. Ordinary life didn't make sense for a while; it was like someone had taken a mallet to a sheet of glass and when you looked at the shards you couldn't see any way of putting it back together. Practical things helped, like getting BT to put an intercept on the phone so journalists couldn't get through, stopping the papers so we didn't have to read about it, but then one night I was flicking through the channels and there was a picture of them on the news. I couldn't turn it off. It was their wedding photo and they looked like any other happy couple on their wedding day. Like Nat and me.

I tried to keep up the front. I briefed my PA about what was going on and she told everyone I'd had to go to Tokyo to sort out the distribution problem, so that gave me a week's grace. When I was a teenager, a friend of mine had to have barrier nursing when he went into hospital and that's what I tried to do for my family, put up a cordon sanitaire so that none of the evil could leak into us. But one time I went to take the baby from Nat and I thought Best not, I haven't disinfected my hands and she saw the look on my face. I didn't tell her what was in my head because she'd think I'd gone mad, but I'd catch her looking at me sometimes and I'd be convinced she was thinking It's in him too. He's his stepbrother, it must have rubbed off.

I hung on to absurd hooks, like when Nat said How could he do that to his daughter? And I'd say He's *alleged* to have done it, Nat, he's not guilty yet, because I had to believe that there was some system, some order, that carried on being rational in the face of this insane thing. I had to believe that the court would sift through the evidence, hear from the witnesses, consider its judgement; had to believe it was incorruptible. Apart from the press, no one outside was going to associate me with him because we'd never taken Finn's name, but inside I knew I was implicated. I tried to keep strong for my family, but sometimes when Sophie'd fallen over and hurt herself in the garden, I felt like sitting on the grass with her and howling.

Marilyn and Sherilyn

Dear Linda,

I have to stick to Linda, I'm afraid, even though I know you changed your name, because when I see Sherilyn splashed all over the papers, I like to pretend it's not you. Not my daughter. You were such a quiet and obedient child it's beyond me to believe you could have committed any crime, let alone this one. Since this bombshell exploded in my head, quite a lot is beyond me, frankly. Sometimes picking up a tube of toothpaste in the morning is beyond me.

When the two of you were little, I had to keep reminding myself that you were sisters, because you could have been beamed down from different planets. Ann Marie was such a poppet right from the beginning that even her naughtiness was part of her charm. She could be a right little madam sometimes, bless her heart, Do you remember that time when you brought home a cake you'd made at school with 'too dere mummy I love you' on the top in blue icing? And Annie carried on and on at you till you gave it to her? She always wanted what you had, but you didn't complain. You're like Daddy that way, he's not a complainer either. But then, seeing Ann Marie's face light up when you handed over the cake made it all worth while, didn't it? We used to call her Little Miss Sunshine because she could brighten up the darkest day. You could never be depressed when she was around.

It's probably my fault we've been out of touch for so long, but I'm kept so busy with Annie's brood I'm always scurrying

here and there with one or other of them. And then Daddy's
under my feet all day since he retired, although thankfully he
spends a lot of time doing his thing in the study and making his
model airoplanes, but he's one more person to think about.

I don't know how people pass the time in prison of course.
No one in our family has ever been in one, so you're something
of a first. I hope you're keeping busy, because when you've got
time on your hands you can brood and things can get ugly.
They do for me anyway. I can usually cheer myself up by
making one of my famous cakes, so I made a pineapple
upside-down cake yesterday, even though I'm supposed to be
on a diet. Annie and I have been doing the tomato sandwich
diet recently and I've managed to shed two and a quarter
pounds. As usual, she's better than me – she's lost six and a half
– but it doesn't bother me. I was obviously meant to be a
porker. Daddy hates it when I talk like that. He says, 'You're
not a porker, Marilyn, you're just well built – and lovely with
it,' but he's just being kind. I expect prison food is pretty
inedible – you see it in films being dumped in those metal
containers like pigswill – but since you're not that interested in
food, it probably doesn't bother you.

I had to make another cake the other day for Frannie
because she'd got the results of her ballet exam. I took her
there a few weeks ago, and she looked gorgeous. She wanted
me to pin her hair on top of her head in my special 'nanny
plaits', so I did, and what with the pink headband and grips and
the pink costume and shoes, she looked like a little pink ice
cream. She got a merit, so I iced the cake with pink rosettes and
piped 'Our Little Winner' on the top in a darker pink. I have to
say she went pretty pink with excitement when she saw it too!!!

Joey had me going the other day – he's such a little terror,
that boy!! I was making my bed after breakfast and as I pulled
the sheet back, there was a pile of dog poo on the bottom one.

As you know, Annette next door has a totally out-of-control dog, and I thought it must have got in and done its business. You probably don't know about Annette's dog, come to think of it. So I'm standing there red-faced, planning what I'm going to say to her, and I hear this noise from my wardrobe. I go over and open it up, and there's Joey trying hard not to giggle. He'd stayed over the night before, as he often does on a Friday – we get in videos and fish and chips and have a lovely snuggly time – and he'd waited until I'd gone down for breakfast to do the dirty deed. He'd bought the plastic poo with the pocket money Daddy and I give him, so I told him he should go next door to Granddad's room and play the same trick on him!!

What else is there to tell you? Oh yes, Donnie. He's turning into quite a little athlete nowadays. Annie and I went to watch him do a cross-country race the other day, and he did so well. There were twenty-three runners and he came in seventh, so it was time for another cake to congratulate him!! He'd trained really hard for weeks. My old mum used to say 'hard work never killed anyone' – do you remember? She'd put on her pinny, roll up her sleeves and get down to whatever it was needed doing. Clearing drains, stripping furniture, she'd have a bash at everything. That's probably how she managed to carry on for ninety-two years, though she wasn't all there for the last seven. It was funny, even when she forgot who I was when I went to visit, she'd go on about you. 'When's Linda coming?' she'd say in her poor quivery voice, 'My blonde curly bab', my little blue eyed darlin' – who's took her away?' Of course you were never a blondie like Ann Marie and me, and it was hard to pin down the colour of your eyes, but it was definitely you she asked after. She was a good mum to me.

And Ann Marie is a good mum too. The best. Better than I ever was. It was what she was put on God's earth for. The other day when it was Mother's Day Frannie, Donnie and Joey made her this big card. They'd stuck sequins and love hearts and glitter all over it, and they'd written this little poem inside which went 'Here's to our mum, Who gives us lots of fun, And juicy currant buns, Aren't we the lucky ones!' It was gorgeous. And then they made me cry because they'd made another one, not quite so ornate, for me. 'For the best Nan in the universe', only they'd spelled 'universe' wrong. I was over the moon.

I was surprised when you sent us that card when Samantha was born, because I'd honestly never seen you as a mum. You always seemed set on bettering yourself, and children are very time-consuming, aren't they? They said in the paper you were some kind of manager – I didn't get what kind – so you must have been several rungs above Daddy. He was never very ambitious, never wanted to rise higher in the bank than working at the front desk, which I suppose is admirable in its way. Shows great loyalty, if nothing else.

I can't bring myself to read about what happened to Samantha. Whoever did it. I don't want to have those pictures in my head. Of course I never saw a picture of her anyway, so I don't know what she looked like. Actually that rather helps because then I don't have to imagine her in the cage. Who could have done such a thing? What kind of monster could do that? Not you, Linda. Not you. You might have been a little different from other children when you lived with us, but you weren't a monster. Not in a month of Sundays. I couldn't have given birth to a monster.

And I can't come to visit you – I'm very sorry. If you were seriously ill in intensive care, I'd come and see you wherever the hospital was, because you're my flesh and blood. But not in prison. Not locked up like a common criminal. It would break my heart, Linda, and to tell you the truth I'm feeling a bit wobbly at the moment. If you're acquitted – I should say <u>when</u> you're acquitted – perhaps we could all make more of an effort and try and see each other sometimes. See each other at all, more like. Play your cards right and you might even get a cake – you never know your luck!!!

Well, that's all our news so I'll sign off now – I hope you're well.

Your loving Mummy

P.S: I know you like to call me 'Mother', but I prefer 'Mummy' myself.

Mother,

How kind of you to write telling me all your news. I loved hearing about Joey and Donnie and Frannie and all the interesting things they're doing. What busy children they are! And then there's Ann Marie running for Best Mother In The World – you must be so proud of her and all her achievements. And Father with his hobby and you with your cake-making – what a picture of domestic bliss! Everything's very nice here too. My room has a lovely view of the exercise yard and the garden. When you've been here for a while you can do gardening with the other ladies, so I'm looking forward to spending a bit more time here so I can get out in the fresh air a little. Maybe get a suntan – you never know. I can wear what I like, since I'm on remand, but the prison clothes really aren't too bad. I rather like baggy sweatshirts and of course the nice thing about uniforms is, you don't have that horrible thing in the morning when you can't decide what to wear – what a relief that is!

The food's fine too. Someone's obviously put a lot of thought into making sure the menu's well balanced. No need for faddy diets here, I can tell you! Actually, I'm considering turning vegetarian because sometimes the meat smells a bit peculiar and there's always a vegetarian option, but I know what you think of vegetarians, so perhaps I won't go on about that here.

There's some very nice ladies on the landing with me. They're here for all sorts of reasons and it's terribly interesting to hear their stories. Donatella comes from Liverpool and she's on remand for smuggling heroin from Colombia. She didn't do it of course, so she's looking forward to seeing her kiddies when she gets out in six months or so. They're so adorable. She showed me photographs. Except that they're half caste, one of them looks a lot like Donnie. Last time I saw a photo of Donnie anyway. Then there's Jasmine, she's in for drugs too and Sammie. Sammie's short for Samantha – that's a coincidence, isn't it? – and she's in for murder. She killed one of her parents – she won't tell me which one – and she cries quite a lot. I'm very sorry for her.

Here's a funny thing that really makes me laugh. We're all remanded in custody and guess what people here call it? It's a sort of slang, I suppose. They call it being 'in custard' – isn't that funny? So perhaps you can imagine me swimming around in a giant bowl of custard while I'm here!

I'm going to close now – I'd better dash because I'll miss the post otherwise. Just remember, I never want to hear from you or Father again. Don't write to me or send me things or come and visit me. Ever. And don't come to court for the trial either. Save yourselves the train fare and spend it on a nice hat.

Yours sincerely,

Sherilyn Gutteridge

Sharon

I've never voted, even though I've had it for three years – the vote, I mean. Never seen the point. All those politicians are alike – I see their faces on the telly and they've all got that same dopey look, like Hello Vote For Me Because I'm Mr Sincere. Load of bollocks. They couldn't give a monkey's, most of them – just in it for the money and the fame. And they get these long holidays too, longer even than when I was at school. When my nan wanted rehousing, do you think anybody gave a stuff? She's living in this shithole, she's got mould on the walls and ceiling of her bedroom – we took pictures – and she's nearly eighty, for God's sake, so eventually Mum went to the MP. Ormsby-whatsisface. She said he looked right through her like she was made of cling film or something. Bollocksed on about how he cared so much about his voters, how he was going to speak to Housing and everything, but did he? Did he shit. Mum went to the local paper in the end and they did this big exposé thing with pictures and everything. Got Nan's name wrong. And her age too, come to think of it, but it did the trick. She got this sheltered housing flat place and she was dead chuffed. She had a good couple of years there with all the other old biddies till she pegged it. I miss her. She loved me, my nan.

But even though the MP was so crap, Mum still nagged at me to vote. Use it or lose it, she said, and blahed on about suffragettes killing themselves to get women the vote. Well, I didn't ask them to, did I? I bet they had better politicians back then anyway because there wasn't any telly, so they'd have to try harder in person. Like standing on street corners and stuff. It's your civic duty, Mum said, whatever that means, but I don't reckon one more or less vote's going to make a difference. They're all big fat posh men anyway, aren't they? Well, except for Maggie, she's a woman. Or so they say.

So this big envelope arrives and Mum brings it up to me. I'm in bed. Between jobs. Her face is all twitchy, like she thinks I'm in trouble or something and I want to say That's all over now, OK? I was fifteen, for God's sake – everybody goes a bit loopy when they're young and it's not as though the police were involved or anything, but I don't. Best let sleeping dogs lie, I think. It's jury service. Oh. My. God. Like *Kavanagh QC* or something. Mum's smiling then. It'll give you something to do, she says, Get you out of the house for a bit, like I'm cluttering it up or something. It's your civic duty, she says. I can't be bothered to point out to her she said that before about voting.

It's lucky I'm not working so I don't have to ask my boss or anything. I've been doing office work for a bit since I dropped out of hairdressing, but that's boring as shit. Mum's on at me to go back to college, but there's no point. Don't know what I want to do yet, but I'm only young. Perhaps I'll go to politician's school. Change the world for people like my nan. Bet politicians don't have to do jury service.

I wonder what to wear. It's not exactly the kind of thing you get in magazines – that'd be a laugh. What To Wear On A Jury instead of What Is A Female Orgasm? I think, If I was Julia Roberts, what would I wear? It'd be thigh-length boots if I was doing *Pretty Woman*, I suppose, but even I don't think that's right – I reckon you've got to look sort of serious and clever. So I look through my wardrobe and I think, Nothing too sexy – oops, that's eighty per cent gone then. Nothing too bright or too tight – oh shit, that's the rest. But then I find my suit. Mum bought it for me when we buried Nan and it looks really expensive, so I think, That'll do. Bit of class going in and out of court through the paparazzi. Perhaps I'll wear my sunglasses with the jewels on and I'll stick my hands over the cameras like celebs do – *No publicity, please!* Only if I get something juicy though, something the press'll be interested in. In this town? I don't think so. My friend Bianca did jury service once and all she got was a load of wanky shoplifters.

I get up early on the first day just to make sure I look my best. Don't want to put the barristers off their lunch 'cause they might turn me down, like object or something – I don't think they have to give any reasons. I mean, they don't have to say We're not having that girl with the wonky eye make-up, or Not that one with the massive bum – but that's what they'll be thinking. Hope I don't get the giggles when I see them poncing about in their wigs and things – they'll definitely chuck me out for that. Probably put me in prison for disrespect. So I practise looking serious in the mirror, and I'm thinking, Looking good, girl, but bloody Robert sneaks in and starts falling about. You look like Miss Piggy on a bad day, he says. I throw my hairbrush at him and it leaves a mark under his eye. Brothers! He'll probably tell his mates some made-up story, like he was in a fight or something. Macho bullshit.

I'm OK till I get to Crown Court – it's all a bit of a laugh still – and then I sober up. It feels like falling out of a bar when you've had a few and it's suddenly thundering and lightning or something. This guy in a black cloak thing – well, it's more like a robe, I suppose, like an old-fashioned teacher – he takes my letter and finds my name on this list. Over here, he says, and takes me to the jury room. God, there's tons of us! I thought there'd be fourteen, sixteen max, like you've probably got to have subs, but there must be thirty or forty. They're all older than me, but there's this black girl sitting in a corner who could be my age, but you can't always tell with them. There's another one of those court people there – she's a kind-looking woman in a black robe like the first guy. Bit like Mum. I start thinking, Maybe that's what I could do and I ask her what she's called. Like her job description. Usher, she says, and I say Do you have to do usher's exams for that? and she laughs. Bet you see a fair bit, I say, and she says Yeah. And we've got a rough old day today. That's the first I hear of it. Don't read the newspapers – unless Nan's in it, of course – so I've got no idea what's coming up. I'd have called in sick if I'd known.

They give us loads of disgusting coffee while we're waiting, and some of them are chatting away about the dead kid. Older lady says Hope I don't get that one, my daughter's just had a baby. I suddenly think, Oh Christ, this is serious. I'm going to be in a murder, and I feel like I'm going to chuck. It might be the coffee, but it's making me think maybe I could be responsible for making a big mistake. One of those miscarriage-of-justice things, and I think, But I'm only twenty-one, what do I know?

We spend all morning hanging about, then most of the afternoon till we're called into court, just twelve of us, and we sit in the box. It's not like on telly: for one thing, it's quite modern and bright and from where I'm sitting I can smell one of the barristers. His aftershave I mean. He's well up himself, actually, and looks us over like we're just some boggy old rabble that's walked in off the streets or something. All that coffee's starting to work on me and I'm thinking, What if I need to pee? Do I have to put my hand up, like in school? Mr Bastard Harrison would never let you go and I wet myself once. So I'm wiggling a bit and I think no one can see, but this big bloke two people down from me turns and gives me this look, like, Behave. Go fuck yourself, I think, and I cross my legs.

Then it's all over and we're the jury. Oh my God. I'm the bollocking jury. We're sent home for the day, but only after the judge has given us this lecture: Don't Talk To Anyone About The Case, This Is A Serious Business, It's For You To Decide

About The Defendants' Innocence Or Guilt, all that stuff, and I'm pissing myself. This is more scary than that time I got stuck in the lift at Debenham's. More terrifying even than when that plane's engine fucked up coming home from Majorca. I feel like I'm about ten and someone's asking me to run the country, or like I can't even tie up my shoelaces and I'm being asked to send a rocket into space. And we're warned this is going to take two weeks or so and to tell our employers. I'll just tell my mum.

When I get back, she's all excited and she says What? What? She's heard it's the case about that little dead girl and she says What do they look like? Are they really evil? I'm about to say I haven't seen them and to tell her all about that snotty barrister – I think he's the prosecutor – but I suddenly think, Oh shit, I'm not supposed to say anything, so I tell her that. She looks like she's going to laugh at me, so I say You'd better get used to this, it's important, there's lives at stake and she looks at me in this really strange way. Like I've grown another head.

The first proper day, we spend the morning banged up in the jury room while the barristers argue among themselves. I don't understand why we can't be in court for that – what do they think we're going to do, throw crisp packets or something? – but after lunch we all troop in and they come in too. I'm gobsmacked. I mean, you'd see them walking down the High Street arm in arm and you wouldn't go Oh look, they must be the murderers. They must be the ones that starved their little girl to death, but that's what they're up for. Murder. You see it all the time in videos and that, and obviously it makes headlines in newspapers, but until you're in the room with them – murderers I mean – you don't really know what it means. It's just words till you look at their hands and think, Oh my God, those hands have killed someone. You start imagining what must've gone through their heads to make them want to wipe someone out. Especially a kid. *Their* kid, for God's sake. But then I say to myself They're not guilty yet, so shut up, Shaz. I probably threaten to kill Robert every other day, but the idea of actually doing it – like stabbing him or something – well, it makes my head go funny. Mind you, if someone else was to do it . . . I suppose I don't even mean that really.

They're completely calm all that day and every day after. There they are, being accused of doing these revolting things – they burned her, for Christ's sake, their own little girl, and poisoned her with drugs and stuff – and they sit there looking straight ahead like they're watching a film, like it's someone else's life. Sometimes they look at each other – it's weird, they look frontways for an hour and a half and then they turn to each other at *exactly* the same time and smile at *exactly* the same time almost with the same smile, even though they're really different-looking. It's like in one of those films with computers and androids and things.

She must have the biggest wardrobe in the world because she wears a different outfit every day. *Every day.* She must be like Onassis or that Getty bloke or something. And she's tiny – so tiny I wonder for a moment whether she was ever actually pregnant. Can't imagine a whole live baby inside her, and one day when some social worker was boring on about files going missing, I get this bonkers idea that maybe the little girl wasn't hers. Has anybody thought about that? Maybe she bought her. It happens – celebrities do it all the time – and in a funny way it might make more sense then, her torturing the kid. It would sort of make it better as well because then she'd just be killing someone else's kid. I can't believe I'm saying that – *just* killing someone else's kid – but the case is driving me crazy. My head's getting stuffed with crazy ideas.

Brendan Gutteridge is quite attractive in a big way. I've always been attracted to big men because you feel they'll look after you, like protect you from rapists and murderers and things. He looks as though he'd do anything for her – like a sort of gentle giant. He's got amazing clothes too – I've never seen that sort of stuff in real life but I've seen them in pictures in glossies down the doctor's. And he's got nice eyes – well, as far as I can see from the jury box he has – and they make him look kind, even though he's a murderer. Shut your mouth, Shaz, he's not a murderer yet. I begin to think, Maybe it was all her because she looks tough as nails even though she's so little – maybe he's covering up for her. Then I think, You're not allowed to have thoughts like that, you've got to listen to the evidence.

Listen to the evidence. Everybody in court's been going on about that. Prosecution's going to show in the evidence that . . . blah blah, defence says there's no evidence that . . . blah blah. I suppose in real life you're not always looking for evidence because you just accept things at face value. But I've got to keep those questions in my head all the time here. It's really hard work.

We get breaks of course, so no worries about peeing myself. I'm peeing a lot, actually. I'm not drinking any more than usual, so it's nerves probably. That black girl's called Claudia and she's on the jury and we keep meeting in the bogs. It's quite funny, really – it's like we're doing parallel peeing. Maybe we're turning into them. The Gutteridges. Bet they do that. Just saying their name makes me shiver.

She's older than me, Claudia, and she's got a kid but no bloke. Says her kid winds her up something criminal sometimes, but the idea of doing anything to him turns her stomach. It's good to have someone young on the jury with me – the others are all really old, like in their forties and fifties. Like my mum. I wonder how she'd cope with all of this. Can't ask her of course. It's weird not being able to tell her anything. I tell her everything usually. Most things anyway – didn't tell her what happened in Majorca that time. So me and Claudia have a laugh together and we sort of team up when we're banged up in the jury room. We had to choose a foreman early on, and that big bloke who glared at me on the first day seemed to assume it was his divine right. He's called Robert, like my brother, but I can't see me throwing a hairbrush at him when he gets up my nose.

It's like we're in a separate bubble from the rest of the world, all doing the same thing, hearing the same stuff, breathing the same air. And there's only one topic of conversation of course, which is not exactly like everyday chit-chat. I know stuff about Claudia – like about her kid, and how she's doing a degree at the same time as being a single mum – but nothing about anyone else. Oh, Robert's got his own business – he made bloody sure we all knew that – so we're supposed to bow down to him like he's the boss. Bollocks to that. He keeps repeating things the barristers say, like it makes him the same as them – stuck-up bastards. The judge keeps going on about *I am minded*, and I think, What's wrong with *I think?* Or, *I want to do?* I am minded. I am minded to scratch my bum. I am minded to get hammered. My mates'd smack me if I tried talking like that.

But the whole court's in the bubble with us. It's probably like being on a film set – you read all that stuff about film stars getting involved with each other when they're making a film and I can sort of understand it now. You lose touch with ordinary life. I mean, I still go to bed, eat my tea, have a shower, paint my toenails, but six hours a day, every day, I'm shut up with these same people, like we're some rare breed at the zoo.

And then we see the photographs. They're just handed out to us like school dinners. In this little book with a plain brown cover, as though it's something normal. I open it and look, and nothing's ever going to be normal again. It feels like when someone asks you if you've had a sudden rush of blood to the head. Like you've suddenly lost the plot or something. My mum says that sometimes. I look at this picture of Samantha in the cage, all dead and dried up like that Bombay Duck stuff you get down the Indian, and my head feels like something just spurted up into it, up against the top of my skull. Like it's going to explode. And I think, My brain's just melted. Don't know where to put myself. I think I make a little sound because the barrister who's asking the questions at the time stops talking and everyone in the court's looking at me. But I don't care. My head's going to blow up and it's going to make a big brain-mess everywhere. Claudia's at the end of my row and I look over to her and she's gone a funny colour. I didn't know black people go pale. I'm going to be sick, I know it. I stick my hand in the air automatically like I'm back in school and the judge, who's got a kind face really, just a funny way of talking, looks at me and says I think we'll have a short adjournment, Mr Gardner – that's the barrister – We'll resume in half an hour, and I'm grateful because he's noticed and I'm desperate, but the usher lady takes us out and I rush to the bogs and I chuck up. Twice.

Claudia's waiting for me outside and when I finally stagger out she puts her arms around me and we both cry. We don't say anything, just cry. There's this other woman from the jury and she comes in too. Can't remember what she's called but it might be Jenny, and she says It's unbearable, isn't it? I keep thinking of my kids when they were that age and that sets Claudia off again because I suppose she's thinking of her kid as well. And at this point I'm thinking, I'm never, *ever* going to have kids because I'm not brave enough. That's how deep it is, the feeling – like grief. As though someone's died in your life. There's suddenly no hope for the world. I know I'm sounding a bit dramatic, like in that film where Julia Roberts dies, I can't remember what it's called, but I don't care, that's what it feels like. I say to the woman, I don't think I can go back in there, do you think they'll let me go home? It's too much for me, all this, and she says this really kind thing. She says I'll get Robert to write a note to the judge and tell him we need to stay out a little longer. You're doing us a favour, you know, we all need a break from this horror. I start crying again.

When we go back into the jury room, Claudia and me, it's like we've walked into a funeral parlour, only without the cheesy music. And the body, I suppose. Everyone's sitting around sort of slumped like they can't hardly hold themselves upright, like they've had their insides scooped out. They look up at us as we walk in and they look really concerned, even Robert. I'm stunned. He's human after all. Someone asks Are you all right? And I say No not really, and that seems to do the trick. Suddenly everybody's talking, but it's not the kind of talking we did before, it's real talking like you'd do with your best mate late at night when you've been out on the piss. Like confiding in each other. Stuff that doesn't come out normally. They're talking about being a mum – or a dad, Robert's talking about his son, how he was disabled in a car accident and how the guy got off and how he's still furious. Jury acquitted him. I could have killed him, he says, I could have. If I'd seen him outside the court I'd have killed him. And I understand. That's what I say, I understand. And he looks at me different and just for a moment I think he's going to cry. It's as though everybody's suddenly realised we're all human. That sounds really stupid – we're not exactly hamsters – but it's like now we know it in a new way. And it makes me feel better about it all, like even though I'm standing on the edge of a cliff, it's OK because there's all these people around and they'll catch me if I fall off. Looks like other people are feeling better too, so we troop back in.

It's really hard to remember all the evidence but I know it's important because whatever it makes me feel isn't the thing. It's all that Innocent Until Proven Guilty stuff – people in *Kavanagh QC* are always going on about that – and the prosecution have got to convince us that they're right. That these people did this thing. That they've got enough people to say enough stuff to make us believe – beyond reasonable doubt, that's what it is – that they're guilty. It's not enough to think, Fuck. Fuck, they look guilty. They're the fucking parents – how could they do that? Because if there isn't the evidence, that's it. We've got to acquit them, like the jury on Robert's son. That's really scary.

So I'm thinking, Just wait till you hear them. Then you'll know if they're telling the truth, if they could do such a thing, but they're not bloody going in the box. Defence barrister gets up on his hind legs and says My Lord, I call no evidence. So does the other one. I'm gobsmacked. It's like getting halfway through a book and finding the rest of the pages are blank. In the break I say to Jenny – she *is* called Jenny, that woman in the bog – So how're we supposed to make up our minds then, if they're not going to give evidence? And she looks really serious and says Well, it just puts the onus (I think that's the word she uses), It just puts the onus on the prosecution to make the case, doesn't it? And I know she's right – perhaps she's something legal, she seems to understand all this stuff – but I can't hardly sleep a wink, worrying that I'm going to get it all wrong and it'll all be my fault someone guilty goes free, or just as bad, someone innocent gets convicted. By me. This is the most important thing I ever did. More important even than GCSEs, and it makes me think maybe I should take everything more seriously, like stop mucking about and decide about my future, because life suddenly feels very short. It's funny, Mum's gone on all my life about It's important this, It's important that, but it's in one ear and out the other. Then this comes along and it's like – bouff! – Oh, that's what she meant.

So it all suddenly shuts down once the defence says that and I'm going, Oh my God, now we've got to decide. The judge gives us this speech about This is what the case is and This is what the law is and he's being really fair, and I think, I've got to be fair as well because at this moment I've got someone's whole future in my hands. Well, our hands anyway. I don't think there's a death penalty nowadays, but suppose there was? Suppose what we decided meant someone got topped? I always thought the death penalty was stupid – it's what backward people do, like Arabs when they cut people's heads off in public and you think, You're just down from the trees, you – but when I look at them, the defendants, I think, Maybe you did it, and if you did I'd want to gas you. It's hanging here though, I think.

I've never talked so much, thought so hard, in my whole life before. We've had two weeks of stuff, people giving evidence, all those experts blahing on about contusions this and enzymes that and I'm supposed to understand it. I buggered up my science GCSE – wasn't hard, crap teacher – but I regret it now. I think of asking for a dictionary, but then I go Nah, don't do it, they'll think you're a div and they won't listen to anything you say. But actually Robert's really good at being the foreman and he makes sure everybody has their say. There's this one time when I'm saying the social worker should've just kept on turning up till she saw Samantha and that fat Les butts in. Robert says You'll have your turn, Les, just listen to Sharon now, and everybody does, like what I've got to say is important. That's a new one on me and my voice wobbles a bit but I say my piece right to the end.

We get food brought in when it's lunchtime but we carry on talking about the case all through eating – it's unbelievable. It's as though there's nothing else going on in the world, just us and the case. England could suddenly decide to drop bombs on some country and we wouldn't know because we're busy deciding about someone's life or death. Well, freedom anyway. After about four hours I know what I think and when Robert goes around the table and asks us, I tell him I think they're both guilty and I tell everybody why. I bring in the evidence from the people who *did* go into the witness box, like those experts and stuff, and all these grown-ups nod their heads and I think, Fuck, they think I'm talking sense.

There's only Les and some woman called Beatrice that are undecided by then – I mean, they don't think they're not guilty or anything, but they're like the Don't Knows in the polls. But about half past three, Beatrice starts shaking all over like she'd plopped into the deep freeze or something, and she says I know what I think now and Robert says What Beatrice? in this really gentle way and she says Guilty. They're both guilty but I think she's more guilty than him because she's the mum, for heaven's sake, she's the mum. And I want to say But he's the dad too, but it's not the time or place, so I keep my trap shut. She gives her reasons really well though, and it's not like she's just been swayed by her emotions even though she feels them strongly, so her vote goes in the guilty box. There isn't a guilty box really, I'm just saying that. And then poor old Les is all out on his own, and he's sweating and sweating even though it's cold in here and I feel sorry for him even though I've mostly thought he's seriously, *seriously* dumb. At two minutes to four, he gives this long sigh that's kind of like a moan as well and says Robert, I've decided. Guilty. Both of them. So Robert does the right thing and asks him his reasons and What is the evidence? and all that, but you can see he's relieved. We all are. It's time to go home. Back out into the real world again.

When Robert says Guilty when we go back in I can't believe it. I expect them to faint, or shout or cry like they do in videos, but there's nothing. They just carry on looking frontways holding each other's hand. Nothing goes across their faces. Not a flicker.

Then suddenly it's all finished. They get life, we get thanked and dismissed and by the time we've said our goodbyes and Keep in touch – (that's me and Claudia, but I don't expect we will) – we leave the court just as the prison vans are taking them away.

There's a little crowd outside and a fair amount of shouting –
Perverts, Sicko, that sort of thing – so no one takes my picture.
I'm not bothered, because I'm not sure I want people to know
I've been linked to the case any more.

But it's made me think that perhaps I *will* vote next time we
have an election. Have my say, like in the jury room. Mum's
right – it's my civic duty.

Lil

I was dreading that day at work, because I'd spoken to the listings officer and I knew what was coming up. I love what I do normally, so it was strange to be walking to court with lead in my shoes, but I made some sugary tea when I got there and told myself to buck up. My friend Judy gave me a big hug in the ushers' room before I went off to find my jurors. See you at lunchtime, chuck, she said, Burgers are on me, OK? Oh, but come to think of it, she said, That's what I've got all this week – load of house burgers! and she snorted at her own joke. I didn't feel much like laughing, so I said Righto, see you later, and went off to gather the troops. Some of the potential jurors knew what they might be facing and this one woman said to me Oh God, I hope I don't get chosen for that one, I don't know if I could be impartial. I'm a paediatric nurse, she said, And when I have to nurse battered children, I could kill the mums and dads – honestly I could. I'd cheerfully strangle them for what they've done. I said Don't worry, you'll be amazed how quickly you put all that to one side when you're sitting on a case – not to say this isn't especially vile, I said, not wanting to underplay it, But you'll be fine, really you will.

Mostly the jurors were older, but there were these two young girls, one of whom looked really bothered when she came in. I was a hairdresser for twenty-five years before I became an usher, so the old professional instincts kick in when I see someone for the first time – she had a lovely head of hair, I must say, very well cut and conditioned. She obviously hadn't known today was the Gutteridges, because she grabbed hold of the back of a chair when I told her. I got her a cup of coffee from the machine and did my best to calm her down, but I couldn't help thinking I wouldn't want one of my daughters to be in her place.

Unfortunately for her she was selected, as was the other girl, so I made it my business to keep an eye on them and hoped the older women on the jury might look out for them too. It's almost worse to do this sort of case if you haven't had kids, because you've got no idea of what your kids can drive you to. Not killing them, obviously, but they can push you pretty close to the edge. The other girl was more mature – turned out she had a kid of her own – so I wasn't so concerned about her, but Sharon, the dark-haired one, did seem very young despite her smart suit.

Part of my job is to explain court procedures to the jurors because it can be very bewildering. There's a lot of hanging about to begin with and some of them find it a bit strange that there's stuff they can't hear, like legal submissions and things. This one juror, Robert Trilling, strutted around as though he knew it all – there's always one – and I thought he'd probably make it his business to get himself elected foreman when it came to it. Didn't bother chatting to me. I expect he thought he belonged in the robing room with the barristers. But Sharon asked me loads of intelligent questions and I could see she was trying to get her head around her role in all this. I was pleased to see her and the other girl were palling up, because they were going to need each other's support during this one, for sure. When the trial proper began, I was sat by the jury box, so I could keep an eye on the girls and I had a good view of the defendants too.

I've watched child-killers of all shapes and sizes squirming through the evidence over the years and mostly you can see they know what they've done. Mostly they do feel some remorse. But not these two. They sat there in the dock day in day out, staring ahead when they weren't locking eyes. They could have been sitting on deckchairs in the garden enjoying the sun or watching something stupid on the telly. It turned out neither of them had any previous, not even a parking ticket, so you'd expect them to look scared sometimes even if they didn't know what happens to sex offenders and child-killers in the nick. They mostly go on Rule 43 – segregated with their own kind – and they don't exactly have a happy time. If any normal con gets anywhere near them, they often have a go – I knew of one who got acid chucked in his face – and sometimes they even get murdered.

Mr Justice Braithwaite was presiding – I always liked it when he was sitting here. He does that judgey look they all do, peering over his glasses like a bony bird of prey, but he's got a good heart, both on the job and backstage. Obviously he's the big cheese in court, but when you see him in his civvies he's this little springy man with a big grin. Slightly thinning dark hair. He's always dead friendly to us ushers. Not all of them are. He was totally professional all through this case of course, but every now and again you'd see his eyebrows go red and his mouth stretch into a thin line like he was struggling to keep something from bursting out.

My friend Bobby was the other usher in court that day and I have to say he's not Social Services's greatest fan, so when the social worker was called he looked like he'd slipped in sick. She stumbled in, her buttons done up all wrong and her skirt hem drooping like a toddler's knickers. Looked as though she'd for-gotten how to get dressed, poor woman. She had the kind of hair that needs a lot of attention, a lot of product, but she'd left it to sprout around her head like a patch of weeds. Social workers always get the blame in these cases, but I doubt any of us would want to do their job, so I always give them the benefit of the doubt. Innocent until proved guilty, after all. She just about made it through her evidence, but it was like she was burping back bits of a report that she'd swallowed whole, as though it was too painful to think any more about what had happened.

I scanned the Gutteridges for the giveaway tics that would tell me what they were thinking. There's always some. There was this serial rapist once – didn't look like a rapist, they never do – and all through his trial he kept checking the knot in his tie, like he was afraid he might slip up and reveal something. Went down for fifteen years. Not long enough in my humble opinion. The Gutteridges gave nothing away. They couldn't have been more different physically but you could tell there was something connecting them deep inside. As though there was no room for anyone else. As though you couldn't have slid a piece of tissue between them. Sometimes they'd cross their legs at the same time and at other times when someone was giving evidence, like the social worker saying that the first time she went round, Mrs Gutteridge said they were on their way out to lunch, they'd both cock their heads. Her blonde one, his sandy one, both to the same side, both at the same angle. It reminded me of my sister's twins except with them their closeness makes you smile.

And they did this thing when the policeman was giving his evidence. Poor sod had had a breakdown and was on heavy tranks, so when he spoke it was as though he was pulling words out of a box and slotting them together like Lego. As though he'd only got them out on temporary loan. He was talking about the moment he and the woman officer broke into Samantha's room and found her body. He said she had her arms around her legs and her head had fallen back and her mouth was open like she was screaming. The public gallery went into deep freeze. I looked at the Gutteridges and they were applauding. Not out loud, there was no sound, but they both had their hands in their laps, heels joined, fingers stretched flat and they were clapping. *Good job. Well done us.*

I like a woman to look good, but Sherilyn Gutteridge was so immaculate it unsettled me. She wore her hair all these different ways: sometimes piled up on top in curls, sometimes pinned back in a French pleat, and a couple of times she had it loose, but it didn't move when she stood up or sat down or turned her head to Brendan. Her nails were perfectly manicured and she'd matched the lacquer to her clothes: three days of pink clothes, four of blue, five of black. When my youngest was little she was into Barbies in a big way – she had one in every colour, had all the costumes and accessories, so for a while there you couldn't have a pee in our house without Barbie sticking her hand up your bum. Sherilyn was like a Barbie: you'd change her outfit, redo her hair, move her limbs about, but her face stayed put. You could spend a day with her and wouldn't know any more in the evening than you'd known in the morning. You'd look at her and see nothing.

Most child-killers are men, and over the years I've struggled to understand how they could do such a thing. But I suppose men don't have the kids. They don't know how it feels to have your baby tumbling around in your belly, tearing its way out of you into the outside world. Maybe that's how come they can kick it out of their way like an old tin can in the street. When it's a woman that's killed her child, even if she swears blind she didn't do it, you can see something's collapsed inside her. You can see she's barely holding on because her kid's still dead even if she did the killing. Not Sherilyn Gutteridge. The only thing she was holding on to was her husband.

It was easier to believe Brendan was a killer because he looked like a thug. Not his clothes, which were dead smart, but if you looked at the size of his hands you could imagine him throwing Samantha around like a bag of beans. It was probably his idea to make the cage. Probably made it by himself. She didn't look strong enough to use a hammer or a drill. Would've broken those perfect nails. When he held her hand in the dock it disappeared, so it was like her arm ended at the wrist. Should've been romantic, but it made my flesh crawl. I expect he wanted her all to himself and the baby got in the way. You meet men like that, jealous types, and they go into one when they see what the baby's getting. You could see Brendan throwing a wobbly, like the terrible twos. There was something dead in his eyes too. My mum used to say eyes are the windows of the soul, but his had the curtains drawn. I'd see him cross his legs with those massive thighs and I'd think, Bet you played rugby. Bet you grabbed the ball and smashed into the opposition. Bet you pounded down the pitch splattered with their blood. Bet you never looked back.

But I'm struggling to describe them, even though I was sat looking at them six hours a day, every day. I'm a good reader of people normally but they defeated me. I've been around criminals long enough to know monsters don't look like monsters in real life. Myra Hindley only looks like a witch because they keep printing her mug shot – she's probably quite pretty when you meet her. These two gave nothing away. There they were, accused of these monstrous things, but they could have been in Madame Tussaud's. Could have been on display as model citizens.

We always segregate the families in this sort of trial, and while it protects them from being jostled or spat at, it also marks them out, like there's this giant neon finger pointing at them: *Here they are, folks! Roll up, roll up – killer's mum over here! See the sister sob!* We put the Gutteridges and the Millers in the press box, just behind and to the right of the dock. Sherilyn's mother was badly overweight, but she flopped like a boneless chicken; her sister and father had positioned themselves on either side of her to prop her up. The other two women, Brendan's stepmothers, wore the kind of brown that's pretending it's not there. They sat bolt upright but so close to each other they could have been sharing an arm. While Mrs Miller seemed to be not quite on planet earth, the other four were obviously struggling not to give anything away. And failing. You could practically smell their distress. I looked over at this odd little clan and wondered who did what. What these perfectly ordinary-looking people had done to turn their innocent babies into the evil adults in the dock.

I had to do a fair bit of mopping up when the defence offered no evidence. It particularly shocked Sharon, poor lamb. Sometimes jurors are holding their breath all through the trial waiting for the defendant to speak, as though that'll be the deciding factor, so it's hard on them when all they've got is the prosecution case. After the judge's summing up, I was sworn in. My turn to be the jury bailiff. I love all that business. All that *I shall keep the jury in some convenient and private place. I shall not speak to them without leave of the court, unless it be to ask them if they are agreed on a verdict.* It suddenly makes you an important part of dispensing justice. As though you're not just an ex-hairdresser in a black robe.

Your bum can sometimes get a bit numb sitting outside the jury room when they're taking their time, but this lot were pretty fast. It was just after four when I took their note into court saying they'd reached their verdict.

There are two moments in any trial when it's as though all the bells in the world have just tolled: verdict and sentence. As I thought, Robert Trilling had managed to get himself elected foreman and he rose very slowly to his feet, as though to eke out the moment when he had the court's full attention. But then I noticed his hands were shaking and the corners of his mouth twitched downwards as he said Guilty in a voice that sounded like sandpaper. The public gallery rippled, the families slumped, but Brendan and Sherilyn could have been two icicles hanging off a gutter. That must have been how they were with Samantha. I'm really not a violent person, but I felt this surge welling up inside me and I wanted to break into them, stuff what they'd done down their throats like dogshit, because *they didn't know. They didn't know what they'd done.*

My friend Judy took me to the pub that evening. My hubby had to come and pick me up at closing time.

Peter

The house is double-fronted, Georgian, placid. A mature Virginia creeper has taken over the left flank and facade, and there's a buddleia on the roof that's cracking the rendering beneath. Someone in the grip of horticultural fashion at the turn of the century has planted a monkey puzzle tree at the front gate, its sea-urchin spikes at odds with the graceful elegance of the building. When the last dipsomaniacal scion of the original family died, the Lord Chancellor's Department bought their country seat for judges' lodgings. When High Court judges ride into town in their regal red robes to try weighty cases, they take up residence in the house, attended by a full complement of staff. It is, in truth, like well-appointed judges' digs and is occupied for a scant six months a year. Currently Sir Peter Braithwaite is staying there, in a bedroom overlooking the knot garden at the rear of the house.

He stands in the drawing room, leaning against the fireplace. A log fire burns in the grate: its smoky fragrance makes him think it must be fruitwood. It reminds him of sitting in the pear tree in the back garden as a boy, idly picking off bits of bark and throwing them at the wasps. The little boy in a pear tree had always wanted to be a lawyer: under the aegis of the law he thought he could lead an ethical life, a generous life, a life that contributed to the common good.

He is a small, sinewy man with a bouncy gait: when *The Magic Roundabout* was required viewing for the nation, his children took to calling him Zebedee. Latterly, since presiding over the Gutteridge case, his feet have filled with granite and he walks as though, like Atlas, the responsibility bearing down on his shoulders is nearly insupportable. During adjournments in the case, he takes his wig off and puts it on the bookshelf in his chambers. Bareheaded, he can feel like an ordinary man strolling down to the end of the street to post a letter, sniffing at the autumnal air. Sometimes in court when he's been breathing in the foetid stench of this case, he wants to suggest everybody downs tools and wanders over to the pub together: jury, ushers, clerks, barristers, denizens of the public gallery. Not the defendants' families. They'll never laugh again, he thinks; this little girl's tragedy will dog their steps forever.

Over the years since he was called to the Bar, he has learned to rein in his quick temper and tendency to tears. A police officer made an official complaint against him when he was a very junior barrister for being pushed up against a wall outside court. He was representing a woman whose partner had abused her for fifteen years – quite inventively for a Neanderthal. His favourite trick was to spray her legs with hair lacquer, tie her to a chair and spend the evening flicking lighted matches at her sticky shins. By that point, she was so brainwashed she hardly knew it was wrong. He was new to this sort of work at the time and could feel the rage building in his belly as the day progressed; he thought he could keep it capped. But when he heard the officers chortling together during an adjournment, calling his client a fat slag, he lost it. He couldn't remember what he'd yelled at the officer, but he was told afterwards that he called him a callous cunt and a lame-brained fucker. It was a yellow card, however, and he was careful never to provoke the red.

He has represented them all: thieves, fraudsters, murderers, rapists; has convinced juries black was beyond reasonable doubt white; has charmed irascible judges, hostile witnesses and intransigent police officers and now sits at the top of his professional tree. When the Gutteridges were picked up he wondered on whose watch they would pitch up. Not his, he thought, because he wasn't due to sit on that circuit again, but then the case was moved to his patch when it became too hot a local potato to manage.

He's been for a run this evening and had a long shower. Often he doesn't know whether he's running towards something or away from something, but since he's been trying this case he knows he's running to escape. He picks up the cut-glass tumbler of single malt on the side table and rolls the dregs around the bottom, debating whether to have a third. He's promised his wife he'll cut down, but he thinks she'd understand why one more Scotch seems life-preserving tonight. If the phone goes in the next half hour, he tells himself, I can have another one. This is a bargain he's likely to win since all his calls tend to come in the early evening. A minute later the phone shrills.

He hears his clerk's voice murmuring in the hall and he smiles and sits down in the unappealing winged chair by the fire. There's a knock on the door and he calls Come! His clerk comes in. It's Lady Antonia, sir, he says. Thanks, Geoffrey, he says, holding out his glass, Another one please, and he picks up the phone by his chair.

Hello darling, how are you? . . . What happened with the contract, did you manage to get it out? . . . Oh, well done! They didn't quibble about the indemnity clause then? – you were worried about that last evening . . . You must be exhausted – have a stiff drink, why don't you, and make it an early night . . . I've only had the one. I said I'd cut down, didn't I? . . . O ye of little faith . . . No, no, really I'm fine – it hasn't gone beyond the aggravating snuffle stage, I'm glad to say. Bit sneezy at lunchtime, but the building works down the corridor generate a fair amount of dust. Nothing a good bottle of claret over dinner won't fix – although I'll bloody well have to share it with Jonathan Fairfax, who's just come up here. I think I've told you about him before, he can bore for England on just about every subject. My head starts to nod when he bangs on about cases he's tried – brilliantly of course – and it's in the soup when he starts in on golf. One so longs for a bit of intelligent conversation at the end of the day, but one's never going to get it from Fairfax. He doesn't seem interested in books or music or politics or anything of substance outside the law. I suspect he can barely read or write, actually . . . Oh come on, I think I'm allowed the odd bitch. I've got to live with the bugger for the next fortnight, after all . . . No, you're right. I think I am a little bad tempered. This case is all pretty grim . . . No nothing particular, funnily enough. I think it's cumulative. The evidence is so unremittingly dreadful. I don't know if I told you, I caught a glimpse of the duty probation officer's face yesterday . . . I did? Oh sorry, darling. Repeating things may be a way of exorcising some of the demons, but it must be a pain in the neck for you . . . Thanks. I know you are. So, just to repeat myself: she's got a very rosy face normally – like that greengrocer in Wales, do you remember? The one we said looked like one of her own shiny apples . . . Well, when it came to the forensics, she went the colour of old bread, as though she'd suddenly been drained. Fortunately Lil, my lovely usher, noticed it too and brought her a glass of water. But sometimes the horror of it all seems to drench the whole court. I've never known a public gallery quite so silent. You know I said the police officer who found her was a bit peculiar? Gave his evidence OK, stood up to cross-examination OK, but there was something missing . . . I don't think I called him that, did I? Oh dear. Well, the poor chap's apparently had some sort of breakdown and had to be stuffed with drugs to get him through it at all. His career's down the drain too – he's been put on permanent sick leave. I'm not sure you'd ever recover from something like that, would you? . . . Well, it's different for me, isn't it? I keep telling myself to get a grip. It's my court, for Christ's sake, and it's up to me to stay steady, especially when people are coming to bits all around me. You should see the jury. There's one little girl – must be of age, but she looks about twelve – keeps putting her head in her hands as though she's trying to keep it attached to her neck. I do sometimes wonder how ethical it is having really young people sitting on cases like this. It must be particularly affecting to an inexperienced mind . . . Yes, but I'm an adult, aren't I? . . . Well, Geoffrey's fine, he's very reliable but it's not exactly part of his job to prop me up, is it? . . . I know you do. I couldn't get through all this without you . . . No, Tonia, don't do that. I'll be fine, honestly. It's a long old way to come and you'd have to scoot back at sparrow's fart the next day, but thank you for offering . . . Yes, yes, I am, but loneliness goes with the territory, doesn't it? I knew that before I accepted the job. But I can't stop thinking about the little girl. In her cage, alone and desperate and slowly dying.

He begins to cry softly.

. . . No, it's a relief to cry, actually . . . I know you do, darling. It's just, all day long in court I hold it in and hold it in and keep the mask glued to my face when all I really want to do is howl. Or hit someone – one of the child's parents, probably – but when I let myself imagine that, I keep going till I've beaten them to death. I don't think you'd ordinarily call me a violent man . . . Yes, but Simon was being provocative, and it was only a flowerpot . . . Well, OK, there was that as well but it was a long time ago and I wasn't so good at keeping my temper then. But I woke up this morning from a dream that really disturbed me. Can't remember the details, but it had something to do with smashing someone's head with a tent pole and enjoying it. One of those dreams that linger all day, you know? Colouring everything with its atmosphere . . . No, I can't talk about it really because I've forgotten most of it, but at one point when I was standing over the body of the guy I'd attacked, I remember wiping the blood on my hands down the front of my trousers and thinking This is me! This is me! in a sort of triumphant way . . . No, I know I'm not, and when I'm awake and in control, I don't ever think I would, but I felt really sick over breakfast. As though I was only semi-civilised. As though it wouldn't take much to turn me into a savage. Capable of doing the kind of things the Gutteridges are accused of. I told you about the cigarette burns, didn't I? Forensic expert said they'd gone on over some time and I was remembering the tenderness of the kids' flesh when they were little and how scared we were when Jemmie fell off that wall that time, do you remember? She was so brave and you said it wouldn't scar, but I couldn't bear the thought that her perfect skin was so damaged. And that's another thing.

He begins to cry again.

I wake in the night sometimes absolutely swamped with the thought that I might unwittingly have damaged the kids. Not deliberately of course – I don't think I was ever deliberately cruel to them, was I? . . . Well, I don't know about lovely, but I always thought I was doing my best. I felt like calling them the other evening to tell them how much I love them, but I didn't because they'd probably think I was crackers and I'd have to tell them why I needed to phone. And then they'd have all this shit in their minds too. But I try to calm myself in the night by thinking, Well, I've never burned them with fag ends, I've never overdosed them with steroids, but suppose they're psychologically wounded by me in some way? That might be almost worse than physical abuse . . . Yes, I hope they do know how much I love them. I know I'm a little hard on Simon sometimes and now I'm wondering if I'm the reason he can't seem to hold a job down . . . But Tonia, how long can we go on saying that? He's twenty-six, for Christ's sake! . . . No, he hasn't got all the time in the world – he needs to pull his finger out and focus! Oh Lord, now I'm shouting at you. I'm sorry, darling, I'm really sorry, but who else can I tell about this stuff? I do the impassive authority bit in court, make sure everyone's as comfortable as possible – you remember I sent the jury out the other day when that young juror looked on the verge of collapse – then come back here alone. At least when I'm alone I can let go a bit. Geoffrey's very discreet and takes himself off when he sees I need to unbutton, but now fucking Fairfax is here, I'll have to keep up the front. Can't exactly see him putting his hand on my shoulder and saying Tell me about it, Peter. Let it all out, son. He's about as sensitive as the average rock face. But I feel implicated, you know? As though I'm linked to these monstrous people by the accident of our shared humanity. As though I'm debased by that coincidence. And telling you about it implicates you too . . . I know you can. I know you understand, and you'll understand too how I'm plagued by thoughts about the last weeks of her life. Samantha. I think, What was she feeling? What was she feeling? Was she panicking when her jailers stopped pitching up? Was she screaming and no one was listening? Or was she so formed by this life of deprivation and pain that she accepted the final stages as just another part of her existence . . . Well, that's right. Absolutely. She exemplifies everything Hobbes was talking about when he described a man's life as being – what was it? – 'solitary, poor, nasty, brutish and short'. I find myself thinking it was a good thing she died, really, and then I'm appalled. Appalled at myself for having that thought. But I suppose four years of torture is marginally better than forty, though that's not an especially comforting thought either. Oh Christ! That's Fairfax coming in. I'd better pull myself together, stop whingeing . . . yes, I'd like that – you're in all evening, are you? I'll call you after dinner – hello, Jonathan, I'm just talking to my wife. Be with you shortly. OK darling, we'll talk later.

He puts the phone down and gesticulates to the stocky man

with a florid face who's standing in the doorway. Come in and sit down, Jonathan, he says. Geoffrey's just bringing me a drink – what will you have?

Ronald

Dr Marcus has been and gone, and after Ronald's made himself a toasted sandwich with some tinned ham he found at the back of the cupboard, he sits in the kitchen with a cup of tea and the paper. In other times, better times, he might have been shocked by how quickly they got their pictures. He's unshockable now. They're on the front page and inside; pages three, four, five and six, with an editorial on page twelve. He's not going to read that. Load of rubbish, he tells himself. Linda and Brendan are on the front page of course, under the banner headline MONSTERS, but the inside pages feature him and his family. There's him, Marilyn and Ann Marie going into court, Marilyn sandwiched between the two of them, her face fixed by the formaldehyde of shame. His parting does an unexpected zigzag in the picture. He's wearing his work suit so he looks quite tidy, but the wayward line in his hair bothers him. It gives the game away. They've got the Gutteridges too: Rita and Shirley walking along arm in arm, heads high, unsmiling. Shit doesn't stick to Rita, he thinks, she's Teflon woman. Marilyn could do with some of that, coat her like a frying pan so shit can't stick.

The paper's got hold of pictures of Linda and Brendan as children. He was quite a chunky boy, but there's something fearful in his eyes that's at odds with his powerful body. Linda's photograph is one taken on a school trip. She's at the back of a large group of children, her face circled. The other kids' faces are crazed by giggles, but Linda's face is blurry, illegible. He wonders where the photos came from. Maybe someone stole them. Someone's making money out of his daughter's life. And Samantha's death.

The ham sandwich is sitting in the pit of his stomach, taking up residence. I'm possessed by a ham sandwich, he thinks, and he giggles. It's OK to giggle, no one can hear. Marilyn's beyond unconsciousness upstairs. He thinks he'd better check on her even though Dr Magnus said she'd be out till the morning, so he puts the plate in the dishwasher and goes upstairs.

Standing by her bed, he looks down at her face, its ridges and furrows levelled by the drugs, and the ham sandwich dissolves in a flood of longing. Longing for the Marilyn he loved before the babies, before their lives crawled around in thrall to her womb; longing for things to go straight, like his orderly parting, his job at the bank. He can do this when she's knocked out or incarcerated in hospital. He can yearn, hope, envy, lust, even hate. Hate feels good sometimes, like taking a shower so hot it melts the veneer of good manners: I hate you, hate you, hate.

Marilyn moans slightly and her head rolls to the right on her ruffled pillows, but she hasn't woken. There's a renegade lock of hair sticking to a pool of mascara under her eye; he pulls it away and returns it to its place over her ear. It's been a long time since he wound her hair around his fingers. He used to wrap a piece of it around the third finger, left hand when they were courting. Just practising, he'd say, and she'd laugh. There were lots of laughs before the first Linda, but they've wasted away over the years. He misses the heartiness of the before-Linda laughs. He wonders if she misses it too.

But he's got his ways of filling the gap, and he stops off in his bedroom to pick up a couple of handkerchiefs on his way to the study. He favours white ones, but Marilyn has taken to buying him blue: she says they're more fun to iron and there's no point making a fuss about hankies. Not that he makes a fuss about anything very much, apart from his private space. She knows now not to touch anything when she's cleaning the study. Sometimes when he hears her hoovering his bedroom he allows himself the wistful thought that she might sleep there with him, but she never does.

When the room turned into his study he left the ceramic plate on the door: *Ann Marie's Room* it says in curly writing with ivy around the edge. He took down the other sign, *Danger: Sulky Teenager Ahead*, although he liked the idea of sulking.

As he goes in, he flicks a switch and two pools of light float out of the darkness, flooding his favourite places. The business of the room gets done in his favourite places. Not the bills and the insurance and sending off for plane parts, but the real business of being Mr Ronald C. Miller. His desk sits in one pool of light, his armchair in the other. He locks the door behind him.

The room used to be pink and purple in Ann Marie's day – he can't remember what colour it was when it was Linda's – but when he took it over, he painted it brown. A brown study, he'd joked to Marilyn, but he'd had to explain the joke. The letter from the bank on the occasion of his retirement hangs on the wall. Marilyn had it framed for his birthday. I'm so proud of you, Ronnie, she said, Only you would stay in the same place, in the same job, for forty-five years.

He closes the curtains carefully so he doesn't disturb the plane he's suspended from the ceiling. It's a WWII Hurricane Spitfire, which has sentimental memories draped over its wings. One came down in a field in Suffolk when he was a boy and he was the one who spotted it and raised the alarm. They said the pilot might have died if he hadn't been so prompt, and they gave him a certificate. That's been framed too. When the pilot had recovered, he made a special journey from his home in Scotland to meet the little boy who'd saved his life. Fancy, said his mother, All the way from Scotland, but Ronald couldn't look at him because his face looked like spaghetti from the burns. The plane moves on its string in the draught, swinging its wings like a woman's hips – *You after business, darlin'?* Roxana, that was her name. Only twice, just after Linda died, but her damp smells and sharp teeth still haunt his dreams.

He has a routine when he arrives, when he's locked the door, when he's preparing the stage. He has to touch things in a ritual with all the cadences of a spell. It's vital to focus, because if his concentration cracks at any point he has to start again. Once when he'd been worried about Marilyn he'd had to do it five times. He's worried about her now. She hasn't said a word since the verdict, she's just making these weird guttural noises and he wonders if it'll be back to the bin again. He doesn't exactly want her back in the bin, but it might be a relief. He can have these thoughts in here. Disloyal thoughts.

He stands, ramrod straight, in the middle of the room and prepares. Takes nine deep breaths. He balls his hands into fists, flexes the fingers thirteen times: fists, flex, fists, flex, fists, flex, and he's ready. First the glass. He draws his fingers together, flattens his hand – left hand, to make it special – and marks each piece of glass in the room with a smeary wave. Bank letter: smear; pilot citation: smear; photograph of Marilyn and Ann Marie: smear; window panes: smear smear smear – pause – smear smear smear. The knuckles register the wood, and he raps his way around the room from door to skirting to window to desk to chair. Don't forget the wastepaper basket. Marilyn fucked up his routine once by changing the metal bin to a wooden one without telling him. He could have killed her. She never knew of course, because what would he say? I'm putting weedkiller in your cornflakes, pet, because you changed my bin. Sounds insane, and he's not the one who's insane. He goes over to the wooden bin and knocks three times.

Now his stage is set. Everything tickety-boo. He checks the lock on the door one more time in case Dr Marcus hasn't given Marilyn enough drugs. She knows she's only allowed to tap on the door when there's a real emergency. There have been three of these over the years: once when she started having hallucinations – she had her tablets tweaked and they went away; once when Ann Marie went into labour – he told her that really wasn't an emergency – and of course the third time was when she heard The News. It's always The News for him, not like the news of a branch closure or a neighbour's move or a new model aeroplane supplier: The News exploded at the centre of his life like Krakatoa. He thought maybe war had been declared when he heard her scream. She was washing up after lunch and he'd nearly finished the knocking on wood when he heard the noise from the kitchen. It had a wild edge to it, like a rabid dog snapping, and he froze mid-knock. How she reached his study so quickly, he never knew. He'd read about people developing superhuman powers in life-threatening situations, so perhaps that was it. Like the Incredible Hulk. He calls her the Hulk in his diary.

When she banged on the door he checked the room briefly and unlocked his sanctum. She looked like seaweed moving in the ocean. Her hands were describing waves of perplexity and her head was shaking in a weird slow motion that strangely didn't strike him as mad. He led her to her bedroom and sat her on the bed, which had been stripped. That's how he felt when she managed finally to tell him what she'd heard on the radio: stripped. As though his skin had been torn from him, leaving his complex systems glistening in the light, smarting in the air.

The impact of The News shut down his diary for nearly six weeks. When he was finally able to write anything, it had a curiously stilted quality, as though to let rip might set fire to the page. *Marilyn is fairly comfortable* he wrote in his first post-News entry, *Thank goodness. Her health has been causing some concern since we found out that Linda has been accused of committing this dreadful crime. Naturally we cannot believe in her guilt . . .* In succeeding months, as his diary recovered its own voice, small fragments of ungovernable feeling would burst out from time to time, like boils that had finally come to a head. *You're fucking doing it again – sucking up all the light, sapping all my energies. It's all Marilyn, Marilyn, Marilyn, isn't it? Fucking give me something back for once, can't you? You make me sick. You make me puke.* And then: *How the fuck could you do this to me? Everyone's blaming me as if I did something to make you a monster. It's always the parents, isn't it? You deserve to die. I'd do it, I'd kill you – but slowly. I want you to suffer.* Linda and Marilyn moved in and out of his words, in and out of his sights, but looking back at the entries he always knows who's who. His girls: Marilyn, two Lindas, one Ann Marie, the miscarriages he's always imagined were girls and his son. Kenneth. He should have been here. Should have cleaved to life. Should have grown up to be a man to stand next to his dad in that courtroom.

He sits down on the desk chair, the castors sighing dispiritedly as they take his weight. At the back of the kneehole, concealed by the ornate edge, is a tiny drawer he made and installed himself. It has dovetail joints, quite tricky in such a small structure, and they interlock like anxious fingers under the three coats of varnish. He bends over, opens the drawer and retrieves a key. The soft sound of the ratchets turning in the lock of the desk drawer pleases him and he smiles slightly.

In the drawer forty years of silent dialogue with himself huddle together in books reflecting the passage of time and taste and technology. The earliest ones are leather-bound, the edges of the pages nicotine-brown. The years of babies dying are recorded in stark black books like ledgers. For a while after Ann Marie was born the books celebrated his life between exuberant covers of cerise and turquoise and orange, but when she left home, the books settled back into sobriety. He pulls out the current book – navy-blue, with bevelled edges – and as he does, he sees something poking out of a diary right at the back. He brings it out and sets it on top of today's diary, like history's silt.

Over thirty years ago, Linda drew him this picture and he opens it out now, careful not to tear it. On a piece of blue sugar paper she's drawn mummy-daddy-linda, in a wobbly frame with a house to one side. The house is nothing like their bay-fronted Victorian terrace, which has been mortgage-free since his retirement. He's proud of that. The pictured house is double-fronted with big windows and a deep roof topped by lazily smoking chimneys. The Linda in the picture has a bow in her hair that dwarfs her head, like a giant butterfly about to take flight. It's dark pink. The garden dress was dark pink. Linda's got this funny look in the picture. Her eyebrows are angled upwards in the middle, so she looks worried. The daddy isn't worried though – he's got a big grin that goes from one side of his face to the other and his mouth is open, showing rows of pointed teeth. He remembers saying to her You'll have to be a dentist when you grow up. See to my teeth. She said No, Daddy, I'm going to be a policeman. Lock up bad peoples. The daddy's next to Linda and he's almost as tall as the house. The mummy's tiny. It's like she's way off in the distance and there's a circle around her as though she's in a balloon, or a bubble. She's not smiling. He remembers helping her with the writing and she's written MUMMY in pink and DADDY and LINDA in black. He hasn't looked at the picture for years but it reminds him that the woman in a suit who went down for life today was once a little girl who drew pictures and couldn't write Daddy by herself. He strokes Linda's hair in the picture, then slides it back into the book. He slides the book back in its chronological place.

He's been recording the case since it began and it's colonising the book. He flips back a few pages and reads: *I've been watching the jury – carefully, obviously, because I bet they're waiting for me to crack. Foreman's very respectable-looking – could be a businessman, or maybe something in finance. Most of the jury's quite mature, fortunately, but there are these young two girls who bother me, one white*

*and one black. As you know, diary, I've got nothing against blacks –
we had these two coloured customers at the bank for years, and they
were very well mannered, not rowdy at all – but I wonder if the black
girl can understand a white person like Linda. I wonder if she's got a
job? Mostly they haven't, but she dresses quite nicely, so maybe she
has. She seems to be paying attention, as far as I can see – mind you,
she's sitting next to the foreman so he's probably keeping her in order.*

*It's the other girl I watch mostly though. She's gorgeous. She's
wearing a dark suit but you can tell she's got a lovely figure. Big tits.
Probably she's not wearing a bra and her nipples are pushing against
her shirt and it's making them hard and I've got the horn now thinking
what I'd like to do to her. She's sitting on my lap and I can feel her
cheeks jiggling on my thighs and they're hard and soft all at once and
I'm undoing her jacket and shirt and sliding them down off her
shoulders and I'm licking down her chest and I'm right she's not
wearing a bra and I'm right she's got huge nipples and they're erect
and firm like her body. I want you now, Daddy, she says, and she puts
two fingers in her mouth and sucks. I push her off my lap and I say
Take your clothes off, baby, pull them down slowly and she slides her
skirt and panties down her hips with her long red nails and her pubes
are dark like my hair and thick and curly. I say Come here, come over
here and I lick my middle finger and I push it up her push it up into
her cunt and she's saying Do me, Daddy, do me. And she's bending
over the desk and her buttocks are round and smooth like apples and I
lift myself up over her and her hands are gripping the edge of the desk
and she says Fuck me, Daddy, and I fuck her till she screams till the
blood runs till I'm finished and she says You're the first. You'll always
be the first.*

The last line dangles in mid-air halfway down the page. He'd
had to pause when he'd finished writing it.

He turns the page to where he started writing again: *My little
juror looked pale today and she's getting dark circles under her eyes.
Halfway through the morning they passed the jury these books of photos*

and she held her copy in her hands like a little brown bomb. She stroked the cover before she opened it, and then she looked. She made this faint sound like a baby animal and everybody's head turned. Even the barrister who was on his feet at the time faltered. Her pretty face collapsed and I thought Oh my God, she's going to pass out and I almost jumped to my feet and rushed over, because I wanted to hold her. I'd have been able to get my arms right around her, unlike the Hulk.

She put her hand in the air and it broke my heart because suddenly she looked like a little girl asking the teacher if she could go to the toilet. The judge noticed she was having a moment, and called for a break. He's really poker-faced so you can't tell if any of this is affecting him, but his head's probably too full of the law to let it get in. Probably hasn't even got any children because he's been too busy making his career and earning pots of money.

Our lives have been blighted by children. Not Ann Marie of course, she's different, but the others, the living and the dead. Sometimes I think to myself if Marilyn hadn't been such a failure at having babies, where would I be now? Might have taken those banking exams. Might have become a branch manager even. What if I'd left her when she went mad that first time? I bet other men would have. I might have fetched up with someone like my little juror and we might have gone abroad to live, like Spain or something. Or the Canaries. She looks like she knows how to have a good time, even though she wasn't exactly having fun today.

He lets the book rest on his knees, his hands flat on the open pages, and leans back in the chair. He looks at the photo of Marilyn and Ann Marie on his desk. He took it when they went on a package to the Costa Blanca and he's captured them sitting with their arms around each other in front of an overblown hibiscus. Ann Marie must have been about seventeen: she looked voluptuous in her Hawaiian-print bikini. He says it out loud, rolling the word around in his mouth like a boiled sweet: vol-uptu-ous. Another word for sexy. He'd never say that to her of course, he limits himself to You look nice, Annie, or That's a nice skirt, if he comments on her appearance at all. But he watched her breasts falling sideways when she lay on the sunbed and imagined touching the fleshy spillage from the cups when he was alone in his bedroom touching himself. Marilyn hasn't touched him once since Ann Marie was born.

He sits back up, puts the diary on his desk and flips the pages to the last entry. Time for today. A red pen for today.

Tuesday, March 18th

She was sent down this morning. I half expected the judge to put on one of those black cap things and say You will be taken from here and hanged by the neck until you are dead, like they used to. I'm in favour of capital punishment – what's the point in obeying the law if there's no penalty for doing terrible things? – but I suddenly felt sick at the thought that Linda could have been executed.

Once they handed the verdict down, any remaining hope was sucked down the drain. We couldn't pretend there'd been a miscarriage of justice or that it had all been a horrible dream. Our daughter's a murderer. You think you'll never know a murderer in a month of Sundays and then, bang, the killer's your daughter and the dead body's your granddaughter.

When the jury came back in, you could see on their faces it was Guilty. One of the women – I'd say she was in her fifties, with mousy frizzy hair – she looked like she'd had an electric shock and she put her hands right over her face when the foreman stood up. Sherilyn didn't react, or not so I could see. She was holding Brendan's hand and looking straight ahead, and I suddenly thought, My baby and I wanted to give her a cuddle. And then I wanted to smack her and it was all getting muddled in my head, I was going cuddle smack, cuddle smack, cuddle smack and I didn't know where I was. Marilyn was

175

slumped against me, so at least she didn't make a scene, but I'm sure it's all to come. I dread what's to come. We've been down this road so many times – cracking up, back in the bin, cracking up, back in the bin – but maybe she won't recover this time. How do you recover from being the mother of a murderer? Or father, for that matter. I saw this bloke on the jury look over at me after the foreman gave the verdict and he looked like he was sympathising. Maybe he's a father too. You grab whatever comfort you can at moments like these. What am I saying? Moments like these? – there's never been a moment like this!

All I ever wanted was a quiet life. I never wanted any dramas or disruptions and I've ended up with this life stuffed with breakdowns and deaths and grief and now a dead grandchild and a killer daughter. I don't deserve this. I've lived an orderly life, I've always done the right thing, never broken the law. I know life isn't fair, but it feels like I'm being punished for something I didn't do.

Marilyn insisted on sending Linda a good luck card yesterday, silly cow, but she didn't reply. Why would she? We're nothing to her. She's even dumped the Christian name we gave her, for God's sake, so it couldn't be clearer. I wish I could surgically remove her from my head, but the suit she was wearing today was dark pink, so that took me back.

The judge looked very serious when he talked to them before he said Life. He told them that in all his years in the law he'd never come across anyone who'd done anything so evil – well, he put it better than that, in legal language – and that he was going to make sure that life meant a good long time. Then he said Take them down and I got this chill all through me because it was like the warders were taking them down into hell.

So that's it. Now we've all been sentenced with no time off for good behaviour and I can't even escape to my job. At least when I was working I could always leave Marilyn at home and have my normal eight hours in the bank with my normal colleagues and normal customers till it was time to go back to the madhouse. That's not fair, she wasn't always mad, but even when things are all right there's this voice in my head going Any day now. Keep your eyes open, Ronald, because there's always a chance she'll blow again. And now she has. There's no one to talk to: David phoned me the other day and we went out for a drink, but it got quite awkward because all we had to talk about was the bank and I'm a bit out of touch now. I don't think we'll meet up again.

I don't ever feel like killing myself exactly, but sometimes I wonder what it's all been for. What's the point of carrying on. Then I think of Annie and the kids and I think, Well, OK, maybe that's what it's all about. Frannie likes to come in the shed with me and hold the parts and the glue when I make the model planes, strange thing for a girl, but she's good company. And Donnie loves his sports so we can watch the athletics on the telly together, so that's something. But I'm grabbing at straws. Annie's asked Marilyn to come and stay for a bit, to help with the kids she said, but I know she's really giving me a break, and I'm grateful. She's a good girl.

I've got that pain in my chest today. It comes and goes but when Marilyn's sorted I'll get Dr Marcus to check it out. Probably nothing, but it's been bothering me for three or four months now. It's stress maybe. You don't die from stress or I'd have died several times before. Linda wouldn't even have been born because I'd have died from stress when Linda Alison died. That would have saved a lot of bother because if I was dead then Linda wouldn't have happened and Marilyn might have had a happier life.

I'd definitely have had a happier life up there in heaven! Lots of lovely girls in heaven. Sex on tap, like best bitter.

He closes the book and settles it back in its place in the drawer. Time for the famous final scene.

The special book has a black cover like its contemporaries, but it's been pulled out and put back in so many times over the last thirty-five years its spine is cracking wearily. Although it's in the same series as the others, it feels heavier, as though what it contains isn't paper, but gold. He holds it against his chest like a baby and goes over to his armchair. He pulls out his hankies and puts them on the table beside it. When he's sitting down, he slips off his black moccasins, his retirement shoes. Casuals, after a lifetime of formals. He leans forwards a little to catch a whiff of his damp-cheese footsmell. He loves it. In here, he loves all the sticky emanations of his body. He sits back. He knows what's coming so he savours the anticipation, like smelling a delicious dinner in the next room. Letting the cumin and coriander and garlic purl around his nose, setting the saliva off from the sides of his tongue, knowing all he has to do is open the book when he's ready.

Now he's ready.

His hands with their savagely bitten nails are trembling slightly as he opens it. Must be the events of the day, he thinks. The book obediently flops open at the page; it knows what it's supposed to deliver. What it delivers every time.

Saturday August 12th

What a day! What a beautiful lovely gorgeous day! I'm never going to forget today!

Crap night's sleep because Marilyn was up and down like a bloody yo-yo. I heard her get up three or four times, but she didn't call out to me so I turned over and went back to sleep. I had that dream again, the one where I'm a giant striding around crushing things under my feet, and various others I can't remember, so it was a busy night what with one thing and another. After one of her walkabout nights she needs to spend most of the day in bed, so I was jolly pleased that the sun was shining when I woke up. Meant I could get out of the house. She was sitting in the chair by the window when I opened my eyes, looking at me with that blank face. I asked her how she was and she shook her

*head. Then I asked her if she wanted breakfast and she shook her head.
Asked her if she wanted to get back into bed and she shook her head. I
thought, Oh shit, here we go again and I said I'll go and see to Linda,
pet, you sit still. Linda was awake of course, but she just sits quietly
in her bed till I come and get her. Lucky she's such a good girl.*

*We got through breakfast fine, because I asked her what she wanted
and she said Torn flakes and I put all three of her bowls in front of her
so she could choose which one. I got the quantities right this time, so
no fusses. I thought, This is starting well and nipped upstairs to
Marilyn with her tea on a tray and her tablets. She was still sitting on
the chair, so I put the tray down on the dressing table, said Come on,
pet, and took her over to the bed. She's so skinny she scares me.
Sometimes I imagine I can hear her bones scraping against each other
when she moves, but I can't force-feed her. I said that to her psychiatrist.
I can't force-feed her, I said. She can manage a little soup usually,
but I have to feed her really slowly with a teaspoon because otherwise
she spits it out. Strange to be feeding your wife upstairs when your
little daughter's downstairs feeding herself. She took her tablets like a
good girl and I made sure she drank all her tea because that way she
has a bit of milk to build her up. I said Night night, and she lay down
and closed her eyes, so that was one job done.*

*I cleared away the breakfast things and did the washing-up, but I
cut myself on a knife, which upset Linda. She hates the sight of blood.
I sat her in front of the telly for a while so I could put in the washing
and do some hoovering; she never stirs when you settle her in her chair
and turn on children's telly. She'll stay put through the news too, and
the sport.*

*When I was finished, I got her dressed in that dark-pink dress – it's
my favourite, nice embroidery, frilly collar, really feminine – and we
went to the park. I took some bread for the ducks and my camera
because it was already beginning to feel like a day I wanted to record.
We walked around, she had a bit of a swing and we pootled down to
the pond. I got her to stand near the edge and I took a quick snap of*

her. She absolutely will not smile to order, so it may not be one of the best, but never mind. She wanted to get the bread ready, so I sat on the bench and watched her. She had this little frown on her face as she made sure every piece of bread was exactly the same size, and wouldn't let me give anything to the ducks until she was satisfied she'd done it properly. Just like me. She'll probably make a good accountant when she grows up. Famous last words – she'll probably be an axe murderer when she grows up!

He's considered scribbling out that last sentence, but he let it stay because it was part of the historical record. But he knows it's coming and skips it.

We had lunch in the café by the library – I organised the plate carefully before I brought it to the table, so she'd eat it – and toddled off home after I'd picked up a couple of plane books I'd ordered. Marilyn was in the lounge when we came in, still in her nightie, sitting on the couch like a statue. Linda pulled her hand away from mine and went over. She stood right in front of her, sort of leaning into her legs, and she said Mummy, Mummy, Mummy? like a question, like she wasn't quite sure. Marilyn looked down at her, but she could have been looking at an empty space. This happens all the time so I'm astonished Linda still persists. I said Come on, pet, I'll look after Mummy now, time for some telly, and settled her down in front of the box.

When I pulled Marilyn up off the couch to take her into the kitchen, I saw she'd wet herself again. It's always on that same cushion, so if I can find a replacement, I won't have to get a new couch – that'll save a bit. Took her upstairs, hosed her down, got a clean nightie, dressed her, brought her to the kitchen and sat her at the table. Stuck the cushion cover in the machine and rinsed the cushion through under the shower. It takes a couple of days to dry, but I don't sit on the couch anyway. I always watch telly on Mum's chair.

He strokes the seat of his chair fondly. He brought it up here as soon as this room became his. That way, no one else sits in it.

I got some tomato soup down her and she managed most of a Ryvita, so that was a bit of a result. Fed her the lunchtime tablets and took her back upstairs. As I was tucking her up, there was suddenly a sort of light in her eyes and she said Thank you, Ronnie. I nearly burst into tears. They said she'd come back to the land of the living eventually, but I didn't quite believe them. I said That's all right, pet, and patted her hand. The light went out of her eyes, but that's OK. She's on her way back.

It was still really sunny, so I filled up the paddling pool in the garden and called to Linda to come out. She stood in the doorway for a minute and she looked so pretty I just blurted out You look lovely in that dress, pet. She gave me one of her funny looks. She can freeze you in your tracks with that look, but the sun was shining and Marilyn had said Thank you, so I said Come over here and we'll get your clothes off. I stripped her down and she stepped into the pool gingerly so she didn't get all over wet straight off. I went to get a towel and the toys she likes to play with in the bath and on the way back through the kitchen, I picked up a beer. Bugger it, I said to myself, it's Saturday. I settled myself in the garden seat and watched Linda in the pool. She doesn't do any of that running in and out like some children do, she sits tight, pouring water from one container to the other, making sure it doesn't spill over. Then she puts them very carefully on the grass when they're full, in descending order of height. If anything spills while she's doing it, she empties them all and starts again. Then she takes her dollies and puts them in the containers head first, so she's got this little row of pink plastic legs sticking up into the air. She can amuse herself for hours, so I sat there and drank my beer and I was beginning to feel really relaxed when she stood up and said Got to do wee wee, Daddy. As she turned round to get out of the pool, I looked at her little bum and the cheeks were like perfect round apples. They were slightly red where she'd been sitting and as the water dripped off them, my cock stirred in my pants.

His cock stirs and he puts his hand under the book, over his flies.

I followed her into the house and she stopped in the middle of the kitchen and said No, Daddy, in this firm voice, so I went and got myself another beer and she trotted off to the loo. I was sat back on my seat when she came out again and I said You OK, pet? and she nodded her head and got back into the pool. I must have dozed off because the sun was getting low in the sky when I opened my eyes and she was sitting in the water staring at me in that way she has. Like she's scanning you with radar. I said Time for tea and bed now, pet, and went over and lifted her out. I rubbed her down with the towel, drying all the nooks and crannies, especially between her legs. I let the towel slip off my little finger when I was drying her cunt and I slipped it, just a little bit of it, up her crack. When she was dry, I didn't bother with her knickers, just popped her dress back on and after I'd done the buttons up at the back I put my hand over her bum. It curved into my palm, fitting as snugly as an acorn in its cup. I said to her Come and sit on Daddy's lap, pet, and I took her over to the seat and lifted her on to my lap and I could feel her little bum hard and soft all at once and she jiggled a bit and my cock got hard. I could feel it pushing against my zip.

He unzips his flies and puts his hand in. It's hot and stiff.

I moved her about a bit like I was playing and I thought, This is good, this is very good, and she was staring at me with her lizard stare so I closed my eyes and it didn't take long, just a bit more jiggling,

His hand moves up and down the shaft more urgently.

up and down and up and down and anyone who saw us would have thought I was just doing a nursery rhyme with her and she's not very heavy but she's warm,

Up to the tip, down to the balls, blood pounding.

and I'm bouncing her faster and faster and I couldn't stop couldn't stop myself and I carried on till I came and came.

He comes, his head jerking forwards as he groans, the book sliding sideways. This always happens, and he catches it before it falls. He sinks back against his chair and rests.

The two hankies do their clean-up job, the book cover is wiped dry and it goes back to its special place in the drawer. He locks the drawer and puts the key back in its hiding place. He pushes the desk chair back into the kneehole, plumps up the cushion in the armchair, turns the light off, opens the curtains and leaves the room. He's put Linda back in her place under lock and key. She can't kill anyone there.

Marilyn

I'm thinking of dying. Of making sure I die. I don't want to cause any trouble, especially to Ronald, who's been so good to me, but if I die, Linda won't be my fault any more. The guilt is slowly killing me anyway. The grandchildren will miss me for a bit – especially my cakes – but they're better off without a nan with blood on her hands.

Blood. I've got blood on my hands. When my skin turns transparent, like it is now, I can see it racing around and down the tubes, through my belly, curdling in my guts like cake mixture if you add the eggs too fast. My heart's gone this funny shape, not like a heart at all. Like a spiky ball. Like a bright red conker in its shell and it's beating like hearts are supposed to do, but it's ripping my insides, poking holes in my organs, mashing up my lungs. It knows what to do, it knows it's not to keep me alive any more. I wrote it a letter yesterday. Dear Heart, I said, it's time to stop what you're doing. Time to give up the ghost, put down your tools, cash in your chips. You've done me proud: filled up with love for my babies, broken when I killed them, stopped at times of shock and pleasure, and now you've got this final job, so do it calmly and well. It bridled at first when it got the letter. Can't do that, it said, My job is to keep you alive, keep the organs grinding, the bellows pumping. You have your instructions, I said in the letter, quite coldly for me, Do what you're told. All I've got to do now is prepare.

I've written other letters too. I've been busy. Written to the living and the dead. Written to Linda Alison saying I'm sorry I killed you but it was nice knowing you, I said, Even for that short time. I saw her the other day, she had these six children toddling along behind her, like a stream of chicks in their mother's wake. I'd have had six if I hadn't been a killer, but mustn't cry over spilt milk. Mustn't grumble. Worse things happen at sea. Wrote to Ann Marie congratulating her for surviving my mothering. You must have been very strong, I said to her in the letter, must have had mysterious powers like Supergirl or Catwoman, because she seems normal, seems to be able to hold her children without puncturing them with her spiky heart. Perhaps she wasn't really mine after all. Perhaps Ronald found her on the doorstep after my two half-formed babies fought their way out of me in a torrent of blood: *get out get out she's toxic.*

I never had names for them, couldn't risk it, but I can name them now they're flushed away. Topsy and Turvy. Namby and Pamby. Pinky and Perky.

Kenneth says he's sorry he can't stay, but he has pressing business elsewhere. He reads my letter, written in blood on sheets of skin torn from my inner thighs and he smiles in relief that he won't have to deal with me any more, won't have to worry each time he turns a corner that I might be waiting on the other side with my hatchet and my tears. He's the spit of his dad, except he's big. He's a real man with a dark shiny pelt on his chest and his arms and he has a wolfish grin.

I don't need to write to Linda because she's inside my head, sitting in the middle of my brain, chiselling away with the truth. You killed Samantha, she hisses, Just as surely as you killed your own babies. When you were born with that serial-killer look on your face, your mother should have held you underwater till you stopped struggling. Samantha would be alive now, would be free and fine and fertile. Her children would have their children and would know that cages are for animals, for the wild things that threaten to unseat us.

I'm looking at my hands, which are resting in my lap. If I keep them clasped no one will see the blood, no one will know that my palms are awash. The other day when I was peeling potatoes, I saw a hint of pink in the water that blossomed into a full-hearted crimson and I nearly called out to Ronald to rescue me, to pull his dinner out of the swill of my guilt. I pushed the floor cloth into my mouth to stop myself from screaming and the grit from the tiles ground against my teeth. I must go in my own time. Mustn't let them take me away this time. I'll choose carefully, run through the options, select the place and the method, but there must be blood. When I'm dead, they'll finally understand that I did it – that I massacred my children before they had time to step out of innocence, and they'll condemn me. But maybe then they'll find it in them to forgive and they'll scrape off the crusted gore, sluice me down, and I'll be clean again. Sins expiated, crimes erased, they might even inter my bones with my babies. We can rot and dry and crumble into the earth together. Separated at birth. Together in death.

I look at Ronald sometimes and can see straight into his head. Can see the disappointment turning everything grey. All the roots and shoots of what his life might have been, poisoned before they had time to mature. His hands have always been full of me, holding me like a cupful of dirty water, swivelling his eyes neither to the right nor the left in case I seeped through his fingers. When I melt into madness, he mops me up with husbandly concern and never complains. I've never heard him complain, never heard his voice turn reedy with resentment. I must have been what he wanted. God knows why.

Brendan and Sherilyn

The prison officers had obviously been genetically modified to expunge anything remotely feminine. They looked like big burly men and had the manners of navvies. As the van pulled out of the prison gates, one of them took her jacket off and the wet patches under her arms made my stomach heave. At court, she shackled my wrist to hers like some insane wedding, and I held my breath so I wouldn't have to take in any of her stink. Inhaling her would have implicated me in the legal process and I refused to be party to our destruction. Fortunately while I was on remand I could wear my own clothes and have my own toiletries, so at least I could look and smell like me. That kept me afloat – that and knowing I was going back to him every day. I could persuade myself that prison and its inhabitants was some nightmarish film I'd wandered into by mistake as long as I could escape to him. Obviously I knew we were in the dock, in the court, but feeling our pulses march in step, hearing him breathing my breath, wiped out everything else. My heart would somersault when I knew we were approaching the court, him in his van, me in mine, and I'd start counting seconds: one to sixty, one to sixty, tapping each minute against my breast with my ring finger. I'd be taken out of the van along with the other women – 'produced' as though we were eggs a chicken had laid – and I'd fold myself on to the bench in the court cell, hungry for the man who was only minutes away.

My other half.

★

I didn't think I could love her more, but each day when I saw
her, every day when they produced us, was like the first time I'd
noticed her in the corridor at work. At night she walked in my
dreams, but when I woke up alone in my cell, she'd been
abducted. Not left me – she'd never have left me – but amputated
like my arm or my leg. Missing a limb unbalances your whole
life. If you fall, you can't save yourself as you tip and spin and
topple to the ground. Without Sherilyn I was paralysed. Stealing
her from me was a criminal act of such cruelty it took my breath
away. I caught the relish in the officers' eyes as they watched me
struggling to remain upright without the woman who gave me
life. But each day during the trial, my life was restored. We'd
meet at the bottom of the stairs that led to the dock, she with
her prison officer, me with mine, and the blood started coursing
through my veins again. When she smiled I was invincible.

My other half.

They saw themselves as bold hunters in pursuit of the truth, but
they couldn't see what was under their noses: the only truth was
us. The only living, breathing thing in that court was Brendalyn.
Sheridan. They droned on like bees – lawyers talking, talking,
witnesses spinning their idiot yarns, the public gallery behind us
shifting and sighing – but all we heard was the sound of our legs
crossing, the crisp *tsk* hanging in the air like sparks from a fire-
work. We stood up and sat down with everyone else when the
judge appeared, but the only movement that mattered was our
hands coming together like an oyster, the pearl of our life resting
at its centre. Our hearts pumped in the pulse of the clasp, and
when we turned our heads, our eyes sucked each other in like
sponges. We were taken down separately for the breaks, but the
bond between us was infinitely elastic and wound its serpentine
way between our cells. Sometimes our lawyers would come down
to discuss something. Insanely, we hadn't been allowed to have

the same lawyer, but we knew that we were saying the same thing to both legal teams. Our story couldn't be told any other way. Brendalyn began the story and Sheridan had the last word.

One day we'd been sent out for an adjournment and I was sitting with a couple of prison officers who were sprawled against the wall, gossiping about nothing of any great consequence. One of them suddenly said Have you seen this? and pulled out one of the gutter papers from her bag. There was a banner headline: Skeleton Child Dies 'Like Rat In A Cage', and I remembered that that was what the policeman had said in court the day before. Underneath there was a blank square and the screw started reading out loud. *We would show you a picture of little Samantha,* she read, *But none exist. No one cared enough to take her photograph. No one framed a photo of her smiling at her birthday party, taking her first step, hugging her puppy.* She looked over at me, giving me the evil eye, *But we can show you her parents, currently on trial for her murder,* she read, and turned the page. She held the paper up so the screw and I could see. They had my wedding photo. My big day. I felt like I'd been violated, like I'd been tied to a bed so anyone passing could take a look, have a feel. That must have cost a bob or two, that dress, the screw said, Could have spent some of that on her baby, and they both stared at me. I kept my face straight.

If they thought they could touch us, they were wrong.

My QC told me there'd been a lot of tabloid spreads about us. I said to her Am I supposed to care about that? and she looked perplexed. Some people would, she said. Some people might mind being portrayed as a monster. That puzzled me. But I'm not a monster, I said, I'm an accountant. That was the one time she lost her composure – she'd been very dignified until then, very professional, but she seemed to be struggling to keep herself

189

under control. Halfway through the prosecution case, she said she thought I should plead. Guilty, that is. But I'm not, I said, I didn't kill the girl. She died, but I didn't kill her, and after some argy-bargy, she said she'd follow my instructions. That was her job, to follow instructions. It gave me a bit of a kick to be instructing someone like her because QCs are pretty grand and I was just Brendan Nobody Gutteridge. Unless I was with Lyn and then I was Superman.

   If they thought they could touch us, they were wrong.

We'd never courted fame, but now we were in the spotlight, the public were mysteriously blind to our rarity. They seemed not to see that we were as exquisite as an endangered orchid, choosing instead to adopt the views of a hostile press, but we didn't let it get to us. They kept going on in court about Samantha this and Samantha that, but the words clattered on the ground like empty shells. We didn't need words. Words would have interrupted what made us the same. Samantha was just a word for the thing that had threatened to make us different, so of course we had to stop it. Both of our QCs were singing from the same hymn sheet: if convicted, we'd get life with a punitive minimum recommendation, plead guilty and the minimum would be considerably reduced and blah and blah and blah. No one seemed to consider that we might not be guilty and some-times the tragedy of it all was overwhelming. They were doing their best to destroy us, like dropping a light bulb on to a stone floor and watching it shatter into a million fragments. They were trying to smash up the one thing that made it possible for us to see we existed, trying to cast us back into the squalid darkness where we'd been crouching in shit until we met.

   The dock officers kept going on about how our families were coming to court every day and how all we had to do was turn our heads and we'd see them. Look to your right when you go down to the cells, one of them said, They're all sitting in that box over there. Look, he said, Over there. We didn't move. It would have been more interesting to count the hairs on our heads; at least then we'd know one more detail about us. We took the smell of us back to our prisons.

When I got back at night, I'd look over at him to see what he was doing. We'd both been put in single cells, so I was blessedly free of cell mates complaining and could concentrate on Brendan. My love. I saw him sit on the edge of his bed and pick at the blanket. He'd discovered that when you rubbed at its surface hard enough, it made little balls of wool which he then stacked in pyramid shapes, twenty-seven in each one. He arranged them on his table in the exact position of the pyramids in the Valley of the Kings. Ancient Egypt fascinated him. Sometimes I'd go into the study and he'd be sitting in the chair with his books around his feet, on the desk, on his lap, and he'd look like a cat swimming serenely in a vat of cream. He had a collection of scarab beetles in the desk drawers, each one with its own handwritten label which said where it had originated, what its dimensions were, where he'd got it and how I'd reacted when he showed me. Mostly what I said was pretty unremarkable: *That's a nice one. What a pretty blue. Where did you get it?* but he said it was important to record the fact that I was always there whatever he did because he'd been so alone with his feathers as a boy, as with everything else. When he'd finished making his pyramids, he did his exercises, twice a day: 200 sit-ups, 30 lunges, 100 press-ups. He took his shirt off and I watched the muscles in his back playing and twitching like small creatures. His sit-ups created ridges on his belly that my fingers tripped over, tracking the strength under his satiny skin. When we played doctors and nurses, I'd pop the nipple buttons on his uniform one by one and run my tongue down his hairless chest to his belly. I'd circle around his navel slowly,

slowly, a snake waiting for the moment to jab its head, stabbing my tongue into the salty, dusty dent, rooting its tip into the hard centre as though it could grow there, sending out rootlets into his liver, his lungs, his heart. The memory's making me wet and I undo the top buttons of my blouse. I slide my hand up the inside of my thigh, down under my knickers. I look over to him in his cell and he's undone his flies; he's holding his dick, rampant with sex. My fingers stroke and pull and flick. I straddle his body and his eyes gorge on me, suck me in. My thighs judder as I sink on to his mouth, holding me in its pillowy heat while his tongue flutters and laps, and my belly, my groin, trembles with desire. I slip like a whisper down his front and draw him into me, watching between our bodies as his dick pulls out with its collar of sticky shine, plunging in again fifteen, sixteen, twenty times and my belly holds itself tight till it's time to let go, and I'm coming in red rhythms, pooling into him, the him and me melt.

There's no higher peak.

Alfie had a picture of the woman he called his missus on the wall of his cell. It was one of those makeover photos plain girls have done, handing over a fortune to a bunch of poofs to tart them up so they can look halfway decent. Alfie's girl still looked like a slapper. I wasn't about to put Sherilyn up on the wall for other men to ogle, and anyway I could look over at her any time I chose, but I kept my favourite photo of her under my pillow. I took it when we were in Egypt, in the Valley of the Kings. She was wearing a canary-yellow sundress which hung off the edges of her shoulders, her delicate collarbones floating in the light. The dress was very tight to the waist that I could girdle with my hands, then billowed like an upside-down tulip to her knees. She was standing next to one pyramid, with two others in the background and she looked so fragile, almost translucent, my heart flooded with tenderness every time I looked at it. There loomed these huge monuments to ancient potentates, and there she stood, my thumbnail queen. I called her Sherititi while we were there and she said on a bright day, with the Egyptian sun in my eyes, I looked like one of the pharaohs in the wall paintings. She didn't share my fascination with Ancient Egypt, but she was interested that I was interested and that was enough. She never once complained when I dragged her around the museums in Luxor and Cairo, and when I bought her a very expensive scarab ring she said Do you think I need to be bribed? But she loved it. She kept it in the onyx jewellery box I bought her in Kashmir. I look over to her in her cell and I feel myself getting hard when she looks back and undoes her blouse a little, just to tease me. She catches my smile in her eyes like a lake captures the moon and as she unpops the last five buttons, her smooth belly emerges gracefully from the fabric's shadows. I run my palm over first one breast, then the other, her blushing nipples brushing my skin like feathers. My other hand's around my dick, moving faster as she slides her skirt down slowly, with that little wiggle when it comes to her hips. She keeps her knickers on because she likes me to take them off with my teeth, and I seduce them down her thighs; when I reach her ankles she steps lightly out of the froth of lace, and smiles. I lie on the ground and she's standing over me and I look up into her, look up into the rosy wet ruffles promising me the taste of her, the smell of her, and she lowers herself slowly; my tongue opens her out, burrows into the place where she tastes salty and creamy all at once. She's ready for me and she slides down my front, slides me into her, holding me safe, throwing her head back when she comes, her neck naked and vulnerable and I push harder, my hips lifting her up and she's pinned to them, she's part of me and my dick's drenched with her cum. My cum. Our cum.

There's no higher peak.

*

The day of the verdict was torture because we were trapped in the same building all day, but separated. It was like seeing a delectable meal laid out on a table, but it's behind glass and you press your face against it, tantalised, starving. From time to time our solicitors would come down to the cells and say It's a good sign, them staying out all this time – they'd be back by now if they were certain. We knew by then that they were going to find us guilty and we were impatient for the verdict, longing to be together again in the dock. The jury came back just after four in the afternoon, so we'd had to wade through court food and moronic prison-officer chat, but our hearts lifted when we met at the bottom of the stairs. It was as though we were getting married again, both of us dressed to kill in our coordinated outfits of black and taupe linen. We climbed the stairs together, our footsteps falling on the treads without a trace of syncopation: one pair of feet, one pair of hands, one head, one heart. We held hands up the stairs, into the box, sitting down, standing up when the judge came in, sitting down when the jury was sent for, standing up for the verdict, which was Guilty. We looked at each other and smiled. One verdict. One Brendalyn. There were muffled noises from the public gallery: something that might have been a sob, something else that was probably the rustle of agreement, the sound of something falling. We knew we were going to get life, but our life continued wherever we were. They could have sent one of us to Siberia and packed the other off to Patagonia, and they'd have said Good. Good, that's them separated, but they'd be wrong. You can't take somebody's mind away and that's where we lived, where we'd laugh, dream, grow old, where we'd flourish in death together. The judge looked over his half-moon glasses, trying to intimidate us. Failing. He cast each word into the air as though it were worth catching and droned on about the heinous nature of the crime, how Samantha had been cruelly this and cruelly that, and we thought, You don't understand. You don't understand that it was self-defence: we had to protect ourselves from her. If we'd pushed a burglar downstairs who was trying to steal our valuables, we'd have been applauded, but no one could see that we were the victims here. The girl was a thief, she wanted to steal our most valuable thing – us – so she had to be stopped. This was a success story, not a crime.

The judge said he was recommending a minimum of twenty years.

My QC came down to my cell with the other barrister and the solicitor, interrupting my conversation with Brendan. The solicitor had this pitying look on her face and I wanted to grab her cheeks and say Fuck off. Fuck off, you're a fool. They can take our house, our money, all our possessions, but they can't take us away from us. The QC said I'm sorry, Mrs Gutteridge, I'd thought there was a slim chance of an acquittal, but I don't think we have grounds for an appeal. I said Fine. That's OK. Thanks for your help. I expect you've got lots to do now. They looked startled but didn't make a move, so I said There's nothing else we have to discuss, is there? The QC turned to the other barrister and said Anything you want to raise, Andrew? And Andrew said No I don't think so, Bradley. The solicitor turned on her heels and went out of the cell, looking upset. I had to say goodbye twice to the other two because they didn't seem to be getting the hint, but finally they shook my hand and left. The court day had finished, so I was taken off straight away in the van, along with an older woman who'd been given eighteen months for prostitution. She was so obscenely fat she could barely fit into her cubicle, and she wasn't wearing any make-up. Her roots were showing and her nails looked like she'd been using them to dig up the road, so I said to Brendan Bet her customers had white sticks, and we laughed. You could see out of your darkened window in the van, but no one could see in, and there were lots of flashes outside as we raced out of the courtyard. I think the press were trying to take photographs. I'd have been furious if they printed a picture of the fat tart and said it was me, but even that wouldn't have been as bad as publishing my wedding photo. Don't worry, love, said Hilda, one of the prison officers at the front, They never get anything clear enough to print, and I said I'm not worried, Hilda, just thirsty. The afternoon tea hadn't arrived for some reason. Brendan looked cool and relaxed in his van, as though he were sitting at a café table in the sunshine, sipping a glass of Veuve Clicquot. I wondered what it would be like if we were in the same cubicle. Rather sweaty, I thought, and I remembered the time we'd had sex in the hall cupboard. It was the last place in the house we'd tried and it began as a game of sardines. I'd taken all my clothes off when I got in there and wrapped myself in one of Brendan's coats; the Harris tweed teased my nipples into readiness for Brendan's mouth when he found me. It was the most exciting sex we'd had since our wedding night.

I settled in for the ride.

After the sentencing they took me back down and as we came towards my cell, this guy James – good-looking, younger than me, glossy black curls – was being brought out. I'd noticed him in the sweat box on the way to court. He'd been remanded for reports and now he was going back upstairs to be sentenced. As we passed, he grinned and said What you get, mate? I grinned back and said Life. That's a fuck, he said, They're going to chuck the book at me too. Maybe we'll meet up. Yeah, yeah, why not, I said, and for a moment Sherilyn wasn't uppermost in my head. You won't, the screw said when he'd gone. Won't what? I said. Won't be in the same nick, he said, He's mental – they'll bang him up in a nutters' nick. Won't stop the bum boys getting to him though – he's just their type. Sherilyn turned her back to me and looked over her shoulder. She was wearing tight white jeans that cupped her buttocks, and she patted her left cheek with her hand. The diamonds in her engagement ring winked at me and I winked back. My QC and her team stuck their heads briefly round my cell door to tell me I shouldn't bother thinking of an appeal, and I said That's fine, OK and Thanks a lot. They couldn't get out of there fast enough. There was some cock-up with the transport, so I had to wait to be shipped out, but Sherilyn was stroking the kinky bit of hair at the front of my head, so I didn't mind. When the transport finally turned up, James was loaded in the van with me. He looked pale as he was brought in and when I looked over at him, he said Twenty. Twenty fucking years for that. I already knew you didn't ask what anyone was in for, so I just nodded. The driver said Not long enough, you fucking nonce – they should throw away the key, and James leaned his head against the window. He suddenly looked very young and I wanted to kiss the back of his neck. I looked out of my window to see if Sherilyn's van was still there, but the yard was empty. You looking for your old lady? the screw said. Don't bother. She'll be under a pile of lesbos by now, loving every minute. Here we go. As we sped out of the yard, there were thumps on the side of the van and voices shouted Sickos, Perverts, Monsters, but I was watching Sherilyn in her van. She was sitting in her cubicle with her legs crossed, one hand resting on the other, moving the engagement ring up and down her finger; there was a soft click every time it met her wedding ring. Never Apart, I'd had engraved inside it, and she'd had Always Together engraved inside mine.

I settled in for the ride.

Now we were sentenced, they moved us from the remand wing. It was felt that we would be in jeopardy were we to be held in the general prison population, so they transferred us to the VP wing. Vulnerable Prisoners. We joked that it was more like a VIP wing but without the room service because, banged up behind impenetrable metal doors, we were spared the idiot ramblings of the ordinary cons. The so-called normals. We were in constant contact with each other of course, but all day we looked forward to the evening, after we'd finished the gruesome dinner and were locked in our cells for the night. Often we'd rerun our wedding day.

Since this was only going to happen once in my life, I'd been determined to do things properly, so I'd been scrupulous about not seeing Sherilyn in her dress, and we'd stayed in different hotels the night before. Without her next to me I was plagued by dreams of being alone in a room made of feathers, the sounds of family hilarity drifting in through the locked door. When she stepped out of the limousine at the registry office, I had to hold on to the balustrade because in her dress, and with her hair pinned to the top of her head with tiny pearl and diamanté pins, she looked like a graceful ripple in a stream. Her shoes were fragile wisps of silver around her feet and her toes were painted the colour of summer clouds; around her neck she wore the tear-shaped diamond that I'd given her in Buenos Aires. In her face I saw a future more permanent than the ice cap, and the muted hubbub of the wedding business melted away as we slipped into each other. I stood with her in front of the registrar's desk and parroted the required phrases, but I could have been speaking Martian. We'd been wedded since we'd met, so the formalities were simply a matter of acquiring tax advantages.

We'd hired a photographer who did all the big society weddings and while he was a bit full of himself, he captured us perfectly on film. His lens must have seen that we were blind to anything outside our borders, so while he was obliged to take ordinary pictures of our guests, his photographs of us were magical. Our wedding album contains only those. We binned the pictures of our families and kept the ones of our colleagues in a shoebox in case they might be useful to us one day.

I organised the reception at the restaurant where we'd had our third date, both because that was the evening we'd discovered neither of us wanted children and because the owner thought Bren could walk on water. The food was magnificent. Plump pillows of vegetable purées lolled in pastry cases shaped like flowers, next to morsels of tender meats and fine slivers of tropical fish flown in especially for the party. There was a blue crystal bowl of caviar – Diana's favourite – and bundles of asparagus, salsify and mooli with rare and subtle dips and sauces. I'd put the families together on one table so they could talk their nonsense to each other; that way they wouldn't bother the others and draw attention to themselves. When Mum waddled to her seat, I whispered to Bren They'd better watch out or she'll have them on toast, and we laughed. When she saw the food her face was a picture. Her culinary ambitions peaked at pies and cakes – for her, smoked salmon smacked of the exotic – so the succession of exquisite delicacies that floated across the linen was like Russian to a Kalahari tribesman.

Neither the Gutteridges nor the Millers had any idea how to eat food like this and we hoped people at the other tables weren't watching as they hacked at the meat with their fruit knives. We watched, aghast, as Marilyn carefully scraped all the contents of the pastry shells on to her plate and sandwiched them together with slabs of butter: she could have been eating McDonald's. Fortunately, our colleagues and partners were too absorbed in their own conversations to notice the families, though we did see Shirley trying to make small talk with Anthony and Diana before the meal. As usual she'd had a skinful, and the top two buttons of her blouse had popped open so her cleavage was on display like some cheap Soho slut. She must have dressed up for the occasion, but the ill-fitting suit she was wearing was made of salmon-pink polyester and looked like it came from Bhs.

The pretty woman I remembered from when she married my dad had disappeared into this cackling, hooting embarrassment with the intelligence of a fruit fly. Rita wasn't much better, but at least she was sober. She'd gone in for chiffon with ruffles and too many buttons and she was so skinny it looked like the dress was wearing her, like a fussy tent hanging off a maypole. She had on her usual pink lipstick, the same shade she'd worn as long as I'd known her, applied with the subtlety of a bricklayer's trowel, and her mouth stretched into a thin line of bitterness when she was told she'd have to go outside to smoke. When I was a kid, I used to sneak into her handbag sometimes and try on her lipstick; I could do the lippie stretch and the thing where she moved her tongue from side to side under her lip, licking off the pink debris she always managed to leave on her teeth. She kept my dad in order though – something Shirley had never been able to do. She'd look at him with eyes like bullets and say Finn. Don't. That voice used to scare the shit out of me when I lived with her but it stopped Dad from thumping her like he used to thump Shirley. I used to wonder if he'd hit my mum. Sometimes I used to wonder if she'd died from a brain tumour at all – maybe Dad hit her in the head too hard once and killed her. With me too his speciality was going for my head, usually with a book, but often with whatever was in his hand at the time – a bag of horse manure on one occasion when he was in the garden, and a little Hoover thing when he was cleaning the car. He barely said ten words the whole of the wedding day. He was a brawny man with hair he kept so short his head looked like sandpaper and huge hands that when I was a little boy I used to think could lift up a house. But that day he looked like a tyre without an inner tube. I knew his business had gone belly-up of course, because I'd handled the receivership, but he'd seemed invincible to me when I was growing up. It was strange to see him now so powerless. Strange, but something of a relief. He sat at the table propped up by an ex-wife on one side and the current wife on the other like a pair of crude buttresses, and ate nothing. He was less abstemious with the whisky.

The only reason the families were there at all was because the other guests might have thought us weird if we hadn't produced a single relative. It would have been tricky to claim mysterious localised holocausts in Norwich and Exeter, or that both families had been tragically lost at sea. Fortunately we were spared having to invite Rita or Shirley's children because they'd made no effort to stay in touch over the years, but Ann Marie was still centre stage, so she had to come.

She sat herself next to Mum, which wasn't where I'd placed her, so the boy-girl-boy-girl arrangement I'd spent days planning was buggered at a single stroke. It was what she was good at, buggering things up. Sticking herself where she wasn't wanted. All through the meal, the two of them had their heads together like a pair of blonde peas in a pod, giggling and gossiping and grabbing each other. They kept patting an arm or tucking a bit of hair behind the ear or putting a hand on a shoulder and I had to look away every time I saw it happening. Dad was wallpaper. His life's task was to attend to Mum like one of Cleopatra's handmaidens in the Liz Taylor film, so he fetched her things when she needed them, gave her plate to the waiter when he came to clear the table and rummaged around in her handbag for her glasses when she wanted to read the menu. Mum took up a lot of space, sucking up all the air, draining all the colour, reducing Dad to a pallid cipher useful only for mopping up her messes. I pared conversation with them down to the bare minimum: *Hello, how are you? Fine, and you? Fine. Congratulations then. Thanks. Here's a present. Thanks.* Apart from the families, everybody else had bought gifts from the Harrods list, but Anthony and Diana's choice was surprising. They'd gone for one of the cheapest things, a Bodum cafetière with two matching cups – we'd expected them to buy us the Rosenthal china or the Tiffany dish at least. Perhaps having come from moneyed backgrounds they didn't need to show off, unlike our families. Mum and Dad bought us a china tea set, showing a failure of taste that beggared belief. It was white with gold edges and fussy rosebuds and violets all over it. They had a set like that themselves, which was brought out of the repro glass cabinet only on special occasions. It had been one of their wedding presents. I remembered being told to raise my little finger when I was holding the cup and sometimes biting the edge to see if I could break it, because Mum swore it was porcelain. I never could. They'd chosen the china thinking I'd like it. Thinking I'd use it. Thinking I'd even have given it houseroom. I'd never invited them to come and visit us, but the calibre of the invitations and the wedding list would have given them some idea of my lifestyle. The wedding was the last time I saw them before they showed up in court. During the trial, my mother sent me a good luck card, which I put in a file with her other letter and my case papers. Her good luck was of no use to me. There was a girl in the next cell to me who called out *Mam, Mam, pick me up, Mam!* in the night sometimes. She used to read her mother's letters aloud during Association to anyone who'd listen, and I'd think, Why would you want anybody to know all that? Her mum must have written twice a day. The girl tried to

come into my cell once, but I said very quietly I have absolutely
no interest in anything you or your mother have to say, thank
you, and she turned tail and left. She was pretty disturbed and
sometimes when I passed her cell I'd see her sitting on the floor
rocking backwards and forwards, hitting her head on the toilet.
From the sound of those bloody letters her mother wasn't all
there either. She went on and on about how this girl was the
light of her life, the icing on her cake, the sun in her sky, and I
amused myself thinking about what I'd write to my mother: You
are the birdshit on my windscreen, the hair in my drain, the
mould on my cheese. People who'd read about me in the papers,
mostly lunatics, wrote me letters, and in one post alone I got
three marriage proposals, including one from someone who said
he was a Saudi prince. One woman wrote to me saying she was
my real daughter, and she could only tell me now because MI5
had suppressed her identity until last week, on her birthday –
coincidentally the same day as mine. It wasn't. She signed herself
Your loving daughter, Samantha, and wanted me to send her a
visiting order so we could get to know each other properly. I
didn't write back. They said I could write to Brendan, but that
was superfluous: we were in touch twenty-four hours a day.

They moved me to another prison after the first ten days.

Once the news about us broke, I started getting letters. Sack-
loads of them. On the out I'd never got any personal letters, only
business ones, so it was weird having all these people pouring
their hearts out to me. They ranged from hate mail through the
'I'm-in-such-pain-only-you-would-understand' sob stories, to the
romantic, the kinky and the plain crazy. I liked these best: they
were very entertaining. One woman wrote to tell me that she
was called Samantha and she knew that I hadn't killed my
daughter because she *was* my daughter. It may not seem very
likely, she said, because I'm the same age as you, but I'm the

result of a scientific experiment where they took nail clippings from newborns in hospital and turned them into other babies. It was all very hush-hush, she said, because it was during the Cold War and they thought Khrushchev could make use of the technology to attack America. I'm only able to speak of it now because the Cold War's thawed. I look just like you, she said, except of course that I'm a woman, but the minute I saw your wedding photo in the paper, I knew you were my real daddy. She then recited her entire life history: brutal adoptive father who drank and womanised, sexual abuse by her mother and uncles, drugs at thirteen, abortion at fourteen, anorexia at fifteen – nearly died – and it made me wonder what else she was about to throw into the mix: gang rape by bikers? Sold to a sultan as a sex slave? It kept me amused for days. Some of the other cons got into regular correspondence with the nutters, usually because they didn't have anyone else in their lives, but Sherilyn and I were in constant contact, so I filed the letters in chronological order in scrapbooks

They moved me to another prison after the first ten days.

Xandra

Linda Gutteridge (AN 2314)

Transferred from:	**Age:** 38
Holloway, March 25th	
	Ethnicity: White British
Offence:	
Murder (victim:	**Height:** 5' 1''
4-year-old daughter)	
	Weight: 6st 12lbs
Sentence:	
Life (min. 20 years)	**Hair:** Fair
Special Needs:	**Eyes:** Blue/grey/hazel
Rule 43	

March 30th

Initial interview. Welfare provision explained.
VP wing explained. Education explained. VOs
explained. Parole explained. Health explained. No
work preferences expressed.

Xandra Cannon, Senior Probation Officer

She needed nothing. I've been doing this for fourteen years, the
last six of them here, seen all sorts and sizes, but Sherilyn was a
first. In the first interview there's usually some affective response
to the circumstances, but Sherilyn – she corrected me briskly

205

when I called her Linda – was impassive. I asked her if she was angry to have been transferred so far away from friends and family: No. Sad? No. Happy? No. OK, I said, You've got a heavy tariff, that must be tough. No. Perhaps you feel you deserved it? No. Obviously I'd seen the press reports and the television news, so I asked her how it felt to be notorious. How it felt to be demonised. Am I? she said with about as much interest as you might show a house fly. Yes, I said, You've been turned into monsters by the press, and she said Really? I wonder why? There seemed little point in pushing anything on that first occasion because she wasn't engaging with me at all, so I left it there and said we'd meet again in a few weeks when she'd settled in.

Shock does strange things to people and the combination of what she'd done – what they'd done – and what she had in prospect could have shut her down, I thought, but over the succeeding weeks, she never wavered. One day I'd gone down to see another girl whose daughter had just been taken into care and when I'd mopped her up – this was the daughter whose dad she'd killed – I sat and had a cup of tea with Jean in the office. She was great, Jean, she'd been in the Prison Service for twenty years since leaving the army and while you might have thought she was a rigid old boot, she was soft as butter inside. It wasn't every prison officer would volunteer to work on the VP wing, but she managed to combine pragmatism with a very subtle emotional understanding of these women who'd had to be segregated.

She's a weird one, she said as Sherilyn went past the window on her way to the shower. Can't work her out. Doesn't come in for Association, never asks for anything, never complains – she's very polite and everything, but there's nothing there. No one home, you know? Just then there were raised voices on the landing and we went to the door to look. Two women were having a bit of a ruck outside the shower room, but Sherilyn went round them as though she were just stepping round a bollard. She does that, said Jean. Nothing gets to her. The other evening Eva goes into one because there's something on the telly about cot deaths, and she's rolling around on the floor and everyone knows about her babies so there's three or four of them squatting around her trying to calm her down. Sherilyn comes out of her cell and watches what's going on from the landing. She takes out a tissue and puts it under her nose like she's smelling something really nasty, and stays there till Eva's quiet. Then she turns on her heel and catches my eye. She raises her eyebrows, like she's saying You got a problem? And just for a moment I feel like I'm the con and she's the officer, it was dead uncomfortable. I've had non-joiners before, but sooner or later they've managed to be part of something even if it's only signing their name to a petition, but not her. She's going to find the next twenty years very slow if she doesn't find some way of participating.

Next time I saw Sherilyn, for her follow-up interview, I asked her how she was fitting in with the others. She said Fine thank you, everybody's very nice. Anyone giving you grief? I asked. Not at all, she said, They seem like a nice group of girls and I'm very pleased to be on this wing. The noise from the rest of the prison can be rather overwhelming. And they'd eat you alive, I thought to myself – though even they might find you indigestible. I said Have you sorted out your VOs yet? You probably know this isn't the easiest place to get to, and your family might need to do a bit of forward planning. My family won't be visiting she said and there was an awkward pause as I waited for her to say why. I said Oh? and she held my gaze, tapping very gently on the arm of her chair with her long nails. I gave it another go, Have you had a falling-out? I asked. Perhaps I can help you build bridges. No, we haven't had a falling-out, she said, still tapping, still gazing. OK, I said. We talked a bit about what she might like to do in the next while, like a degree for example, because she's clearly quite bright, and she said this odd thing. Perhaps something to do with ancient history, she said, Probably Ancient Egypt. I'll speak to Brendan. You'll write to him, will you? I asked. Speak to him, she said and gave me a contented smile.

I didn't think she was suitable for any of the groups I run: Anger Management, Addressing Offending Behaviour, Enhanced Thinking Skills, because I could neither see her contributing herself nor responding to anyone else's contribution, so I adopted a wait-and-see attitude. Quite what I was waiting to see was a bit of a mystery but there was just a chance that time here might erode her defences and she might ask for help. I wasn't holding my breath.

Jean

Xandra's one of the better POs – I've seen a fair few in my time in the Prison Service, and they're mostly pretty wet. Christ knows what they teach them when they're training – I think some of them must have taken a wrong turn and gone to gardening school by mistake. Probably great at pruning roses, but they're crap at dealing with these girls. Had one once kept bursting into tears if one of the girls told her to fuck off. Fuck off's practically affectionate in here, it's like a greeting, but when I told her this she kept saying But it's so rude and I thought, Oh grow up. She didn't last long. Then there was this streak of piss – Jeremy someone or other – southerner, done some sort of psych training, and he just wanted them to tell him about their mothers and how they'd wanted to screw their fathers, and given half the girls in here have been sexually abused, that was well out of order. He was drummed out of the Brownies for forming an 'inappropriate attachment' to an eighteen-year-old junkie, in for prostitution and dealing smack. Wanker.

Mostly they come here fresh from the out and they think they can get out their book-learning and lob it at the girls, who'll just roll over to have their tummies tickled. The poor lambs get very bewildered when they discover most of the girls understand the system much better than they do and know how to milk it dry. Until the day they find themselves on the floor of the office with their arms in a reef knot and their legs pulled off, and it dawns on them that you've got to stay one step ahead or you're fish food.

They start off thinking that prison officers are only slightly more intelligent than pond life, and Nazi pond life at that. Then they learn: this is *our* nick, the girls and us understand each other and the rules and they have to fit in with that or go under. They write their reports and shuffle their papers and go to their meetings, but it's us who have to cut a prisoner down when she's hanged herself, or talk a girl down who's throwing a wobbly in the middle of the night because her daughter's just had her first baby and she wasn't around. The better POs clock the pecking order sharpish and don't fuck with it. That's how it's always been and that's how it's going to stay. We know our place in it – in its way it's as clear as it is in the forces: we're below the AGs, most of whom have never worked at the sharp end, and above the prisoners. The welfare lot can do their job, but it's alongside us, not above.

And the VPs are the lowest of the low, scum of the earth. The normals have a number of choice terms for them – nonce, beast, bacon, that sort of thing – and if we didn't arrange things so they never meet, there'd be tears before bedtime. Can't think what they've got to be so arrogant about – we're talking drug dealers and madams and all sorts on the wings – but they behave like what they did was only human and the VPs are animals. Probably it makes them feel better about themselves, thinking our lot are a bunch of earwigs they could squash underfoot, but that's shit. It's why I chose to work on this wing, because I don't think anyone's an animal and usually what these women have done is so awful they must be a bit touched, so they need careful handling.

You can warm to anyone that's banged up in here because the atmosphere's different from the rest of the nick, less confrontational. Obviously it's smaller than the other wings, which means that there's no such thing as a secret and everyone knows everyone else's business. Including what they're in for. But even if that wasn't the case, Sherilyn wouldn't have had a snowball in hell's chance of keeping it quiet because it was all over the telly. Even hard nuts like Kym were shocked, and she burned down her house and killed her ex and her kids. Said she was only going after him. So when Sherilyn arrived, the whole nick was agog. I happened to be passing Reception when the transport came in and she was put in the Rule 43 cage. There were these three other girls in the normals cage who were yelling stuff at her: Baby-killer bitch, killer cunt, that sort of thing and I muttered to Kylie, who was on duty, Perhaps you'd better cool it down, but I could see she was rather enjoying it. I looked over at Sherilyn because I was concerned for her, but I needn't have been. She looked like a little fairy out somewhere posh, sitting there on the bench completely undisturbed by the ruckus. Give her a pair of white gloves and a cucumber sandwich and she'd be sorted, I thought, so I didn't carry on at Kylie. Once she was on the wing of course, I learned that what I'd seen as cool was actually ice.

She was always perfectly well behaved, never any tantrums or demands, incredibly polite and her cell was immaculate. With no personal touches. All the other girls brought little bits of themselves to their cells: photos of their children, their boy-friends, china ornaments, things that reminded them of their lives outside. One woman even knitted a sort of tea-cosy thing for her toilet. They plastered their walls with pin-ups, either men or women, and quite a lot of them had calendars with dates circled in red and each previous day scratched out. Some of them had quite a lot of calendars to get through. But Sherilyn's cell had nothing in it beyond prison-issue bedding and towels and a row of cosmetics along the back of her table arranged like soldiers on a parade ground. All the girls had make-up – it's one of the little things that makes being banged up a bit more civilised – and quite often Association's full of small groups doing makeovers on each other, but not Sherilyn. She'd slap on that mask – I don't know when, because I never saw her without it – and go about her business, smiling when a smile was called for, looking serious when necessary. It never cracked. There was never a hair out of place and I think she must have done her own roots because I never saw anyone helping her. Even her uniform looked smart. I think she may have put a stitch in it here and there because it was tighter around her body than most of the others', but several of them altered the clothes and we turned a blind eye. Like the make-up, it let them feel more like a woman and made doing their bird a little easier.

In the first few months I noticed most of the others trying one way or the other to befriend her. Especially Charlene who never gave up on anyone. Poor sod, she'd been transferred in from one of the normals' wings because they were giving her such shit. She must have been twenty stone and was pretty weird-looking, with her skew-whiff nose and no eyelashes or eyebrows. She was what we used to call subnormal. I know there's some more acceptable term now, but I can't be bothered learning them because they change every other day. She was very slow anyway. She wanted to be friends with everybody, but had no idea how to keep a distance, so she'd be towering over you yakking away in her thick Glaswegian accent, and you wanted to go Whoa, Charlene, back off. She was very short-sighted and she kept busting her glasses, so she'd stick that nose of hers right up against yours and burble on. If that didn't work, she'd pick you up bodily, dump you in a chair and sit on your lap. I had to rescue several of the girls when she was trying to make friends because she'd have stopped their blood otherwise. I'd seen her making her approaches to Sherilyn and Sherilyn had avoided the crush by slipping under her arms like a puff of smoke, but one day Charlene had her cornered.

Every day when the cells were unlocked, Sherilyn was in the showers so fast you'd think Scottie had beamed her up, but this one day Charlene got there first. She positioned herself so that

not only had she blocked the doorway, she was holding the
railing too, so Sherilyn could neither get into the shower room
nor carry on down the landing. I was watching from the office
because I had no idea how this one was going to pan out. How
come you don't talk to me? Charlene said, You been here ages
and you never chat, you don't want to look at my postcards –
what's wrong with me? I done something wrong? Sherilyn's
glossy lips smiled and she said Yes, it was a very kind offer to
show me your cards, but I need a shower now so perhaps you'll
be good enough to move. Be my friend, said Charlene, I think
you're pretty. You'd better move, said Sherilyn in a voice so
calm she could have been saying Pass the cornflakes or I'll kill
you. The girls say that all the time: Shut the fuck up or I'll
kill you; Carry on like that and you're dead, but it was like
Sherilyn's voice had been sharpened to a point that could slide
itself under your ribs and in a few seconds make you history.
Without thinking, I'd moved to the landing outside my door
ready to jump her, but Charlene's limbs seemed to go soft and
she eased herself out of the doorway. Sherilyn trotted in with
her pink frilled sponge bag. Charlene had gone very pale. She
had an asthma attack an hour later and had to go to the hospital
wing. Obviously it was because of what Sherilyn had said, but I
couldn't put her on a charge, though I thought she was one of
the most dangerous girls I've ever had here. What would I say?
I'd say *On April eleventh, Gutteridge threatened to kill Collins* and
they'd go *Yes, and?* But after that it was like I'd grown special
antennae for her – twitching, twitching, ready to go for her if
she threw one. I kept track of her movements, always knew
where she was on the wing, knew her timetable off by heart;
Monday: gym 9–10, Tuesday: gym 10–11, Education 3–5, Wednesday: Chaplain 9–10, Gym 10–11, and so on. We tried her in the
kitchen on the VP shift, but her presence disturbed the other
girls too much. Theresa said That girl, she turn eggs bad, she

fucking with our heads, man, so we gave her cleaning duties on the wing. She requested silver polish and when I asked her what for, she said the hatches were disgusting, so I got her some. She polished them to within an inch of their lives, so you'd go to look in on a girl and catch yourself checking out your hair. I found her cleaning the inside of the locks once with ear buds and bleach and when I asked her about it, she just said Germs. I don't want to catch something and die here, she said, so I let her be. I think we could have put her in Solitary for the whole of her bird and she wouldn't have noticed. She was in Solitary in her head, it seemed: no one else existed.

With so little going on for her here, you'd have thought she'd have been writing to her old man all the time. Unusually for these kind of cases they hadn't done the 'it-wasn't-me-it-was-him' thing in court, but she made no attempt to contact him. She got the usual letters from the barmies – one was from some nutter claiming to be her daughter, Kylie showed me – but none from anyone in her life. I supposed her family must have disowned her. But sometimes I'd see her in her cell, she'd be sat on her bed looking like she was communing with someone and I'd find it difficult to believe it was the same chilly bitch. She looked like a woman in love.

Brendan and Sherilyn

Finally you're here. I've been waiting. I've bathed my body, oiled my limbs, and I'm wearing that yellow dress you like, my Sherititi dress. It embraces my waist like your hands, in a tender circle of possession. Tiny pools of perfume have settled in the troughs of my collarbones and I see your eyes hood in expectation as my scent licks around your nose.

I could smell you in the air before I got here. Feel the warmth of your flesh softly shunting the temperature up a notch. You unfold yourself from a boulder humming with the song of the sun, and the skirt of your dress billows out from your knees. I kneel to kiss them, my palms sliding down your pale calves to your ankles. I look up at your face and the love in your eyes melts my bones.

You stand and rest your hands around my waist and I lean into you, my face in your chest. You smell like cedarwood, and I inhale you into my centre. You're wearing the silk shirt I had made for you in Bali: tiny invisible stitches made by fleet brown fingers on fabric so soft it could be newborn skin. When we've finished feasting on each other, we will eat.

I lead you to the restaurant dug in the blasted rock, coolly shrugging off the sun's rays, and we go to our table under the jasmine arch. Your dress slips off your shoulder as you sit and I tease it back with my finger to its perch on the soft curve of your flesh. There's no need to order, they know what we want, and soon the dishes whispering with cardamom and coconut steam in front of us.

We break off triangles of warm bread and drench them in the juices; you press yours against my lips and I insinuate mine into your mouth. I select a morsel of fish and hold it on a fork in front of your face. As you bend to eat it, I pull it away and you kiss me instead. The tastes of spices and desire roll around our mouths and slip down our throats. Later, replete, we find our bed where it always is, under the umbrella of the purple jacaranda.

We sit on the bed and I unhook your dress. The fabric sighs down your body and you recline on the tribe of luscious satins, fragile silks and fervent velvets covering the bed, punctuated here and there by traces of lace. Your head lolls back over an embroidered cushion, your throat a lovely arc of innocence. I slip out of my clothes and join you.

Your clothes and mine tangle together at the foot of the bed and I lie on my side observing every second of your life tick under your skin. Your breath mists my face as you move closer and you trace your fingertips down my body, swooping around my breasts, sweeping along my hips, swirling across my belly, leaving an incandescent trail of tiny sparks on my flesh. You are naked, vulnerable, tender – I swim into your eyes which hold me as I dissolve into your soul.

You find the silver bowl of oil by the bed and plunge your hands into its heady fragrance. You sit astride my thighs, your bush teasing my skin, your face radiant with love. You understand my body, you know it like your own and you map its contours with your silky fingers, hold my heart in the curve of your palms, cushioning its beating sides.

Afterwards we lie there, our limbs muddled, our sweat mingled, and talk softly of us, of our present and our future. We understand that this combination that has resulted in our living will include our death. We sleep like lovers do, dreaming the same dreams.

James

James Bracknell (FC 3341)

Transferred from:
HMP Strangeways,
April 29th

Age: 27

Ethnicity: White British

Offence:
8 x sexual abuse of
children

Height: 6' 1''

Weight: 13st

Sentence:
20 years

Hair: Black

Eyes: Blue

Special Needs:
Rule 43

Brendan's manner reminded him of his girlfriend when they encountered each other at court, Gutteridge going down for life, Bracknell going up for sentence, but what was appealing about him was irritating about her. He wished she hadn't come to court every day, wished she hadn't plagued him with her mewling from the public gallery each time a witness spat out some new salacious gob. He wanted to hear what they were saying about him, every lovely detail, and her sobs diverted the court's attention from him. This was his show: the mothers (and a few fathers), the policemen, the doctors and teachers, they'd all come to talk about James and he twirled in the spotlight loving every second.

His barrister loved him too, he could tell. He was a tall man, slightly taller than James, with fetching wings of silver hair just visible under his wig. When they met – conferred – in preparation for the trial, James kept a tally of how many times he made his brief's otherwise serious eyes crinkle in amusement, how expertly his emollient charm softened the lawyer's formality.

He was always going down, he knew that, though he fancied his protestations of innocence were convincing. The police-woman had seemed uncertain during the interviews, but the inspector had remained impassive. That was aggravating. Up till then his record was almost flawless, from the nurses tussling to hold him as a seraphic newborn to the heads turning to admire him as he creamed down the street. Inspector Deardon was a rare failure.

His voice hadn't broken like other boys' at puberty, it had slid gracefully into a lower register where it snared his listeners like flies in maple syrup. When he was out with friends he had a hunter's instinct for mirrors and he would watch himself as he talked, admiring the graceful swoops of his hands. So did his audience. One of his bosses once said James, your body language could seduce fossils out of a rock face, as she promoted him for the second time that year. When he and his mother went to the opera together, the audience rippled as he passed, swivelling in their seats to get a better look. Bette, his mother, was monstrously beautiful; her dangerous radiance lured men, women, children and stray dogs into its vortex, but in James's company its light dimmed. *They only have eyes for you,* she'd say to her son as she lost her fingers in his curls, *They're yours for the taking, darling – which one will you have?*

He'd begun with the girls when he was fifteen and popular in the neighbourhood for his readiness to babysit. Only when they were asleep though, he didn't want to queer his pitch. Once when his hand was approaching a five-year-old's genitals, her eyes had flicked open and he'd pretended he'd seen a giant insect crawling under her bedclothes: I'm just looking for it, he'd said, Don't worry. She'd been mollified with hot chocolate and a story, but it had taught him caution. His mother's voice in his head warned him to be wary. She had always told him only the two of them could be trusted. Once he'd pulled off the impossible feat of leaving home, however, the world was his oyster and he drove long distances in his unremarkable van in pursuit of small-girl satisfaction. He left his convertible at home: too readily identifiable. He could sit in his van on the other side of the road from a school playground and pick out the ones he could have: the dark girl sitting by herself every playtime, knotting the hem of her skirt with her fingers; the skinny blonde one who had to be the centre of attention in all the games, but who sucked her thumb when they lined up to go back in; the child in a short skirt and heels, who sat on the wall as if posing for an invisible camera.

He learned chameleon tricks, pulling hats over his curls, disguising his azure eyes with coloured contacts, bulking up his slender frame with padding, so if they ever told, if they ever looked for him, they'd be in pursuit of a phantom. He was gentle in his approaches, languorous in his movements: a sudden gesture and they'd flee, even the most desperate. He didn't suggest going anywhere in his van until he knew they trusted him, after he'd retrieved their ball, steadied them on their bikes, heard their stories of bullying and isolation. He was that longed-for thing, a special friend, a listening ear, and hand in hand they stepped into the van and drove to the woods, his stereo playing nursery rhymes and shallow pop.

He never had a straightforward refusal because he'd earned their compliance, although from time to time he had to use a silk scarf as a gag or a blindfold or a bond. He found the sight of a blinded and bound girl especially exciting, but he was careful not to lose control. He wanted them to come again. Except for that one time. She'd turned out to be a screamer, so he'd tied the scarf tightly over her face and she'd become unconscious. This made it easier for him to do what he wanted and when she'd come to, he'd snapped her neck. He found it surprisingly easy.

He didn't repeat the experience because, as with all child murders, this one caused a brief national furore. Politicians and pundits ranted on about society's decadence and children's innocence, so he kept his head down until it ran its course. The perpetrator was never found and the child's death became just another entry in the annals of crime. But as a result, he started hunting in the northeast, mostly in small coastal towns with nothing much for anyone to do, and for a while he found rich pickings. It helped him, when having sex with a girlfriend, to imagine one of his little-girl encounters. Without the fantasy, he knew he'd have difficulty getting it up and his great beauty would be traduced. He went through women like an eel through water and coasted on his reputation as a Lothario; he knew his girlfriends would forgive him when he left, because they'd know they'd supped at a royal table.

The one he had on the go when they caught him, Amanda, wouldn't have lasted longer than a week or two more, a month at the outside, because her plaintive demands were exasperating, but his arrest sealed the relationship in amber. On the other hand it did no harm to have her agonised face spread over the newspapers during the trial because she was from respectable minor aristocracy, so her protestations of his innocence carried some clout. She gave one journalist a photograph of them in Sardinia relaxing on board a yacht, and they looked like a poised young couple in love; it was endlessly reprinted and only added to his glamour. He didn't look like a sleazeball pervert, so he thought that that, coupled with Amanda's very public keening, might get him off. It was a mistake to have become too confident and to have moved closer to home, but his job had become quite stressful and he'd wanted to conserve his energies. One of his exes saw him with a young girl and wasn't fooled by his disguise.

Once he'd been implicated in one assault, several of the others came out of the woodwork. On remand, he totted up how many they'd got and he was pleased that it amounted to less than a third. The dead girl wasn't on the list: the year before, a child-killer had hanged himself in prison and the press concluded he'd probably murdered the screamer, so he was safe on that count. Bette had become hysterical when he told her that he'd been charged and what with. He was used to that. His growing up in the sticky grip of her adoration had been punctuated by her outbursts and he was no longer cowed by the extravagance of her passions. He knew that the tempest would move on as swiftly as it had blown in, and that he'd once again be her beloved. Her perfect little plaything.

The worst had been when he told her he was leaving home. In an hour. She had run from room to room, tearing at her clothes like an Old Testament prophet, hurling herself against walls and holding a knife to her throat in the kitchen. As he turned to pick up his suitcase, she'd slipped down the wall next to the giant American fridge and screamed, simultaneously hitting her knees with her forehead and her temples with her fists. She was still doing it when the taxi arrived and he answered the driver's quizzical look with an elegant shrug. Mothers, he said, Who'd have them?

But once the case had to be made, her money was useful and she did her research with the same obsessional attention to detail that had made her business so successful. The dream team of big-bucks solicitors and barristers put in interminable hours, so if anyone was going to get him off it was them. He knew he was guilty – or at least, he knew he'd done the things on the indictment – so he had to work hard to keep up his mask of injured innocence. Behind the mask he was planning his life in prison.

He thought it probably wouldn't be that bad – food, shelter, education, all on tap – and he imagined publishing a successful novel about villains when he emerged some years down the line. He might even publish it himself, armed with the MBA he'd have acquired inside. His public-school background had enrolled him in a monochromatic social circle and the prospect of hob-nobbing with real criminals was intriguing. He imagined the stories he'd have to tell when he was back in his world; it could only enhance his celebrity.

When he'd seen Brendan in passing during their respective trials, he'd looked like the kind of council-estate lout he'd expected to meet. Expensive-looking suit housing a brutish frame: an absurd attempt to look respectable, he'd thought. But when they'd passed a few words – What you get, mate? Life. That's a fuck, they're gonna throw the book at me, maybe we'll meet up. Yeah, yeah, why not? – he hadn't sounded coarse at all. A well-spoken southerner, clearly not a welfare scrounger, and he hadn't known whether to be disappointed or relieved. But the sentence was a head-fuck. He'd be middle-aged by the time he finished, and while the combination of good genes and groom-ing had made Bette queen of the cocktail-party circuit, he imag-ined maintaining his looks might be tricky inside. Taunts from the screws about predatory buggers in prison didn't faze him: he'd been king of the castle on the out, so he didn't see why he shouldn't be king of the cons inside.

He was Category A of course – Cat. A they called it – which made him Top Cat: *You're my special boy. My special little man, darling.* He understood about the Rule 43 thing and while some of his fellows were a bit drippy, he liked the fact that they had something in common. They were all special. When he was shipped into Brendan's prison six weeks after sentence, he already knew he was going to meet up with him again because news zipped through the system faster than a silver bullet going for the heart. All the cons knew who was coming in and going out, who was on the punishment block and why and who was whose bitch. There were no secrets on the VP wing, that was one of its pleasures.

When he arrived on the wing, it was empty. The VPs had been decanted to their morning's activities so he set about arranging his cell. Posters first, because that set the tone. He wanted any casual visitor, any door-peeping screw to see a red-blooded male, so he covered one wall with silicone-stuffed women. The phwoar factor. Then the books. He'd discovered the Russians while on remand – a bent solicitor had recommended them – and he was now midway through *Crime and Punishment*. It was whetting his appetite for moral philosophy and with time on his hands he thought he'd try that next. Start with Bertrand Russell, the solicitor had said, so he'd ordered them from the library. The books filled up the back of the table, although the Brothers Karamazov kept suicidally throwing themselves off the end.

There'd been several suicides in the last nick, some of them men who'd looked as though they could chew through concrete. One, a burly South Londoner, had swallowed bleach when he'd got a Dear John. That had surprised James because the guy had strutted about, cock of the walk, regaling them with his tales of a high-octane life that seemed to be one long fuck-fest. He'd offered James introductions when he eventually got out, but James said he thought he could find his own women, thanks very much, mate.

He was well into his first novel, working title *Wing Nuts*, which at the moment was a series of character studies. The Russians were teaching him about plot development, so when he was ready he'd loop his characters together in an elegant arc. Brendan hadn't yet appeared on the page, but there'd been something about him when he'd looked at him in the prison van that made him think they'd be close. He'd had a dream in the last nick where he'd been the size he was now but young, about ten or so, and he'd been sitting on Brendan's knee. Brendan's hands were an exaggerated size, and when they'd ruffled James's hair, he'd sobbed. He'd never known his own father – Bette called him Barclays because she'd made a withdrawal from his sperm bank – but when he was little he used to wonder if he was the prime minister. Or an astronaut.

When the other VPs came back for lunch, he went to his door and watched their orderly entry. Brendan was immediately visible, partly because he towered over the others and partly because he was still in his gym gear. His hairless skin was the colour of oats, so from this distance he looked waxen. He turned away from his conversation with a small black man James vaguely remembered from remand. James caught his eye and they both nodded with enough recognition to be civil.

At lunch, he noticed Brendan's plate was loaded with carbs: he'd taken both rice and potatoes and he'd obviously done a deal with someone for their helping of bread, so when he went over to the table he said In training? And Brendan said Yeah – there's a good gym here. You work out too? and James sat down next to him.

Brendan and Sherilyn

I knew I'd been dreaming when I woke up in the morning, but it melted away like frost on a sunny windowpane. I knew Brendan had been in the dream and usually when he featured I could remember every turn of the story, but this one vanished. All that remained was a disquieting mixture of excitement and grief which I struggled to place. But I hadn't forgotten what day it was. When I was growing up, Mum had a passion for calendars, which she stacked on the kitchen shelf like books. As though she read books. They're my history, she'd say, looking at the dates and green-inked appointments on page after page of the cute and the twee. I'd always kept a diary, but calendars were ungainly things that became a dog-eared mess by July, so I left them to Mum and her kitchen. Today was October 21st. I closed my eyes again and remembered the first time I went to his office. Ten days later, my fingers were exploring the muscled swells of his back, but then all I saw was the seagull-grey jacket and its careful seams. Once we were in the same skin he said he'd known I was there because he could smell his future, and for my part I had the feeling as I walked towards him that the tides of my life were reversing. I sat down on the other side of his desk and tried to examine my file, but my eyes kept flicking to his face. I sucked him in like a blind girl who can suddenly see, heady with wonder. I saw grey, slightly hooded eyes, a generous mouth and that kink in the front of his hair: it was all I could do to stop myself leaning across the desk and stroking it. I cleared my throat a few times, as though to clear my head. I put the personnel file on his desk and rested my hands on it. I looked at him. All the ordinary sounds of an office – someone barking down the phone, paper rustling, files shifting – were tuned out, like when Tony and Maria meet at the dance in *West Side Story*. Except he was bigger than Tony and I was never attractive enough to sing 'I Feel Pretty'. He hadn't even tried to speak – he sat there looking astonished, as though he'd seen a tropical flower bloom on a stick. From that moment we took the ordinary words of love and recast them. From that moment we were no longer dead flesh. I was about to celebrate that moment. When I heard the cell doors being opened along the landing, I got up to the prison's day, but I floated through the first hours of the morning empty-headed, conserving my energies. At 10.19, I stepped off the treadmill and went over to the mirror; I closed my eyes and leaned into it. There was no clock in the gym but my blood knew when it was 10.21. I saw him coming towards me with that slightly goofy smile he had when things are just too marvellous to speak. I put my arms out towards him, barely able to breathe. He shook his head, turned his back on me and walked away. I slid down the mirror to the floor.

James said he hadn't done much in the gym before, which was barely credible because when I saw him for the first time in the changing room, he looked like the gym rat to end all gym rats. He wasn't one of those pumped Schwarzenegger clones, stuffing yet another muscle under their sausage skins: James was strong in an understated way, like a man who doesn't have to wear loud checked suits to be noticed. He was tall and slender and his long muscles rested on his frame like leopards on a branch: one pounce and you'd be dead. When I slid my gaze around his nipples and down the smattering of curly black hair on his belly, my fingers itched. His olive skin looked like virgin snow and I engineered a brief contact with it as I appeared to turn awkwardly at the locker. The back of my hand glided across the small of his back like a feather on a breeze and I said Sorry, sorry. He said Don't worry, holding my gaze tight. We took to working out five times a week and he put himself in my hands. Standing by the machines, I touched the parts of his body they were working, telling him Here are your quads, your dorsals, your glutes, and he nodded and thanked me, smiling. As I bent over him to settle his hands in the right place for the bench press, I inhaled the spicy tang of his body. I could have buried my face in his groin. I could have licked my way up his legs to the dark patch of sweat on his shorts. I could have tasted his body from the damp curls fused to his forehead to the arches of his feet. I counted the reps for him as he pushed against his limits: *15, 16, 17 – c'mon, James, do it for me!* When it was my turn, he lifted the weights on to the bars and said Christ you're a big guy, Gutteridge. You could lift me over your head, no problem. Maybe I'll have a go sometime, I said. When he strode across the gym ten pairs of eyes followed him, but everyone knew we were workout buddies, companion bodies, and kept their distance. One day as he bent to retrieve the soap I'd clumsily passed him in the shower, I had to jam my hands hard into the shampoo suds to stop myself cupping his dark-brown balls. He stood up and looked at me as though I had. Gossip was the way we oiled the cogs of the penal machine, so I knew there was talk on the wing, but I didn't care and I think James relished being its subject. They say I'm your bitch, he told me one day, and we each threw our head back and laughed, keeping our eyes fixed on each other. One morning we were on adjacent treadmills and I watched the sweat clouds billow on James's T-shirt as he pushed himself to run ten miles. How much longer? he panted and I glanced at the clock. It read 10.23 and a fuse blew in my head. James said What's up? as I punched the stop button on the machine. I folded over the bar. I didn't answer. It was October 21st and I'd missed the only moment that had ever mattered in my life. I tried to say sorry to her, tried to explain, but she was weeping too bitterly to hear me, and I knew the cord that joined us was bleeding.

Xandra

It was the only time I ever saw her cry. She came back from the gym with the others looking quite normal; she picked up her dinner and went back to her cell as normal and I was just filling out forms in Jean's office as normal when Kym knocked on the door. The ice queen's melting, she said. What? I said. Sherilyn, she said, She's up there crying her eyes out, go have a shuftie. As I went out into Association, there was a weird silence: Kym had obviously told the others. I looked down as I got to Sherilyn's landing and they'd all stopped mid-bite; twenty-one pairs of eyes stared up at me. As I got closer to the cell, I could hear a soft snuffling. When I was a kid I used to keep rabbits, and the sound reminded me of rabbit babies suckling. I pushed the door open and stuck my head in. Her dinner was on the floor, untouched, and she was lying on the bed with her face in the pillow. Grief was cascading out of her. It didn't stop when I came right in, didn't stop when I pulled the door to, didn't stop when I brought the chair over to her bed and sat down by her head. I rested my hand very gently on her back and I thought, Christ, there's no meat on your bones, as each sob dug her shoulder blades into my palm. She was trying to make words between sobs, so I put my head down next to hers so I could hear. Left, left, left, she was saying, so I said Left what, love? And she said Left me, gone, left, left, left. I knew she hadn't had a Dear John, so I said Who's left you, Sherilyn, is it your family? She made this tragic sound that sounded like a groan. I said, A friend then – maybe one of your friends? and she shook her head. I said You don't mean your husband do you, love? thinking, He's not leaving anyone, mate, and she suddenly sat up. I barely recognised her. Never having seen her without make-up, I had no idea what colour her skin was. She always wore the works: foundation, blusher, powder, so the pallid face with its tiny colonies of spots startled me. The tears hadn't completely washed off the mask and there were pink and peach streaks on her cheeks which made her look strangely vulnerable, like a little girl who's been mucking about with her mother's cosmetics. Her eyes had practically disappeared. Naked of brown and blue goo, and all puffed up from the crying, they looked as if they didn't have any eyelashes at all, but I think they were just very short and very fair. She looked as though she'd been rubbed out. Why don't you write to him? I said, Send him a letter – I bet he'll write back, he must be missing you. She was staring straight ahead and said nothing, so I tried again. You get all sorts of peculiar ideas in here, I said, Everybody gets a bit paranoid about their loved ones, but I bet he's doing the same thing. He probably thinks you're not interested in him any more – you know what men are like when they're not getting any. I left a bit of a pause thinking maybe she needed some space to get herself together, and then I said Look, it helps to talk, you know? If you told me what's going on you might see things a bit more clearly and you'd know he's not going anywhere. She looked at me and for a moment there was a spark in her eyes. You . . . Just . . . Don't . . . Get it, she said in a robotic voice, We're . . . Separate, and she closed her eyes and lay back on the bed. I'd obviously been dismissed. I left the cell quietly and closed the door. The girls hushed as I came out, but all I said was She's OK, just leave her be and finish your dinner. I signed her off sick for the rest of the day and kept an eye on her. She stayed on her bed, in that position, until lights out.

I had a word with Sue when she came in on night duty. I didn't think she needed a suicide watch, just a little closer attention, and Sue said Okey-doke and You mean there's something going on inside her? and laughed. I was on leave for a couple of days and when I went back in I asked about her. She's OK, fine, Gemma said – Why, is something up? Just a bit upset the other day, I said, Not quite sure what about. Well, she's sorted it now, she said, but Gemma's about as sensitive as a Sherman tank, so I thought I'd see for myself. When she came back from the workshop, she looked normal enough – face back on, hair in place – but I thought if I patted her on the back there'd be an echo.

Sherilyn

October 22nd

If he hadn't breathed life into me like Frankenstein into his collection of body parts, today would be another empty day in a week, a month, a year of empty days. As it is, pain ticks at today's heart, as it will tomorrow and the day after. I thought I knew what being alone was: it was the essence of my life, the way I walked, my constant companion, but his betrayal has sucked out my centre and staked me out in a desert. The sand dunes ripple away from me and I close my eyes to avoid seeing his absence. To avoid hope seeping through my skin. To avoid expecting any minute to see him pop his head out of the ground at my feet.

He fooled me into thinking that the future consisted of more than Tuesday following Monday. He fooled me into thinking that ours was an unbreakable bond. I was a willing fool. I haven't needed this diary since we met because he *was* my diary, he *was* my thoughts, he *was* my account of myself. I didn't need to write down my feelings because he felt them; didn't need to look at myself because he saw me; I didn't need to pretend, to hide, to move around among people in disguise. He's robbed me of my future, taken it with him into his new love.

October 23rd

I remember being on holiday once in Wales with my family – and I'd brought my diary with me of course. That year it was padded yellow plastic with a combination padlock. It was a present from my nan. Everyone knew that I kept a diary and one relative or another would give me a new one each Christmas. One day I left the caravan site by myself with my diary, my pencil, my book and a sandwich in my school satchel. I was nine. I walked across eleven fields, wondering if I should scatter breadcrumbs behind me like Hansel and Gretel so I could find my way back, but I wasn't sure I wanted to find my way back. It wasn't raining for once and purple thistles scratched my thighs as I clambered over stiles under a cloudless blue sky. I was looking for a secret place to write my diary and finish my book. I had three more to go.

At the end of the eleventh field there was a stony path and I followed it along the side of a wood until I reached the edge of a cliff. I could see a blue-grey beach at its base and a range of rocks to the right, at the end of which there was a giant stone shaped like a seat. I thought it was a sign from the God-the-Father-God-the-Son-and-God-the-Holy-Ghost that I believed in when I was small. I liked the fact that he apparently loved me unreservedly. Possibly Ann Marie too, but I didn't think about that. I imagined he'd seen me tramping across the eleven fields and had dropped the stone down from heaven because he could see I was getting tired and needed a diary-writing chair. There was a bit of cliff that was less steep than the rest, with what could have been a path leading to the beach, so I made my way over and started climbing down. Loose bits of shale made the descent slippery, so I sat down and scooted myself along on my bum, tearing my new shorts in three places. I knew I had to get to the chair because God-the-Father-God-the-Son-and-God-the-Holy-Ghost had willed it. When I reached the beach, a solitary cloud in the shape of a hand passed over the sun, which I knew was him congratulating me: *This is my beloved daughter, in whom I am well pleased.* I clambered over the rocks to the chair, which had dynasties of limpets around its base. It looked to me like a jewel-encrusted throne waiting quietly for its queen to put on her crown and start ruling. Me. Close up, it was bigger than I'd thought, and I struggled to climb on to the seat, but I managed it and settled, cross-legged, to record that morning and read my book.

I didn't have to mind my manners with my diary, didn't have to mind the p's and q's that littered my days. When I sat down with it on my knee it was as though I plugged into it and it into me, like a shared artery. I never thought about what I wrote, never planned or edited or censored, my life's blood flowed on to the page, which took it in for safekeeping. There hadn't been enough cereal in the packet at breakfast time, so I gave my share to my sister in what I thought was a rather grand gesture of generosity. I think Ann Marie's really, really hungry, Mummy, I said, She can have my Puffed Wheat, I don't mind, and I pushed my bowl across the table to her. When Ann Marie smiled it was as though every bud on a bush had suddenly blossomed at once, as though a meteor had suddenly illuminated the dead dark of the night, and Mum leaned over the table and kissed her head. My angel, she said, Eat up, buttercup and we'll go and play kiss-chase when you're finished.

If it had had lips, my diary would have kissed me on the head a hundred times a day; if it had had legs, it would have chased me round the garden until I flopped, sweaty with laughter, on the grass. It would have wrapped me round with its love and told me I was an angel. In its pages I was queen of my world. On the limpet-encrusted throne I was queen of the sea.

A sudden sharp gust of briny wind threatened to carry my book off and I levered myself out of its pages like a limpet off its rock. The sea was licking hungrily at my throne and the causeway I'd clambered over so confidently had disappeared. The blue-grey beach clattered a taunt to me across the waves: *There's no way home. You'll never get back.*

I stayed there as the sun died slowly behind the cliff, my arms pulling my legs into my chest, my head resting on my knees. It was pointless calling out: the cliff conspired with the sea to send my voice back to me on the wind. I wasn't afraid, I didn't think of death; sitting alone on a rock was familiar to me.

The torches came down the cliff and on to the beach and found me in their cross-hatching. A helicopter stuttered overhead. When I arrived at the caravan, wrapped in a red blanket like a chrysalis in a policeman's arms, my teary mother said We didn't notice she'd gone. We didn't notice she'd gone.

I'm back on that rock, marooned by Brendan's defection. There's no kindly policeman to wrap me in red wool and bring me home to my husband. He didn't notice I'd gone.

He didn't notice I'd gone.

25th October

Father's dead. My daddy.

Xandra

Letter received from Sherilyn's mother. On file.

October 20th

Dear Probation Officer, .

I'm Sherilyn Gutteridge's mother and I'm afraid I'm writing
with bad news. Her father, my husband Ronald, died very
suddenly three weeks ago of a massive heart attack. He was not
an old man, nor had he complained of any aches and pains, so it
was a terrible shock to us all. He collapsed in his study. He'd
been spending more and more time up there of late, but I knew
he needed the peace and solitude, so I didn't disturb him except
when it was time to call him for a meal. That day, he'd been up
there most of the morning with the door locked and he didn't
answer me when I called him down for lunch. At first I thought
he might have fallen asleep at his desk because he hadn't been
sleeping very well, so I went upstairs and banged on the door
quite loudly, trying to wake him up. When he didn't answer,
I started to panic and hit a ceramic plate on the door so hard it
broke and cut my palm. I was covered in blood. I raced
downstairs and called 999 and they sent a fire engine along with
the ambulance. The firemen forced the door open.

He looked very peaceful sitting in his favourite chair with a
large book like a ledger on his lap. It was obvious even to my

untrained eye that he was dead, so there was little point in the paramedics trying to resuscitate him – he could easily have been dead for four hours or so. They carried him to his bedroom and laid him on his bed so that I could have some time alone with him – they were very caring and thoughtful – and then took themselves off. I called Ann Marie, my daughter, and we sat with him for the rest of the day, just the two of us. She loved her dad.

I had another lock put on the study door and I've shut the room up until I can bear to clear it out. It remains as it was when we found him, with the book on the chair and his shoes by its legs. I'll have to go in there sometime, I suppose, but not yet. I'm not ready yet.

When it came to planning the funeral, Ann Marie and I discussed whether to invite Linda – Sherilyn – but we didn't know how to get her out of prison for the day. Ann Marie was sure she wouldn't want to come anyway, and I thought she was probably right. We lost her a long time ago. I don't think it was anything we did – or she did, for that matter – we just drifted apart, as some people do.

But I wanted her to know that there were quite a few people there last week – several from the bank that he served so loyally and for so long – and that we played his favourite music. 'Black Is The Colour Of My True Love's Hair' was a song he used to sing a lot in the old days, so we found a recording and played that in the middle of the service. He had a happy life, even if it wasn't long enough, and took great pleasure in his hobbies and his grandchildren. I'll miss him, but my daughter and her lovely children are around a lot, so I haven't had time to be lonely.

Please tell Linda if she wants anything to remember her father by, I'll gladly sort out something of his that might remind her of him. There was a picture he took of her in a pretty pink dress that she might like. She must be about three or four and she's standing near the pond in the park with a very serious look on her face. It was his favourite picture of her. Of course she can write to us if she wants to, but I don't expect she will.

Yours sincerely,

Marilyn Miller (Mrs)

I went to the wing to tell Sherilyn. She was in her cell eating alone, so I didn't have to siphon her off from the others. I hate this part of the job. The days are hard enough for the poor sods on this wing: it's like they're doubly banged up, doubly excluded from their lives. Even now after six years inside, when the front gates clang behind me in the morning I have to touch the key pouch on my belt to remind myself that I can always leave. Then when you go on the wing, through the doors in the two-storey-high metal wall that separates the VPs from the normals you know you're going beyond any ordinary loss of liberty: they've had what little freedom there is to associate with other prisoners snatched away from them. They're a little colony – like a leper colony, or a cult – sealed up in an impenetrable chamber, cut off both from life outside the prison and life outside the wing.

Sherilyn had given nothing away since she'd been shipped in here, apart from that one fit of weeping, so I had no way of knowing how she'd take the news. She was sitting at her table with her plate in front of her and I was struck by how she'd moved her food around. She'd separated off all the different elements of her meal, so there were peas in one corner, tomatoes in another, celery in a little pile by the side and three potatoes in a neat triangle surrounding a small stack of kidney beans. She'd obviously had the vegetarian meal which was a sort of hotpot, so it must have been quite a job to distinguish one vegetable from the next in the gloopy mess. I said Hi Sherilyn, How's your meal? and she said tightly Oh, it's edible. She put her fork down and turned as I sat on her bed, crossing her legs so precisely she could have been posing for a magazine. I think you haven't been in touch with your family much since you've been here, I began, and she said No, not at all, we're not very close and they're very busy. I've had a letter from your mother, I said, And it's bad news I'm afraid. Her face didn't change. It's your father, I said, He passed away three weeks ago – I'm really sorry to be the bearer of bad tidings. I watched for any sign that the news had impacted on her, but she stayed still on her chair apart from a tiny sigh. Yes that is sad, she said in the same tone you'd use to comment on a bad weather forecast. When will the funeral be held? It has been I'm afraid, I said, It seems to have been last week. You must be sorry to have missed it. Why? she said, and I almost didn't have an answer. B-b-because he's your dad? I said. Because whatever you might have thought of him, it's still a parent's death and that's a terribly painful loss. She smiled. Not for me, she said, We didn't have much of a father–daughter relationship, so it's not as if I've lost anyone important. Not like losing your husband, you mean, I said, rather capitalising on the link. She wrapped her arms around her waist and briefly closed her eyes. But I haven't lost him, she said, After all, I know where he is and who he's with, which is more than some wives can say, so I don't have anything to worry about. I wonder if you want to write to him and tell him about your dad's death, I said, He was his father-in-law, after all. No, she said, I've told you before. That's not what we do. Well you know where I am, I said, Come and see me whenever you need to. She did a nod and smile that owed everything to civility and nothing to sincerity, so I left a copy of the 'Dealing With Bereavement In Prison' leaflet on her bed and took my leave. I almost didn't tell the officers on duty

because the news – a major life event for any normal person –
had passed her by like a whistle in the wind. When my dad died
I had to take compassionate leave. I still cry for him sometimes.

Sherilyn

I wish I could be angry. I've tried it on for size, like a new pair of shoes – *here, Sherilyn, try a bit of anger, see if it works for you –* but it doesn't fit. I need a mind Hoover to suck every trace of Brendan out of my head, every mite hidden in obscure corners, every crumb that's slipped underneath the debris of my past. It would be simpler to saw off my head. Simpler, but just as lethal as losing him. I look at my face in the mirror and I don't recognise it because there's only me there. It's not me-and-Bren. Yesterday's news reminded me that there was a time before me-and-Bren, a time when there was only me except for the moments when it was me-and-him. In that pink dress I'm his-and-his. I'm in the kitchen with him and he's hurt his finger. I see the bleeding blood. Real bleeding blood. I say to him Daddy are you cutted? And he says No no it's just a little bit bleeding, and I don't want him to pick me up like he sometimes does because it'll all get on my dress and today I got a pretty dress on, I like it and Daddy says he likes it too. And we get to the park and I carrying the bread for the ducks and there's Daddy he's over there on the chair because he can't do the bread for the ducks, but I can because I'm a big girl and I know what they like. They don't like big bits because they mouths are very, very little and small so I make the bread little too because that's what they like. And they all come up to me when I give them their dinner and they're very happy and they go quack quack and Daddy stays on the chair because I say to him Daddy stay on the chair, stay over there and I look at him hardly so he stays over there. We have our dinner in a café near the library, only it wasn't bread like the ducks have for dinner, it was carrots and potatoes and pie, and then we go home. Mummy's sitting on the couch and I talk to her but she has to go sleepy-byes because she's very very tired, Daddy says so, and I watch some telly and then we go into the garden. And I'm in the paddling pool and I like the paddling pool because I can play there, and Daddy can stay on the seat and I can see him. He's looking at me and looking at me and I don't like it when he does that, and he must stay on the seat, but then he comes over to the paddling pool and he says Time for tea and bed now, pet, and he's lifting me out and I don't like it when he does dry me with the towel because it scratches me a bit in my wee wee and I'm sitting on his lap and I don't like it when he jiggles me a bit then some more and his eyes go all funny and I look at him, I look at his eyes and he makes this funny noise and I don't like it.

I never told anyone, and since Brendan and I met I rarely thought about it. I was safe inside our stockade, and I forgot how wrong I was. I forgot how it was my fault. I forgot how I made Mummy ill, how Daddy had to punish me because I'd been such a bad girl, how dirty I was. And now that Brendan's gone, now that he's turned his face from me, I'm drowning in blame. I'm bad, I stink, I'm putrefying like dead flesh.

Collum

Brendan GUTTERIDGE (BL 2943)

October 25th

Urgent request from prisoner to see me on October 21st, but away at conference. Called him in today. Request unusual – not seen since induction interview. Arrived on the dot, stood in the doorway, looked as though debating with self whether to come in. Dishevelled – usually one of the better groomed on wing, but stains down sweatshirt, bit malodorous when sat down, strange lock of hair out of place on forehead. Shifting around in chair. Said imperative he speak to his wife – & co-def. – SHERILYN GUTTERIDGE. Matter of life & death. Asked why. Wouldn't be specific. Tried to explore why difficult to tell me. Wouldn't say. Asked: probs with other prisoners? Probs with prison staff? Unwanted sexual approaches? Stopped shifting around in chair, so pursued this – wouldn't go there. Back to shifting. Physical/ medical probs? Muttered something – had to ask 3× to work out what – said 'Wet bed'. Reassured him happens all the time, esp. on VP wing. Said 'Not for years', so tried pursuing history of enuresis. Uncooperative. Asked how things generally – said fine, must speak Sherilyn. Explained regs. re: contact with co-defendant – (maybe forgot to do this at induction?) – wasn't listening. Kept repeating, must see wife, must see Sherilyn etc. etc. Thought iron hot, so struck – join probation group? Explore things with other prisoners/find ways to settle etc. Shook head. Said I had to disappoint him – sorry. Perhaps meet again? Said no & left. On wing later, Rashid on duty, had word. Confirmed

Gutteridge wet bed 3× – tried to hide sheets under bed, but other prisoners complained of stink. Said G's getting close to BRACKNELL (FC 3341), so went to his cell. Not to be trusted – charming, articulate & manipulative – mother on phone constantly demanding special treatment for son. Bracknell complained about state of library, slowness of book requests. Complained about failure of Ed. Dept. to run MBA course (!), complained about standards of food, then complimented self on aftershave (not wearing any) and suit (M&S). Wouldn't help with Gutteridge. Just gym mates, he said. Offer Gutteridge appt. in week's time. Work on getting him into group.

Collum Mackie
Senior Probation Officer

Brendan

He wheedled the stinking sheets out of me. He was the only one who could help me phone Sherilyn so I steeled myself to go to his office. It was all 'Collum' and 'Brendan' in there, like we were mates idly chatting in a bar over a couple of beers. He poked and prodded me till I confessed to the pissing, but even that didn't convince him to bend the fucking rules. This is an emergency, I said. Write to her, he said, You can send her all the letters you want. I'm not a violent man, but I could have killed him. Prison regulations permitted me to call anyone else he said. I could call my parents, though that might be a bit tricky in the circumstances, or I could call a friend when I had an urge to chat, but my own wife, my soulmate – no. He was a runty little bloke with glasses and built-up shoes sitting behind a desk that was too big for him. He knew what he was doing, turning me down. Getting his rocks off on my grief.

James was waiting for me when I got back on the wing and he was so sympathetic I almost cried. His eyes brimmed with tears when I told him how desperate I felt and he said he understood. He talked about his girlfriend, Amanda, and said he'd completely lose the plot if she stopped writing and visiting. She came from a titled family, but it didn't faze her at all, he said, to sit alongside The Great Unwashed in the visitors' room. He grinned when he said that, so I'd know he wasn't referring to him and me. Mother's a different kettle of fish, he said, She's on the phone seventeen times a day and she'd use up all my VOs if I let her. When I told her Mandy took priority she didn't write for four days. Gave me a bit of breathing space, he said. I told him I'd never used any of my VOs and he looked astonished. What, no one you'd want to come and see you? he said, No friends or anything? I shook my head. Sherilyn's my world, I said, I don't need anyone else. A chap needs friends, he said, I'll lend you some of mine when we get out. He put his hand on my shoulder. It felt like hot coals.

I watched him the next day in the workshop. We were making pink plastic address books and he was on the bench in front of me. It was really fiddly work and the size of my hands meant I was constantly dropping bits and pieces on the floor. I was sitting next to Frank who glared at me every time I did it. He was a cop on the out, so old habits died hard. James had this habit of flicking his hair with his fingers when he was either bored or concentrating and as I got back on to my stool after picking up a binder, his left hand was twisting the curls around his forefinger and flicking them free. They caught the light in such a way that they looked like dolphins cresting the waves in the sun and I wanted to lose my fingers in them. He was five or six feet away, but I was sure I could smell him and I imagined nuzzling his neck, the short hairs crisp against my mouth, the curls caressing my cheek. He must have felt my eyes on him, because he turned round on his stool to face me, his legs splayed. His jeans were pulled tight over his crotch and his cock and balls strained against the fabric. It was all I could do to stay behind the bench. Y'OK, cookie? he said, Need a hand? Any time, sunshine I said like a bar-room flirt and I grinned. That kind of banter went on all the time on the wing and no one turned a hair because we were all pervs, but I'd never joined in before. Dumping Sherilyn on our anniversary had opened up a space and James was moving in.

We walked back along the corridors together after work, and his arm kept bumping into mine. We were chatting about books. He'd lent me a huge novel written by a Russian and I was telling him that I was finding the names a bit difficult. I'll come up to your room later, he said – he always called our cells rooms as though we were staying in a hotel – it's not that difficult once you've got the hang of it. I've got something else I want to show you too, he said, and it felt like I had a date. I wanted to have a shower, splash on some aftershave and sit on my bed with a stiff drink, waiting for the doorbell to ring.

James

James had dumped Amanda as soon as he'd been convicted. She'd served her purpose adequately. She'd written him a few tear-stained letters pleading with him to send her a VO so they could at least meet as friends, but he'd ignored them and she'd subsided into silence. Find yourself some nice Guards officer, Amanda, he thought, Revert finally to type. Anyway, he was swamped with letters from his fans, not all of them girls, so he had no need for a real and rather trying girlfriend. He had one regular correspondent who called herself li'l Annie and wrote long letters in a careful italic hand using the language of a ten-year-old. She'd got it spot on and he heard her piping voice inviting him to come and play with her when he wanked over her stories of soaping herself in the bath and doing cartwheels without knickers. He and Brendan laughed together about the more preposterous offers they got in their mail but he didn't tell him about that one. Bizarrely, Brendan had been sent a letter inviting him to join an Irish letter-writing circle. It promised to let him into the secrets of where to eat Irish food in England, where to hear Irish music and see Irish dancing, together with the exchange of cookery hints and parenting tips. Parenting tips, James said, That'll be the one for you then. Share your child-rearing philosophy with the hoi polloi. There was no one else on the wing who attracted him, though there were many who found him attractive. Frank, the bent cop, adored him and had taken to buying him pricey toiletries from the shop; James received them as gracefully as a prince accepts his subjects' obeisance. Buffalo Bill the sheep shagger was a fan too, and James was often aware of him across the gym when he and Brendan were breaking sweat together, laughing and joking together. Bill would lean against a machine between sets, willing James to turn his blue eyes to him and give him a word, a smile, anything. From time to time he threw him a sop, Way to go, Buffalo! he'd call over, or Watch the wrists, Billy, and Bill would gulp it down hungrily.

Brendan was different. There was nothing servile about him – he was as self-sufficient as a bottle garden quietly sucking up its own juices. The density of his body was shocking; nothing could get past that, James thought, and the dream he'd had about Brendan's hands sometimes tickled at his memory like a butterfly glancing off a cheek. But behind the bulk James picked up something of Brendan's history that chimed with his. Neither man had said anything, but sometimes when he watched Brendan pounding seven colours of shit out of a punchball, he'd discern a vulnerability beneath the infrangible surface. It was time to share his special treasure. They shared so much already, it was only right to offer him this feast.

Brendan

I tried to see what Sherilyn was doing, hear what she was saying, but she baffled me. She was punishing me for leaving her and I struggled to keep alive the hope that one day she'd forgive me. When she fell pregnant, I thought she might have blamed me for the girl, like imagining I'd lied about the vasectomy, but after we won our case, the silence between us dispersed like early-morning mist. This silence was different: it felt lethal. Had it not been for James, grief might have suffocated me, but his light-hearted banter was the oxygen I needed. After tea when we'd stacked our plates, he said I'll meet you in your room in five minutes, it's time to talk books. I went to my cell and sat on the bed, *The Idiot* on my lap. I'd felt ignorant reading it but I knew James would guide me through the patronymics and diminutives that kept tripping me up. I planned to try speaking to Sherilyn later, after lights out.

He appeared in my cell with a pink file under his arm. He shut the door behind him. Bit of privacy, he said. His cheeks were rosy with excitement, as though it were Christmas morning and he'd just seen the bulging stocking by the fireplace. When he stood by my bed he towered over me. Standing, I had three or four inches on him at least but looking up at him I felt settled, as though he were my guardian angel. He sat down on the bed. You reckon talking about Dostoyevsky'll scare the bollocks off the others, do you? I said, Some of them even read, James, I wouldn't worry. I caught Skidders with Jackie Collins the other day. James stopped smiling, so I said What's up? Something happened? No, no, he said, It's just – it's the first time I've ever done this, showed this stuff I mean, and it feels a bit weird. What stuff? I said. This, he said patting the file, It's – well showing it to you is like exposing my private life, that's all. I mean, bringing it here means I trust you – I *can* trust you, can't I? I nodded. Good, he said. I just wanted you to share something that does it for me, if you know what I mean. Here, he said, handing over the file, Take your time. It starts off with mine and then goes on with other peoples'. Bought a couple here, but mostly they're from remand and the last nick.

I picked up my pillow and stuffed it between me and the wall like a bulwark, the weight of the file on my lap quadrupling as I moved. You sure you want me to do this? I asked, and he held my eyes and said almost savagely Yes! I want us both to have this – open it! It made me jump and the file fell off my legs on to the floor. A fan of papers slipped out. They looked familiar. I had some of those. As I bent down to pick them up, I could hear James's breathing getting more laboured as though he'd been running. I didn't want to look at his face, so I studied the first page closely. *Witness Statement of Ellie Thompson* it said – she was nine and lived in Saltdean. I'd read these things over and over during the preparation of my own case, so I knew the first bit was just identifying information. I skipped down the page. *He picked me up from school one day, I don't know exactly what day of the week it was, but it was three days after my birthday, so it was May 15th and he told me my mum said I could go and pick mushrooms with him before tea. He held my hand on the way to his van and it was sweaty. I said 'Oh, you're very sweaty' and he said 'Well, it's hot today isn't it?' It was a nice van, very clean and tidy, not like my stepdad's which has got all rubbish in it, and he told me to put my safety belt on because he didn't want me to get hurt. My stepdad never says that. We drove for a bit, I don't know how long it was, and he'd got this big bag of crisps and Coke which was by my feet and he said 'Have as much as you like.' When we passed a chippie he asked me if*

I wanted some chips, but I was stuffed by then so I said 'No, not now, maybe later.' He asked me if I liked music and he let me put whatever music I wanted into the machine. I put the 'Now That's What I Call Music' tape on because it had all my favourites on it. He said he liked it too and we was both singing along as we was driving. He asked me if I was having a nice time, and I said yes, because I was.

We stopped by some woods and he drove his van up this track a bit through some bushes. He said he didn't want to get it robbed. We went down a path and he was telling me the story of Little Red Riding Hood because he said she went to see her nan in a wood like this. I was a bit frightened because I didn't want to see no wolf, but he said 'Don't worry, they don't scare me and anyway I know how to kill wolves.' I didn't see no mushrooms and I was getting a bit tired so I said 'Can we go back now?' and he said 'Not yet, we're going to play a little game.'

He took me over to a tree and made me sit down. He said 'Now, you're Red Riding Hood and I'm the bad wolf and I've tied you to this tree but don't worry because I'll come and rescue you in a minute.' He had these silky scarf things and he tied them around my wrists so I couldn't move and then he tied each of my legs to a bush so they was wide open. He tied another scarf over my head and my face and he said 'Look, there's your hood.' I started to be a bit frightened and he said 'No, don't be frightened, remember I'm coming to kill the wolf soon,' so I stopped wriggling. He was sort of tugging at my knickers and there was a noise and he said 'There, I'm just cutting off your knickers so you can run faster away from the wolf.' I said 'But Mum will be really angry with me for spoiling my knickers' and he said 'I've got some spare ones in the car.' He started sort of panting, like he'd been doing some really hard work and then I felt this hard thing poking on my tummy. It was sort of hot and he said 'Don't worry, it's just the wolf and I'll be along any minute now.' And then the thing was poking in my face, on my mouth and I couldn't see it because of the scarf and he was sort of grunting and . . .

I skipped some pages ahead and waded into the swamp of a second little girl's story. Fifteen pages later he was raping a third. I lifted the main heft of the papers and discovered the statement of another small rape victim – buggery this time – from someone else's case and I turned my head through treacle to look at James. He was looking at me, grinning, his hands barely concealing his erection. Well? he said, What do you think? I collected the papers together slowly so I could collect my thoughts. Do you want to borrow it? he said urgently, I could let you keep it overnight, but only overnight. You could copy it all down and then you'd have your own set. I closed my eyes. It was as though he'd unzipped his beautiful skin and stepped out like some monstrous scaly creature from its chrysalis. I'd never taken drugs, but momentarily it felt like I was tripping, like I'd flipped into some mad universe where raping children was as unremarkable as brushing your teeth. He must have seen something in my face because he said Brendan? You OK? You've gone really white. I said What made you think I'd want to look at this? What kind of perv do you think I am? and I threw the file at him. You'd better go, I said, Take your shit and fuck off back to your sewer. And this too, I said, pushing *The Idiot* into his chest, It fucking stinks, just like you. He seemed to pull himself together. I'm disappointed, Brendan, he said standing up, I thought we were the same, and he left the cell.

After he'd gone, I threw up in the toilet and sat by the bowl watching the red and brown and green vestiges of my tea bobbing in the water. I had this insane idea that if I gathered them up and stuck them in a scrapbook like my feathers when I was a kid, it would all be OK again. I'd write 'Tomato, November 9th, toilet, Gutteridge cell, VP Wing' and give it some fancy Latin name, and I'd be safe. I concentrated on the bits, planning how they'd look on the page because I knew if I let go for a moment, I'd fall apart.

And then I did. I sat on the floor and wept, my head banging on the wall behind me. I was more alone than I'd ever been before. It was as though I'd been flayed and now any worm, any germ, any poison, could get in, and the me that Sherilyn had germinated would die.

Brendan and Sherilyn

It was a Wednesday morning when he came back to me. I was in the shower, trying not to listen to two girls in another cubicle having a revolting conversation about their sex lives, and I felt his hands in the small of my back. They slid down in the soap and came to rest on my buttocks, his palms mapping the curves. I turned to face him and ran the backs of my fingers up his belly to his chest, my skin skating over his. He lifted me so slowly I could feel each single hair on my body standing on end, so gently I could have been thistledown, and I wrapped my legs around his hips. The water flowed on our heads, down our backs, but our fronts were dry. Nothing could come between us. We were back in the place where we lived, loved, felt, thought. The place where we began and ended.

My hands were full of her again as they tracked every pore of the skin that stretched around her. Skin that was continuous with mine. I was merged with her again, her brief disappearance from my life waved away like a bad dream. I had been dazzled by James's toxic charm, but she forgave me and together we forgot. Like the girl, he had tried to slip between us, and like the girl we'd repelled him. Nothing would spoil this again: this one of us. Nothing would dim the light that showed us to us. Showed us our life and our death.

Xandra

I had thought that maybe the shock of her father's sudden death might provoke some affective response in Sherilyn that made her more available to me. I'm still mystified by how heroically I held on to that hope. I remembered what her dad looked like from the photographs in the press. The Gutteridges had been so notorious that for some weeks over the course of their arrest and their trial it seemed like there was nothing else going on in the world. There was a terrible earthquake in Pakistan at the time, in fact, but it didn't appear in the paper until about page fourteen. I remember seeing her family going in and out of court on the news and thinking what a mismatch her parents were. They looked like an Angus McGill postcard, her mum billowing and blowsy and her dad this little scrap of a man. She looked as though she could gobble him up for a mid-morning snack if she felt a bit peckish. He was an office worker of some sort, so far as I remember, and had the pallor of someone who's been kept in a darkened room all his life, let out on a leash only on high days and holy days. He had this funny polished hairstyle from about forty years ago, and delicate facial features, like a doll. He was perpetually scampering along behind Sherilyn's mother in photographs, trailing in her wake, or maybe he was just ready to catch her if she fell, because she didn't look a well woman. I suppose in a Warholian way it was their fifteen minutes of infamy. Naturally I wondered what had gone on in that family to cause Sherilyn's psychopathy, but I never knew because she wasn't telling. From the reports that came in with her, no one else had been able to find out either. After her dad died, I asked the staff from time to time if she'd let anything slip, but nobody noticed anything new.

A couple of the girls were in serious emotional difficulties and for a little while they absorbed all my time and energies, so Sherilyn was a misty figure in my peripheral vision: just another inmate. But when I saw her properly after the crises were over, I was astonished. I'm not a fan of romantic novel slop, but it was as though she'd been lit up from inside: she was radiating happiness. She wasn't a naturally beautiful woman, not like Kym, whose beauty nailed you to the wall, but if you'd bottled what she was giving off, you'd have made a fortune. Any woman would look a million dollars wearing that glow. You're looking well, Sherilyn, I said to her as we passed on the landing. Thank you, I'm feeling well she said. Got over your dad? I asked. That wasn't a problem, she said, I think I told you. Yes you did, I said, But you look especially happy now – what's going on? She smiled. I've got my life back, she said, Of course I'm happy, and she walked on. I didn't think she was doing drugs, though any other girl that euphoric probably was – she wasn't the type. I don't imagine she ever did much more than sip at a glass of champagne on the out, either; it was too important for her to stay in control. I should have been grateful that at least there was one girl who wasn't wanting my full attention all the time, but she was a walking challenge. There's very few I can't get to eventually and she was a rare failure.

The End

Xandra hears about it as soon as she arrives at the front gate. Barry is on duty and tells her the news, skipping any pretence of a greeting. She doesn't bother opening her office and goes straight to the wing. By now, its inmates should have been dispersed to their morning's activities, but they're all out of their cells, leaning into each other's misery. Charlene is sobbing, her head on the table, and two women flank her, their hands stacked on top of each other between her shoulder blades.

She never touched them while she'd lived, but now she's reminding them how fragile they are; grief hangs in the air like a dismal aurora borealis. I'll come back down in a minute, Xandra says, vaguely including everyone in her promise, Who's up there? The medic, Kym whispers, And Jean. In six years on this wing, Xandra has known a cluster of women who have finally given up hope, but she's never been there quite so soon after they've died. Most suicides tend to occur under cover of darkness. She climbs the stairs and stands in Sherilyn's doorway, holding on to the reassuringly solid doorknob. Jean is leaning against the table, the gritty lines of her face softened by sorrow. She hates losing them. Dr Burrows has unbuckled the belts around Sherilyn's neck and removed the two plastic carrier bags from her head. She is kneeling by the bed, sitting back on her heels. About three hours, I'd say – what's the time now? she says, looking at her watch. Eight fifteen – OK, let's say time of death was five a.m., that'll be about right. I don't think I've seen this one, have I? she says, turning to Jean. Shannon must've examined her on intake. Was she seen by Mental Health? Jean shakes her head. She never needed anything from anyone, she says, Couldn't get near her – she was a loner. Dr Burrows grimaces. Well if they won't tell you, you can't know, she says, Don't blame yourself, Jean, you'll have done your best. She stands up, unhooks the stethoscope from her neck and begins coiling its length. You got any light to shed, Xandra? Any indications she was getting ready for this? Her father died a little while ago, Xandra says, But they had no relationship to speak of. Actually she seemed terribly happy recently – almost ecstatic. Often the case, says Dr Burrows, Once they've decided to do it, they feel like their life's sorted – which it is, in a way. She barks a short laugh. Death does have a tendency to sort things, doesn't it? Who is there to tell, Xandra? Xandra? Xandra is looking at the woman on the bunk. She is ugly in death, her face puce, her swollen tongue forcing her mouth open, her eyes punctuated with burst blood vessels. She'd been so careful, in life, never to reveal anything of herself and the bold, bare sight of her death is appalling. I suppose I'd better start with her husband, Xandra says, He was the only person she had any relationship with. They were very close. Jolly good, says Dr Burrows – Well, I'd best be on my way. I'll come down to the office with you, Jean, fill out those ruddy forms. You can get me some tea too, I'm gasping. Jean squeezes her colleague's arm as she passes and the two women smile wanly at each other.

Xandra pulls the cell door to once she's alone and draws the chair over to the bed. Sherilyn's hair is damp and awry. Her fringe sticks to her forehead in jagged clumps and bleached spikes point waywardly from her crown. With a tissue, Xandra gently dries her brow and strokes her hair into a semblance of its usual order. There's a smear of mascara at the corner of each eye and she wipes away the brown tears with another tissue, remembering Sherilyn's one fit of weeping. She's used to tears; sometimes when she gets home she needs a very long bath to soak off the misery she's been coated with during the working day. She hasn't had time to have children of her own, but her charges suck at her like wailing infants. They tell her their stories of abuse and loneliness, abandonment and loss, but she's never met anyone quite so alone as Sherilyn. She picks up the body's left hand and strokes its back, as though she can give her something in death she'd never had in life. There's a smudge of something on her finger, just above her wedding ring. She can see when she looks more closely that it is writing: TEN YEARS, it says in biro.

When she's back in her office, she prepares herself to make some difficult phone calls. Cup of coffee first. The paperwork can wait. Start with Brendan. In the other prison, the probation officer's phone is answered after one ring and Xandra introduces herself. Bugger me, that's a coincidence, says Collum Mackie, I was just going to call you – with bad news I'm afraid. Xandra's heart flutters: she knows what's coming. Brendan Gutteridge killed himself this morning, says Collum – obviously I was going to call you first so you could tell – erm, Linda, is it? Oh no, here it is: Sherilyn. How's she going to take it? She won't take it at all says Xandra breathlessly, She killed herself this morning too. There is a loaded silence at each end of the phone line until Xandra interrupts it by clearing her throat. I'm not sure I can bear to ask you this, she says, But what time did he die? Doc reckons about five this morning, he says, Why? Christ, you don't mean she . . . ? Mmm, same time. And she'd written 'TEN YEARS' on her finger above her wedding ring – you got any idea what that might mean? Yeah, he did too, says Collum, but Bracknell, one of the other cons who was friendly with Gutteridge for a while, told me today's their wedding anniversary. I think we can safely assume it was their tenth.

There's a refuge in the bureaucratic task of bringing Sherilyn's file to an end. Killing it off. It takes her an hour.

When she's done, she goes back to the wing to attend to the survivors.

Brendalyn

I'm walking towards the light. I am intact again, whole again. Since 10.21, this has always nestled in the curve of my mind, this me: death now restores me to me. I am untouchable.

I love. I am loved.

I am Brendalyn.

Acknowledgements

This novel arose, unbidden, while I was at UEA doing the MA in creative writing. In the throes of writing another novel, I found myself writing two maddened pages in the primitive voice of a little girl. It became clear she was in a cage and that her parents had been the carpenters. I was all for dumping what I'd been writing and setting off in search of Samantha, but wiser voices prevailed and I grudgingly finished the first novel and put it in a drawer. It is a strange and terrible irony that Samantha's words were lost again by the time *Monster Love* was finished, but her voice still echoes in my mind. I spent two years at UEA, beetling up to Norwich once a week while working in London, and am especially grateful to Michèle Roberts who tutored me with warmth and good humour and who taught me that writing can be an act of generosity.

Writing the book while conducting a busy psychoanalytic practice, I have been precious about my writing time and timid about asking friends to read the multitudinous words that tipped on to the page, but over and over again I have been reminded of the value and certainties of friendship. Maggie Mills survived an early draft and responded to it with the emotional intelligence I can expect from her. Jan Woolf, Cheryl Moskowitz, Gillian Isaacs Hemmings, Neel Mukherjee, Andrea Mason and Andrew Mackenzie have all been subjected to later drafts and have shuddered, winced and sighed before offering their considered comments. I have benefitted from Wayne Milstead's skills in literary architecture, and the book is better structured as a result. The Julia and David White artists' colony in Costa Rica offered me a month's fellowship and I went there with a novel which I thought needed a little structural tinkering. By the time I came back, it had a new beginning, a new ending, substantially rewritten middle and two new voices – testament to the opportunity the colony offers to dream new writing into being. Royce Clay Snape, the director, brings his own creativity to the table in his running of the colony and is at the heart of experience. While there, I met Nancy Blakey, another writer, over bushes quivering with hummingbirds. I showed her mine, she showed me hers and we embarked on a friendship for life. Jenny Uglow knows about friendship, too, and has encouraged and guided and supported me with her loving wisdom throughout this book's gestation. Sally Sampson, another old and beloved friend, was especially helpful in mapping the way to an agent. I salute Jonny Geller, the agent brave enough to take me on, for holding on to the joy of his new baby while wading through the murky swamps of the novel. Juliet Annan, my publisher, understood immediately what I was trying to write about and has been – as it were – on the same page as me throughout the honing process. Jenny Lord, also of Fig Tree, has been unfailingly enthusiastic and jolly, and the two of them are the very model of professional attentiveness.

Finally, I thank Shah Husain who some years ago told me in a low dive in Soho that I *should* write. And always, always, I thank Michael, Cassie and Clea, who knew that I could.